GW00671801

Wimbledon Village thrives on the edge of a hill, the utmost southern tip of a large high plateau in South West London. Its northern border is dominated by a wasteland known as the Common, mysterious grounds teeming with wilderness. To the west, the Common spreads further like a plague, where Nature lives unruly, until it grinds against the bustling roads, the public buildings, the suburban houses of the village, where men and women live their dreams and nightmares. All along the southern ridge of the hill the Epsom Downs stretch south into Surrey and at the foot of the hill lies modern Wimbledon Town, constantly moving, growing, as it fades into the desolate urban landscape of Merton. The eastern front meets the signs of modern transportation and modern urbanisation until they all step aside to show the green triangle of Wimbledon Park, as it embraces the hill in a cuddle, as it has done since the earliest of times.

Our story starts in Wimbledon Village. But as the pages unfold, as the fog clears, and our characters come into play, it will become clear this is an alternate Wimbledon. It is a Wimbledon where you and I do not exist...

Titles available in the Wynnman series:

Book 1 – The Wynnman and the Black Azalea

Book 2 – The Wynnman and the Crimson Paths

Titles available from the same author:

Il Canto Della Chimera Vergine

Beyond Boundaries

Memento Postridie

Arya

The Misadventures of Mister Fast

THE WYNNMAN AND THE BLACK AZALEA

by
Trevor P. Kwain

Published by Threepeppers Publishing

2nd Edition – June 2020
First published in English in Great Britain in 2019

ISBN: 978-1-9993268-5-2

Cover: Still Life of Wynnman Ep. 1
Drawing © 2020 Trevor P. Kwain

The incidental black and white photo in the cover is taken from "Wimbledon Past" by Richard Millward, published by Historical Publications. Historical Publications did not object to its use. We were not able to trace the copyright holder or photographer. A person with a claim should contact Threepeppers Publishing.

Bread Logo sourced and modified from http://clipart-library.com

www.3peppers.co.uk
www.trevorpkwain.org

#trevorpkwain   #TheWynnman

To Richard Millward and to my parents

The sign at 9b High Street seesawed up, pull after pull, under the strength of the Polish builder. The letters written on it swung sideways, to and fro, until they reached the top of the shop window. Gradually, they no longer blurred at each sway and came together as words comfortable to read from any side of the street.

'Come on... Almost there!' said the man behind him with his arms crossed in contemplation.

The Polish builder pulled with the last strength in his arms. The sign whined against the friction of the ropes. There was a bit of rust on the edges, and the white and red colours already looked old and faded. The man thought it gave a rustic look to the name of the shop.

La Pagnotta

'Is it up, mate?' asked the Polish man without turning.

'*Ci siamo quasi...* We are almost there! One last pull!' replied the man eager to push through with the work.

'This thing is heavy. That is why we needed two people on the job.'

'Too expensive. Stop crying like a *bambino*. You will be proud when it is done.'

The man did not shift from his position below in the middle of the pavement, arms crossed and head high to check the sign was up and aligned. His thick, wavy hair ruffled in the light breeze blowing through the high street. His brown eyes focused on the final touches to the work, seeking a perfect balance, a masterpiece. He wore a white short-sleeved top, red and white chequered trousers. Splashes of paint and dry patches of white dust

9

showed on his bare arms and on his trousers. He was so focused he hardly heard the passers-by complaining he did not budge to let them through. A car passed by at great speed. It swished close to the pavement, close to the man's back. He jumped and took a safe leap forward.

'*Cretino!* Can't you see me on the pavement?' cursed the man waving his hands in disapproval to the car before it disappeared beyond the small roundabout at the end of the high street. He puffed, annoyed. He did not like to be disturbed, or even more, distracted.

'Mister, I think we are done here!' said the Polish man with a final pant.

The man in the chequered trousers looked back at the sign and a grin of satisfaction broadened across his lips.

'*Perfetto!* Now that is what I am talking about.'

The Polish man stepped down the ladder to join the man at his side and finally contemplate his last thirty minutes of sweat. He dried his damp forehead with his forearm and took a deep breath. The sign was now hung nicely above the main shop window, framing it alongside the entrance door next to it. There was a second shop window to the left of the door, a curved-shaped glass tracing its round edge. Opaque plastic sheets covered the large glass frames of the shop from top to bottom, not allowing passers-by to see inside. Only the entrance door allowed to get a closer look inside. If passers-by cupped their hands and stuck their forehead against the cold glass, they would spot the pasty yellow walls and the marble effect of the floor tiles. The shape of an empty counter and showcase shelves behind could be seen against one of the walls while the rest faded into a fog of dust which seemed to have no intention of settling.

The shop was at the end of the row of unique low buildings that made up the Western side of Wimbledon High Street. After it, taller Regent-style buildings broke the pattern and carried on until the end of the high street before it blended with the residential houses of Wimbledon Village.

'So, what is this? A bar?' asked the Polish man to get to know his client.

'This, my friend, is the home of bread and pastries' replied the man with a friendly pat on the Polish's shoulder. 'It will be the best bakery in town.'

'What does *La Pagnotta* mean?'

'The Loaf.'

'Is that it?'

'I'll tell you what, *amico mio*. You clean up the interior and I give you 20% off when we open in a few weeks.'

'Very kind of you, mister…'

'LoTrova, Enrico LoTrova.'

'Are you Italian?'

'You are quite the observer.'

'What brings you here to London?'

'I wanted to move here and open my own bakery. Baking is what I do best.'

'You seem pretty sure of your skills. You do know there are already one or two places selling bread on this high street alone? And you have a few supermarkets down the hill?'

'*Dilettanti!*' dismissed Enrico with a sweep of his hand 'They are not bakeries. They are just amateurs who sell pre-cooked bread. Where is the joy in that? Not everyone can make *ciabatte*, croissants, baguettes and bloomers. Bread is no "loafing" matter, eh?'

'I hope your bread is better than your jokes.'

'Mr Wyczenski,' said Enrico with a slanted nod at the dust inside of the shop 'why don't we get a move on and finish the work? It is past eleven a.m. and perhaps we can finish before lunch. *Dai, su!* Chop chop!'

The Polish man agreed with a grumble and picked up his tools. He then opened the door to the shop and disappeared inside. Enrico smiled, and before he followed him, he turned his head to take in the view of Wimbledon High Street.

The short straight road was the main artery of Wimbledon Village, throbbing with heavy car traffic both up and down. Black cabs and flashing red double-decker buses hurried along up and down the street waving the colours of London. Enrico could not fail to notice how the buildings on both sides of the high street seemed to be out of place with the livelihood of the neighbourhood. They were tiny and narrow, some old, some refurbished, but never higher than four storeys. Wimbledon Village had all the charm of a small secluded village with the thumping upbeat of a London town.

Enrico was simply happy to be here. He knew he had chosen a great spot for his business. Busy street, with many shops on either side. He felt proud after so many weeks of stress and hard work. His parents would be proud. Finally, it was all coming to plan as he wished. He knew there would be more to celebrate with the opening, the first customers, and that first monthly revenue. His gaze shifted to the blue sky above. For once, it was not raining.

Three days later the last boxes arrived. They were mainly food ingredients and a few decorative items to put on the empty shelves Mr Wyczenski had put up. Enrico thought they would bring the cream walls to life. The layout of Enrico's bakery was starting to take form, bringing the opening day closer. The inside of *La Pagnotta* had an odd shape and probably unique on the high street. The curious curve of the low two-storey building Enrico had bought took shape inside a beautiful round alcove, perfect for a few tables, half of which looked onto the street through a curved glass. Enrico looked at it and wondered if he should engrave the name of the bakery onto the glass. He carried on emptying the boxes and putting some of the items on one of the large counters. The opposite end of the shop was more square and symmetrical. As you came in through the entrance, you were welcomed by a black counter with a stone-like finish, running across from right to left, and showcase shelves for the bread were stacked at the back. At one end of the counter, there was a coffee machine with espresso and cappuccino cups. At the other, Enrico had put a second-hand cash till he had been lucky to lay his hands on. The counter then turned at a ninety-degree angle, running away from the entrance, and stopped short of the wall opposite. Enrico had planned this section of the counter for a glass showcase and store some of the pastries he made. At the end of it, a small door led out of the shop floor and up a cranny flight of steps to Enrico's studio apartment on the floor above.

Enrico's lodgings were large enough to suit his solo lifestyle. A pull-down bed, a kitchen corner, a few drawers. The bathroom was on the ground floor before you walked up the stairs. Quite tiny but he knew city houses came in small sizes although he had to disagree on such a generalisation after seeing some of the large mansions in and out of Wimbledon Village. Next to the bathroom, a door opened onto another flight of stairs leading down to the basement. This was where his art and magic came to life. It was his laboratory, if he were to say the right term, or label it more commonly as his kitchen. There was a large stone slab, a mixer and kneading machine to one side to make the dough, a sink for sanitary purposes and last but not least the mighty oven at one end. It was a modern baker's oven, with three flaps each opening onto a metal surface large enough to bake a decent volume. It was as high as the basement ceiling, looking bulky inside the window-less room. Enrico could still not believe how he had managed to get it down there in pieces and put it together. It was a risk and a challenge he had taken without considering whether the stairs or the doors were too small. He had already made a test batch to test power, heat and obviously taste. The oven was ready for production.

Enrico's hands tingled while he pulled out jars, coffee bags, a few empty *fiasco* bottles and small wicker baskets. He had ordered decorative items that would bring colour and some rustic authenticity. However, he could not wait to bake. This is what he enjoyed the most. Prepping the kneading machine, checking the oven thermostat, beating up the dough to those shapes he was fond to make. And there was more to that. Enrico wanted to make good bread, like he had learnt back home, and he was a bit of a perfectionist. His first test batch, with some *filoni* and some bloomer bread, did not produce the greatest results. The dough felt too thick and dense, not light and fluffy enough. He had tried three types of flour, distilled and purified the water twice, reduced salt, added oil, and he even adjusted the temperature of the basement to get a good rise from the dough. Enrico was a man who did not like loose ends. If there was an answer or a solution, he had to find it. The test batch did turn out better but not as perfect as he wanted. He emptied all the boxes as his mind wandered onto the next bread to bake. He knew though the front of the shop needed attention, and being on his own, he had to make fast progress, or he would be there all day. Watching all the items stacked on the counter, waiting to be placed around the shop, almost made Enrico's heart cry out. Opening day was not far away and he had already invested most of his funds into this place. Wimbledonians had better buy his bread or he would close shop before even opening.

By the time it was noon, shelves, cupboards and tables were more than just white blemishes against the pasty yellow walls and the marble texture of the floor. Enrico was no house décor expert, but he did recognise how small additions made a difference. Even the small metal jugs filled with sugar sachets on the round coffee tables made it all stand out better. The shop still felt empty and Enrico thought it could be the bread that was missing. He decided it was time for a coffee. An espresso, to be exact. The LaGaggia machine was ready and operational, and since the first day it had never let Enrico down when he had his three or four coffee breaks while setting up shop. Even Mr Wyczenski enjoyed it in between work schedules. Enrico knew he could not pay him off with coffees alone. Yet, the Polish worker was an honest and reasonable man, affordable too. He was happy not to be paid in full until opening day, and so Enrico agreed to at least cover the material he needed with coffees on the house.

The Italian baker took the steaming espresso cup and leaned against the counter, sipping slowly the bitter caffeine shot. It tasted good. Better than that franchise he went to when he first arrived here. He could not remember the name. Burnt coffee, that's what it was. He chuckled and took another sip. He watched the bustling high street outside through the shop window. A Maserati passed by without hearing its thundering roar, taking over a double-decker bus approaching the nearby stop. A couple of mums pushed their prams and walked by apparently gossiping about the upcoming shop. The sound was down to a bare minimum. The glass he chose kept the place quiet and watching the world outside from where he stood felt like an old silent movie. Enrico felt at home and knew he was doing the right thing. He stood there, still looking out, almost in a trance. The building opposite his bakery was a taller one, similar in style to the one next door. Regent-style, red-bricked, white stone around the high window frames. To its left, an odd Victorian corner building marked the end of the Wimbledon High Street. It could have been taken from a Gothic story with its little turrets and sloping roofs as if it were a castle. To Enrico's surprise, it was the local bank.

The beauty of Wimbledon Village was the lack of high rises or even skyscrapers which let the sun spread its light and warmth across the top of the hill until it set low behind the trees and the residential homes towards the end of the day. Even now, Enrico could see the blue sky reflected against the second-floor windows of the Regent-style building. His gaze moved down to one of the wide square windows on the bank's ground floor and the sun's reflection caught his face unaware. He blinked and moved his head out of the way. Pulling himself out of the trance, Enrico noticed a woman was standing on the pavement across the road waving her hands to catch his attention. He did not flinch at first although there was not anyone on the pavement on his side answering back. The woman slowed down her waving, probably confused. She then crossed the road and came up to the shop's entrance pointing at the door. Enrico realised she was talking to him and was asking to come inside. He had seen her before on the high street, but he could not place his finger on when he had actually met her. He smiled and waved her to come in as the door was open. The tiny brass bell on top of the entrance door rang its cheery tinkle. It rang beautifully as Enrico expected. The woman was wearing a yellow blouse with its sleeves rolled up and a pair of dark blue cigarette pants. Her figure was very slim but not too thin apart from fragile wrists and ankles. Her feet stood in red flat shoes. She knew how to play with colours and her clothes were casual and comfortable but smart enough; no cheap jeans or trainers.

'Hi! I hope I am not disturbing.' said the woman with good enunciated English.

Enrico pulled back from the counter and walked the short distance to the entrance to greet her.

'Hi! Not at all.' reassured Enrico. 'Please come in.'

'I have seen you have been very busy over the last few weeks and did not know when it was right to come over. My name is Viviane. Viviane Leighwood.'

She stretched her hand forward in a welcome gesture and Enrico grabbed it in a friendly shake. Her hand felt cold and bony to the touch, but her skin was soft and her nails well kept. He gulped feeling ashamed he may not have checked if his hands were dirty or covered in flour dust.

'Oh…I am Enrico. Enrico LoTrova. Nice to meet you. Sorry for my hands, I have been busy with handiwork.'

'Don't apologise.' said Viviane with a casual shrug. 'I work across the road and my hands are never clean because of my work. I own the gardening shop over there.'

She turned to point at her shopfront. Outside it was full of green leaves, terracotta pots and the colours of upcoming spring. Enrico looked and then he remembered seeing her coming out often to pot plants or arrange vases here and there not to crowd the side of the pavement too much. Before she turned back, he was quick to notice she was as tall as him, with her auburn hair cut in a nice, voluminous up-do hairstyle to frame her fair complexion and rosy cheeks.

'Flowers and plants are my daily job.' continued Viviane. 'What's yours? I see you are wearing a chef's jacket.'

'I am a baker. Baking is my…well…my bread and jam?' dared Enrico to use some of the English idioms he had already picked up.

'Your bread and butter, you mean.'

Enrico smiled nervously, and so did Viviane wondering if she had offended him.

'Nice. A baker. We have not had one since I remember. Everyone buys bread at the supermarket. I thought it was a bar or café from outside.'

'I make bread and pastries, but I have a coffee machine too. I was told you enjoy coffee in London and not just tea.'

'We do. Too much I think.'

'Well, I thought someone may come in the morning for some bread to take home and they may want something sweet to have with their morning coffee. Why not, maybe even something to accompany your five o'clock tea. Isn't that what you English do?'

Enrico laughed nervously. Viviane returned a cordial smiled.

'I hear you are not English. Let me guess…Spanish? Italian?'

'Italian.'

'Where from?'

'Central part.'

'Near Rome?'

'Sort of. Small village, you know.'

'Well, Enrico. Welcome to Wimbledon Village. Welcome to the neighbourhood!'

She opened her arms wide as if she wanted to take in the surroundings and package them into a wrapped gift box for Enrico to accept. It was a nice gesture from her, and Enrico was happy to finally meet a friendly face that was not a contractor or a council representative. It was probably the first friend he had officially made since landing in London.

'*Grazie mille!*' thanked Enrico.

He thought of living the moment and enjoying it a little longer.

'I was planning to have some lunch,' he continued. 'but I have not thought where. Care for any suggestion and perhaps join me too?'

Enrico felt a bit nervous with his English. He was keen to thank the woman for her hospitality.

'I'd be happy to.' Viviane replied without hesitation.

She found the Italian baker odd but handsome. He brought some fresh air to the staleness of the village, even if he just baked nice, simple bread.

Eric Quercer was on the most expensive black cab journey into London, from Heathrow to Wimbledon. He did not mind. He had the money and the reasons. The driver, coming from the south, took the long bend round Tibbet's Corner roundabout and before it made a full circle, it was out onto Parkside driving down to Wimbledon Village. Eric had never been there. He had been to London many times, but he had to look up where Wimbledon was. First time was when the letter arrived. That same letter he had now in his hands, showing the creases from multiple folding and unfolding. He re-read it a few times and the words were more credible now, especially after the mysterious sender had been kind enough to give him a call. A strange voice, the man had. Maybe it was a long-distance call, or he was simply muffling his voice. Eric was no fool. He checked the facts, double checked them. He could not fault the mysterious sender for the information he had shared with him. It gave Eric hope for something he had been seeking for a long time. Something special for his collection. Something unique. He was renowned, and even mocked at, among his peers at his private club. He just could not help it. He was a horticulturist with great knowledge and skill. His daily job was to collect plants or flowers of unique beauty, the rarities people thought did not exist or assumed had all been discovered. He could not do or think about anything else. Indeed, he got himself into trouble most of the time. He breached security at a Buddhist monk temple for a rare form of Asian flower used in herbal medicine but now down to only two or three specimens. He even bribed officials in Western Africa for the leaf of a rare fruit plant quarantined by the WHO due to possible Ebola contamination from bat's blood. He had to have it. He ensured all safety and containment measures were in place and now he had it on display in his greenhouse back in Toronto. He even enjoyed talking about these rare specimens at dinner parties, bragging in front of his bored friends from the club. Eric Quercer was a born horticulturist. This was his calling.

The black cab sped down the straight road called Parkside, flanked on one side by large mansions and on the other by the high trees and thick woodland of Wimbledon Common. The moment the trees thinned out, the green idyllic patches of Wimbledon appeared and so did the village at the end of the road. Eric glanced at it as the cab turned right, before entering the village. The Duchess Hotel was to the West, right across a triangular green space called Rushmere Green. The mysterious sender advised him to stay here and also requested discretion. Eric Quercer knew what he had to do. He would do anything to lay his hands on another rare plant. Something out of this world.

Viviane banged the pint of ale, full to the brim, down onto the table.

'Pint of beer. And fish 'n' chips coming right away.' she said. 'I hope you enjoy it better than Geppetto's, the Italian restaurant down the road.'

There was a hint of scorn in her voice, meant to humour Enrico following their short, animated discussions. She sat opposite Enrico in defiance as they both settled comfortably on the wooden benches outside the Dog and Fox pub. Viviane took a delicate sip from her glass of Pinot Grigio while watching the people strolling along the high street.

'The man served *pappardelle con pollo*. Pasta with chicken? It's atrocious!' lamented Enrico 'I might have a word with him when he is in the shop.'

'Geppetto's is a chain of restaurants that serve Italian food so there may be some long-forgotten truths. Hey, I am sure there is an old recipe from Ancient Rome.'

'Is this some sort of British joke?'

'Well, you are the one fancying British food over Italian cuisine.'

'*E allora?*' dismissed Enrico gulping down his ale. 'I can make pasta at home. Let's try the local specialities And I fancied fish. Fish is good for memory.'

Viviane took a cigarette from her purse and lit it cocking her head slightly to protect the flame from the wind.

'You smoke?' asked Enrico in rhetoric.

'One of my many vices. Like you and your fish.'

She giggled. Enrico stared at her and followed with a low and soft chuckle.

'I like food made the proper way, and I'm worse when it comes to baking proper bread.' started Enrico with a more sombre tone. 'I do not mean to scare you with my attitude. I must say I get carried away and we've only just met.'

'I take you are passionate like all Italians.'

A Maserati passed by with its engine roaring like a lion.

'I see a lot of those here.' Enrico observed as he took another sip of his beer.

'There are plenty more. Ferrari, Porsche.'

'Nice rich people, eh? Do you think they will buy my bread?'

'They are not all rich, you know. And I don't think being rich changes your taste in bread.'

'True. Are you from Wimbledon?' continued Enrico changing the subject.

'I wish I could say I was born and bred. I am not originally from London. I come from a town called Leicester, north from here. However, I have been living here now for…erm…ten odd years.'

'You have been a gardener for ten years?'

'I am a shop manager, Enrico, and my shop sells flowers and plants.'

Their lunch suddenly arrived at the table. They were served by a young man in t-shirt and jeans. The courtyard was still busy. A few co-workers having a late lunch, two middle-aged men drinking and laughing coarsely, an elderly woman reading a magazine while patting her Yorkshire terrier. The exterior of the pub bore traces of old architecture, another mix of Regent and Victorian styles, which Enrico was starting to recognise as a common pattern across the village. The two facades facing the high street were of different colours, but it did not strip away the charm. There was no modernity creeping in. Even across the street, a strange colourful church-like building broke the dull pattern of the grey tarmac. It was the same for the rows of two -or -three storey buildings leading up north through the second part of the high street.

'Is that all of Wimbledon Village?' commented Enrico.

'If you mean the Wimbledon High Street, yes. Everything else grows around it.'

'Is this also the Broadway?'

'No, that is at the bottom of the hill. Haven't you explored the area yet?'

'No. Busy setting up shop.'

A chirpy ringtone echoed nearby. It sounded clunky like it came out of an eight-bit computer machine. Enrico touched the inside of his chef jacket.

One side, then the other. He then pulled out a dark blue Nokia 3310, but the caller had hung up.

'What is that?' gulped Viviane.

'My phone.'

'From a museum?'

Enrico faked a high-pitched laugh. The woman in front of her was cheeky. Nothing restrained her from slipping in a comment that let her speak her mind. He liked it though. She did not seem to come across as someone with a stiff lip. On the contrary, she spoke the truth with such an elegance.

'It works, no? Makes calls. Receives calls. You can reach me anywhere.'

'Right. Reach you where? In the past?'

'*Finito?*' cut short Enrico. 'I just don't like phones. I don't like technology.'

'Is that why you have that old cash till in the bakery?'

'Yes. Well, it was also cheap to buy. I am just scared of being near electronics. The less I am around them, the better. I get an itchy feeling.'

Viviane rolled her eyes. Enrico saw it with a fleeting glance before checking the missed call.

'You smoke. I hate technology.' he added. 'Match made in heaven. Now, let me see.'

The phone rang again. Same number. Enrico did not recognise it. He answered straight away, worried it could be Mr Wyczenski or one of his suppliers who needed payment.

'Enrico LoTrova?' said the voice on the other line.

'Yes?'

'I am from the Council. Are you at the shop?'

'Not at the moment.'

'Can we meet in front of it in twenty minutes? I have an urgent letter for you.'

Eric Quercer liked the room he had been given on the first floor. Small by North American standards but anything in Europe would be anyway. The view was onto the green park extending behind the Duchess Hotel. The famous Cannizaro Park he had been reading about on the plane. The one he had a month or so to explore while he made the necessary preparations. He laid out his clothes on the bed and went to the bathroom to display his toiletries in one corner. He was careless about it, almost creasing his shirts in doing so or knocking the bottle of aftershave in the sink. Instead, he carefully checked the small indoor palm tree in one corner and the tall philodendron. Eric Quercer was a meticulous man when it came to plants and flowers. He dismissed the rest as less important unless it helped him put his hands on more green and flowery treasures. He did not waste time and left the room quickly counting the doors leading to the end of the corridor towards the south of the building. Close enough but not too close to the room of interest. He then walked back to the grand staircase leading down to the ground floor. The hotel's attempt to revive its neoclassical look and Regent-era memories was impressive. The corridor walls were striped in white and lavender. Idyllic paintings and pencil sketches from centuries ago filled the space in between the white hotel doors and every now and then a small white coffee table was placed below with a nice plant to keep the pale pastel colours from becoming bland and boring. Eric looked closely at one of the plants and then his face turned in disdain. Plastic. It felt wrong. He moved and went down to the bar for a gin and tonic, to gather his thoughts.

'Are you here on business or pleasure?' asked the barman in such a cliché manner.

'Business, mainly.' he replied sipping his drink. 'I heard though Cannizaro Park is a pleasure to enjoy at this time of year.'

'Oh indeed. The festival is only a month away. There is a great build up to it both here at the hotel and also in Wimbledon Village.'

'Oh, a festival? What a joy!' lied Eric Quercer.

The five-day festival he had read about would be his cover. He had all the details in advance thanks to the letter from the mysterious sender. The man who knew about the special flower he was looking for would be attending and by then his trap would be set.

'What is your line of business?' asked the barman.

Eric hid his boredom. He also found the barman's intrusion a little bit irritating.

'I am a horticulturist. Meeting the Royal Horticultural Society in London.'

He did not have to hide who he was. Hiding in plain sight, as they say.

'You could not have chosen a better place. One of the owners of Cannizaro House, what this place was called before it became a hotel, was a member himself and a fine horticulturist too. He brought a lot of new species here to plant in the park. From South America. Canada. Even Japan. Edward Kenneth Wilson.'

'Really?' pretended Eric.

He was not faking his interest. He was simply pretending to ignore knowledge he was fully aware of. He let the barman continue.

'Yes. He made most of the final touches to expand the park as it is today. The side entrance to the park, which is open to the public, has his initials above the iron gate.'

'I'd better check it out.' added Eric.

'Will you be having dinner here?' asked the barman.

'Yes please.'

Eric sipped his drink while the barman put through his reservation. The open space of the ground floor had only a few guests here and there enjoying a chat and drink in peaceful solitude. Eric made a mental note not to sit at the bar next time.

By the time he had finished his drink and walked out into the park, the sky had become a little cloudy and overcast. He put his Barbour jacket on and walked to one side of the hotel, following the paved footpath until it crumbled into a dirty track moving away from the hotel. He turned around and looked up. The window he stared at was easily accessible from here if he had trouble getting through the front door. He only had to be sure the room he was looking at was the one chosen for his target. He glanced around. The park was pretty calm and nobody was in sight. There would be more people during the festival. More suspects to chase while he moved to the second phase of his plan.

He walked on towards a wide, almost circular space of green area. It was the last clearing in this direction before entering the deep woods of the park. He found a bench under a cherry tree and sat down to contemplate the Duchess Hotel. He knew that until he put his hands on the documents he would not know much about where to look. However, he knew the mysterious sender had chosen him for what he was good at. Plants. Eric was sure there were clues in the park he could not miss. Maybe there was a perfect plan in which the gardens, the trees, the flower beds, had all been arranged. He glanced up and the rustling sound of leaves in the gentle breeze in contrast with the cloudy sky reassured him he would savour victory before he knew it. No matter what the friends of the club would say.

Enrico waited for the Council representative for more than twenty minutes. He rushed all the way back from lunch and he was now sitting at one of the tables in the seating area of his bakery. He was still wearing his chef jacket. He had cleared some of the piles of cardboard boxes laid strewn around and even had time to make himself another shot of espresso coffee. His LaGaggia machine did not fail. It grounded the beans as it should, brewing the aroma with a roast flavour not too deep but strong and with enough punch. He wondered if the water used by the machine was different from the one he used for making the dough. Perhaps his Polish helper connected two different water mains. He dismissed the silly thought, glanced at his Nokia 3310 and looked out into the street, still busy with the post-lunch crowd.

Enrico looked at his shop and searched for something to remind him of home. The choices made by the furniture company were not really his thing. Rustic straw baskets, big pepper grinders, jars of chillies in oil which he was advised not to eat, an old Chianti fiasco. They were nice but they felt rather plastic to the touch and they looked worse on the shelf he was now staring at, half decorated, half empty. Enrico reached for the cup of espresso and took a few sips to think it over. Maybe he was overthinking. Things like this took time. He had to settle in. For the second time since meeting Viviane, he thought the florist could be the best person to ask for some advice on how to decorate and perhaps she would be honest with him.

The tiny brass bell at the entrance rang its cheery tinkle again. Its sound echoed in the empty bakery and Enrico woke up from his thoughts. He turned and smiled automatically in the direction of the entrance. A chubby woman in her late thirties had entered the bakery. She wore a flashy pink cardigan and a pair of black leggings, tight in all the wrong places. Her white badge showed a big watermill wheel, but the writing was unreadable from a long distance. Enrico stood up and walked to the counter, to come closer to his new guest.

'Can I speak to Mr Latreva?' said the woman as she smiled broadly.

'LoTrova, *signora*!' replied Enrico with a polite nod hardly masking the annoyance. 'LoTrova. At your service.'

The woman nodded vaguely and took a few shy steps forward. Enrico read discretion in her eyes. She took a few papers from a leather messenger bag and placed some copies on the counter nearby. Enrico walked toward her to get a closer look.

'I am Lorraine. I am from the Council.' resumed the woman. 'I presume you received my emails?'

'Emails? ...emails, emails....err...can't remember...'

Enrico realised he might have struggled to tell her he did not have a computer. Well, he had one he always sat in front of at the Wimbledon Library down the hill. He could not remember though the last time he checked his email account. He did remember her name though.

'Lorraine, you said? About the food and hygiene licensing, right?'

'Correct, Mr Letruova'

'LoTrova!'

'Mr LoTrova,' continued the woman filling her lungs with air of importance. 'I am afraid you have not submitted the forms in full when applying for the license and you have not completed the last checks required before opening.'

'So?' shrugged Enrico.

'You are not technically allowed to open until this is addressed and I see you are already preparing for an opening day. I thought I'd clarify matters before they are source of any disappointment to you.'

'My grand opening isn't probably until another two weeks.' Reassured Enrico. 'I am just trying to get a flavour of the neighbourhood, what people like, what they don't. Do you want to try my *focaccia al rosmarino*? Or one *bicerin*, some espresso coffee with chocolate and cream?'

'I can get a mocha at the coffee shop down the road.' was the woman's dry reply.

Enrico sensed the same tone he heard from Mr Wyczenski. Dismissal in favour of something he could vouch was not as good as his.

'Now you are insulting me!' said Enrico half-joking, half-irritated.

'Here's the official communication from the Council' continued the woman with persistence.

She pointed at the copy of the letter she placed on the counter.

'We request you do not open the bakery until an inspection is scheduled next month or so.'

'A month?' jumped Enrico. 'What am I going to do with a closed shop for a month apart from paying rent for nothing?'

'If you have a complaint to make, phone number and email are on the letter I just gave you. Goodbye!'

The woman from the Council left as swiftly as she came and moved along the high street with an air of self-importance until she was out of view. Enrico was left stranded. He picked up the letter and read and reread the content. A bitter taste formed in his mouth mixed with incredulity. The espresso he had just sipped was now turning too sour or perhaps it was his imagination. The Italian baker could not believe what had just happened in those last few minutes. He wondered what he was going to do now. Waiting another month meant stretching his finances. He stood still looking out of the large window onto the street, the cars, the passers-by, things that were now starting to be familiar. It somehow felt as if the dream of building his home and business was starting to melt. When he read the letter again, he checked the fee he had to pay. It was not a small amount, and the moment it came out of his bank account in a month, or whenever this damned inspection would happen, he would remain in the red for months before he could start making a decent living.

He was about to swear loudly in the loneliness of the bakery when the bell rang again as the door opened for another customer. Enrico froze, unable to accept another surprise.

'Is this how you get things done? Leaning on that counter?'

Viviane's friendly voice came as a refresher. Her rosy looks and the broad, composed smile almost brought in the perfume of her flowers with her. The look on Enrico's face and his muted expression gave it away in no time.

'What's the matter?' enquired Viviane, her smile suddenly clouded. 'Hey, where's all the energy gone?'

'Read this!' said Enrico.

He handed the letter to Viviane. It now looked a little bit crumpled from Enrico's tense grip.

'And I thought I had escaped bureaucracy…' he added looking outside disinterested.

Viviane picked up the Council's letter. Her other arm was wrapped around her waist, giving some support to her stance as she held the letter at eye level. She turned it over to look at the back and then checked the front again.

'Well, these are the regulations, Enrico.' concluded Viviane almost in surrender. 'I also had to fill in tons of paperwork and pay the right licenses for my shop. It was even more complicated back then.'

She glanced at the Italian baker and knew the facts would not help change the preoccupied look on Enrico's face, worried about business failure. She stood there reflecting, her eyes first set on him and then on the letter. She then came up with an idea.

'I tell you what.' she said. 'Why don't you come and join the league of independent shopkeepers from Wimbledon Village?'

'The league? What are you, Batman and Robin?' joked Enrico as he turned around to hear about the latest extravaganza from the village.

'The real name is Wimbledon Association of Independent Shops. WAIS, in short. Actually, I have just dropped in now to invite you to our General Meeting tomorrow night. Maybe someone there may be able to help. What do you think?'

Enrico did not understand how he deserved such cordiality and support from Viviane. She had been very helpful since their first meeting earlier that day, and he did not find her intrusion discomforting. The bakery was the reason he was here and if there was no bakery, there would be no Enrico here in Wimbledon Village. He was figuring out what he had to lose. If he did not take this opportunity, he would face a month of uncertainty.

'What kind of help?'

'They have connections. We can make sure your bakery gets the success it deserves.'

Enrico grinned. This league, or WAIS, as she called it, was shrouded in mystery and he was about to tease if it were a criminal organisation perhaps. He thought not. He needed all the help he could get.

'Dear Viviane, my English shop neighbour,' he replied putting up his best or maybe worst English posh accent. 'you have convinced me. Let's hear what Batman and Robin have to say!'

'Great! And please work on your jokes a bit...'

'Anything else?' commented Enrico as if to stop the commentary.

'Yes! Do you always wear that chef jacket even when you go out?'

The evening was quiet along the Ridgeway and the sky was turning gradually to deep tones of blue. The pale shades of yellow behind Emmanuel Church announced another early Spring day was over and the weak backlight beyond the hill had turned the church and all the surrounding buildings into a black, shapeless shadow burnt against the clear sky. Enrico watched the colours change as he waited on the corner of Lingfield Road. The fresh night air made him shiver slightly, feeling the difference in temperature from the sunny weather of the last few days. He somehow could not bear to part with his baker's outfit and he had carefully picked one of his clean, freshly pressed chef jackets for the occasion. He kept it open this time, to look casual. Underneath he was wearing a light blue shirt. He did change his trousers though and wore a pair of camel colour chino trousers. He looked at his watch and it was almost seven thirty.

The Wimbledon Association of Independent Shops, or WAIS for short, did not have an office per se. On a given weekday they met regularly in the cafeteria of the Wimbledon Village Club on Lingfield Road, preferably when no social events were planned and the building was quieter than usual. Enrico looked at the entrance in front of him and he could see there were no signs outside. Viviane told him they did not do a lot of self-promotion, but they did a lot for local businesses day in day out, discussing issues, organising funds. It was an informal association and everyone who owned a local shop was welcome to join. Viviane had promised Enrico to introduce him to some of the nice folk she knew. Some were Wimbledonians by birth while others came from afar and had been living and breathing Wimbledon for quite a few years. She was sure some of them could help him with his problems with the Council and maybe chip in with ideas on some of his financial worries. Enrico had not dismissed the idea as a stupid one, but as the minutes raced towards seven thirty, he started to question the purpose of it all. Perhaps he would be asked for some favours in return. Maybe he should have brought some sweet pastries or printed a series of discount coupons, to gain favour with the village folk.

Viviane appeared in the distance, walking briskly on the narrow pavement. Her auburn hair and red lipstick flashed intermittently as she passed in front of the window lights from the shops still open along the Ridgeway. She wore a similar pair of cigarette trousers but of an ash grey colour. A light, emerald green cashmere sweater wrapped her body in a gentle cuddle, respecting her full slim figure. She waved at him to announce her arrival from afar. He waved back and then took his time to check the building they were about to enter. It was split into two or three sections, with each having a pointy roof shooting up in the sky, and it bore a dull brown colour. It had nothing to do with some of the buildings on the high street with their flat tops or Regent-like style. Enrico thought half of it looked like a church but then the owner or the builder had changed his mind and built a gothic mansion. Enrico could not see any plaque near the entrance apart from a sign saying 'Museum of Wimbledon'. He waited for Viviane to lead the way.

It turned out there was more than one entrance. She took him around the corner and through a tiny front courtyard guarded by tall and narrow white windows. A door to the right led them into a series of small corridors until they reached a well sized seating area lit by a suffused light. The short light pine bar and the maroon carpet contributed to creating a cosy and warm feeling. Viviane said hello to the man at the bar who gave a friendly reply as he dried a couple of tea cups. Enrico nodded shyly. The place was quiet, but a gentle murmur reminded guests the place was not dead. Most of the customers spread across the seating area looked the same age as Enrico or maybe a little older. Most of them were making their way to one side of the room and queuing to step into another room through a wide double door.

'Are they all there, Frank?' asked Viviane while crossing the seating area.

'I think we are waiting for a few more but everyone is settling in the Lecture Hall. Coffees and teas are on the table.'

He nodded at the wide double door.

'Great. This is Enrico!'

The barman lifted his dirty rag to welcome him. Enrico smiled shyly to acknowledge it. He then followed suit and walked with Viviane towards the entrance to the Lecture Hall. The whole room had the feeling of a cinema or theatre bar and the audience was slowly wandering in to take a seat for the show.

To Enrico's surprise, the size of the hall was daunting compared to the cramped or compact size of the previous room. It was a cavernous hall where you could see the high pointed ceiling with its wooden beams. The noise of simple chatter was amplified loudly and Enrico had to adjust his hearing before he could make out Viviane's instructions to follow him. The hall was long with a gothic style window at one far end and a theatre stage at the other. The length was impressive and it reminded Enrico of a church nave. He thought he visualised the shape from outside and he wondered once again whether this had once been the inside of a church.

The members of the WAIS were a large crowd. They were busy gathering around one end of the hall, underneath the gothic window, where some of the guests scoffed the free coffee, tea and biscuits. The rest of the nave had rows of seats laid out for the occasion, ending up in front of a small space at the feet of the stage where a flip chart and a few long tables were joined together for some sort of presentation. Leaflets were piled on the other end of the tables and there were also copies on each chair. A middle-aged woman was busy finishing the distribution. Enrico could not read them but the four-letter word in capital letters showed him the association, no matter how informal, was well organised in true British efficiency. An elderly man was at the flipchart, busy writing bullet points and some form of agenda.

Viviane kept pulling Enrico forward and he nervously stumbled behind her. She stopped in her tracks as if she knew what she was doing. They were both now standing by the elderly man who had not noticed their arrival. His wrinkled and creased skin on his hands and neck showed a man who had stood the wind of time. Still, his pure white hair was well kept and tidy in a medium-long taper cut. He kept his posture composed as the strong hand delicately shaped the round letters of the words he wished to convey. His blue navy tweed jacket was slightly faded but still looked chic, with a red handkerchief in the left breast pocket and a grey snood giving him a bohemian flair to fight his aging years.

'Hello, Dr Watkins.' said Viviane 'How are you today?'

The elderly man turned politely with an air of mistrust of whoever was interrupting him, but he soon brushed it off when he recognised Viviane's face.

'Miss Leighwood! How nice to see you!' replied Dr Watkins with a warm, paced voice. 'When was the last time you joined us? Flower business doing well, I suppose.'

'Can't complain, Dr Watkins.' chuckled Viviane. 'I actually brought a new arrival to Wimbledon Village with me. Let me introduce you to Enrico LoTrova.'

Viviane moved aside and placed her hand on Enrico's arm to welcome him into the discussion. The Italian baker felt exposed and pulled a nervous smile, raising his hand clumsily. Dr Watkins eyed him with a stern but kind-hearted look. There was an air about him filled with knowledge and savoir faire.

'He is about to open a bakery on the high street.' continued Viviane. 'I thought he may find our meetings useful.'

'How wonderful!' burst out Dr Watkins with a controlled tone of voice.

His face suddenly lit up, showing a white smile, and his wrinkled cheeks seemed to take some colouring from the excitement.

'It is always nice to meet new people joining the community. I am Dr John Watkins, nice to meet you. I head the WAIS as chairman, but I am also the curator of the Museum of Wimbledon.'

'*Piacere!*' replied Enrico. 'Pleasure is all mine! Viviane spoke about you and your association, and I thought, why not.'

'Why not indeed? Your accent is familiar. Italian?'

'Yes I am. Just been here a few months and I hope to open my bakery pretty soon. *La Pagnotta.* Did you notice it by any chance at number 9/b?'

'Oh yes, I did.'

Dr Watkins was not a man shy to hide his excitement.

'Oh, my goodness. Our association is definitely becoming more and more international. We have a few people from other parts of the world. We all share the same interest. We all do what we can to keep independent trade alive here. Would you care for a chocolate digestive biscuit?'

Dr Watkins put the marker down and slowly turned to reach the nearby table.

'What's a *d-a-i-j-ai-stive*?' whispered Enrico to Viviane as they started to make way to follow him.

Enrico did not manage to finish his comment or wait for Viviane's answer. All of a sudden two small plates were pushed in front of them with two oatmeal biscuits covered in chocolate on one side.

'Here. Please try it.' offered Dr Watkins.

Enrico took the plate observing the food offered under Viviane's watchful eye. She smirked at the oddity surrounding the Italian baker.

'It's a biscuit, Enrico. Not a cake.' she joked with a mouth half-full and crumbs at the corner of her mouth.

'Very nice…' answered Enrico taking small bites.

He felt the semi-sweet crumbs softening on his tongue, leaving the oat and chocolate aftertaste in his mouth. Dr Watkins's eager eye made him think he was expecting an opinion sooner than later.

'Very very nice! Thank you!' he repeated keeping eye contact with Dr Watkins.

'Glad you like it!'

'Dr Watkins is a big chocolate digestive fan, if you had not realised Enrico.' added Viviane to make Enrico less confused. 'He eats them any time of the day and makes desserts out of them too. Dr Watkins, I don't think they have digestive biscuits in Italy.'

'Shame, it would be a great addition to their heritage. Whereabouts are you from, Mr LoTrova?'

'Central part of Italy.'

'Nice. How come you have travelled all the way to Wimbledon?'

'My work led me here. Opening a bakery was my dream and here I had the chance.'

'Fine, noble reason.' replied Mr Watkins. 'Say, shall we get ready and take a seat? The group will definitely want to know what you do and how we can help, Mr LoTrova.'

Enrico was happy to have made this rather unusual acquaintance with Dr Watkins. The elderly gentleman pointed at a few seats in the middle row nearby, reminding them again to make themselves more comfortable, get a cup of tea or coffee or help themselves to more digestive biscuits. He then moved back to the flip chart to finish the last bullet point and with an agile twist of his body he turned around to face the audience, who by now was settling in or grabbing the last cups of tea. He clapped his hands to get everyone's attention. The meeting was about to start.

The WAIS was modest in numbers but still larger than what Enrico had expected. He could not fathom the number of independent shops scattered on and around the one mile stretch of Wimbledon High Street. Hairdressers, tradesmen, pub landlords, restaurant owners, property realtors, specialist physicians. Enrico recognised a self-sufficient community that found strength in numbers. As Dr Watkins went through the agenda, from presenting a new discount scheme for restaurants to an open discussion on whether to allow the opening of another estate agent franchise, Enrico realised Viviane was right. The association was indeed well organised and strong enough to support one another. Almost all of them had a business they found safe and enjoyable to run. The Italian baker recognised himself in that. He recognised the possibility.

'And now let's move to the last item of the agenda.' announced Dr Watkins after a short ten-minute break. 'We have the Cannizaro Festival coming up next month, as you all know. The Duchess Hotel has informed us of the participation quota for the WAIS for this year, of course a higher one, God bless them. Enrolment is open for any independent business to have a stall on the grounds of Cannizaro Park...'

'This is what I was talking about.' whispered Viviane to Enrico.

'What? A festival? How is that going to solve my problems?'

'Don't despise it, mister. Four or five days of events and music. There are many people coming to this fair and it is a great chance for you to show off your trade. I will be there.'

Viviane went back to listening to Dr Watkins going through the details. Enrico kept his eyes on her. The English florist was resourceful. He toyed briefly with the idea. A fair where you had your own stall. Perhaps she was right. It could work.

'…Remember we have limited numbers, carried on Dr Watkins. You can come and see me once we finish but I would not mind running a quick poll by raise of hand. Who in the room is likely to enrol?'

Viviane put her hand up decisively, followed by a few other shy ones. Enrico looked around and then he crossed Viviane's gaze. Her smug face told him she was expecting something.

'You have bread to sell, Enrico.' she added.

The Italian baker wavered. He did not have much to lose and by the number of hands raised, he could tell this was a popular choice and that places were numbered. He raised his hand, looking at Viviane rather than at the stage ahead. He had made his choice.

The rest of the evening was left to idle chat in the lecture hall. Enrico followed Viviane around, dropping in on half-started conversations and listening to what he could follow. He met one of the local reverends from St Mary's Church, who organised market fairs on the grounds outside the church. There was also a representative from the bar at the Royal Wimbledon Golf Course. He also met someone from the Dog and Fox pub, which apparently was one of the two oldest pubs in Wimbledon with the second being the Rose and Crown. Enrico was surprised to meet Mr Wyczenski at some point. The tradesman had been a member of the association for a few years and he was happy to meet the Italian baker outside working hours.

'You are in good hands. Great place to start from!' he commented, giving Enrico a strong pat on his back that pushed him forward and knocked him off balance.

He laughed coarsely showing his yellow teeth. Enrico wondered if he should mention his financial trouble. However, there was something in Mr Wyczenski's attitude that told him the tradesman himself must have also gone through this before. They probably all had. The association was indeed a mix of different people from different backgrounds and trades, but they all had something in common.

The chatter in the lecture hall buzzed for another hour or so and it slowly died out as people finally left to go home. By then, Enrico's memory was just a fuzzy picture of names he had heard or faces he had met. The Italian baker stuck around until closing time, mainly because Viviane insisted on helping Dr Watkins wrap up before going for a drink at the bar nearby. She was close to him and there was probably a friendship going back some time. He longed to join this family of theirs too and throughout the evening he did not miss a chance to say thank you to the kind florist.

'So, did it all make sense?' asked Dr Watkins as all three sat at a small table.

The bar was not completely empty. A few associated members were sitting at the other tables, having changed their mind to get a drink before leaving. One for the road, they said. There were others Enrico did not recognise, probably locals hanging around.

'Yes. And thank you.' added Enrico in appreciation. 'Is this your club then?'

'Not mine although I am a member by default. This building has many purposes, but it shares a common history. This is where the Wimbledon Village Club has stood since 1858 thanks to Joseph Toynbee. A place for the community to thrive together. It makes sense that the WAIS, a Wimbledon institution like many others, meets here.'

'How long have you been leading the WAIS?' asked Enrico. 'Do you have a shop of your own?'

'The museum is his shop!' joked Viviane.

'That is true.' replied Dr Watkins. 'But they needed someone independent to chair the WAIS. Someone with less self-interest perhaps. I was happy to be that someone, so I said yes and that was ten or fifteen years ago. I remember Viviane opening her flower shop, but I guess from my looks you could tell I have lived in Wimbledon for a while.'

He let a light chuckle out after his own joke. He did not jolt. His hair did not move. It stayed composed like the gentleman that he was.

'Is the museum here too?' Enrico wondered.

'Yes. Upstairs. This place sometimes looks bigger than it is. Would you care to have a look?'

Enrico and Viviane agreed to the offer full of curiosity and complicity. Viviane had seen it before. Yet, she did not mind a visit, especially if led by Dr Watkins. When you had been in Wimbledon for a while, it was easy to forget they had a museum and some history to talk about, no matter how brief it may be.

Dr Watkins led them out of the bar and into the main entry corridor of the Wimbledon Club. The museum was up two narrow flights of stairs. The entrance at the top of the stairs was an arched solid wooden door and to Enrico it looked like the secret entrance to an attic. The Museum of Wimbledon was a large room taking space under the bare wooden beams supporting the tilted Gothic roofs of the building. It was an open space divided into smaller sections with glass displays and movable partitions, from which multiple corridors formed and led in different directions. Colourful rug runners snaked through, building you a path which probably followed some chronological order or theme telling the story of Wimbledon from its prehistoric era to modern times. Enrico could spot wooden artefacts and old black and white photographs. For a small place, it seemed Dr Watkins had been able to gather a lot of history into it.

'Welcome to my humble abode!' announced Dr Watkins turning the lights on.

There was a short desk by the entrance with an empty cup. The ticket office, Enrico guessed, by seeing the cash registry and a small pop-up shelf covered with leaflets repeating the word 'Wimbledon' all over.

'A lot of stuff, Dr Watkins!' commented Enrico as he and Viviane stepped further inside, each taking a different route of the museum.

'I have grown fond of this place, so I am always looking for new clues from Wimbledon's past. One day this place may not be big enough.'

His voice echoed around the attic room, nice and clear, while Enrico looked at a series of flint stones from the Stone Age, then some rust-coloured pieces of what seemed iron knives and oxidised brooches.

'It is nice to come here again. I always forget.' said Viviane looking at a picture of Queen Victoria's and the German Kaiser's visit on Wimbledon Common in the nineteenth century.

'Well, just like your shops out there, I also need visitors to keep things running. It is not bad. We get by.'

'Does the name Wimbledon mean anything?' shouted Enrico not sure if he was too far away to be heard.

'The most recent name we have, dating from 967, is a mix of Anglo-Saxon and Celtic. *Wimbedounyng* or something like that. It means "Wynnman's Hill".'

'Who is Wynnman?' asked Viviane

'Probably a local chieftain. We have no record of that. All of Wimbledon history becomes more detailed after 1086 when it appears in the Domesday Book and from there we have more written evidence.'

Both Viviane and Enrico wandered around the museum, bumping into each other from time to time. As they followed the history of Wimbledon to more recent times, the amount of written evidence and genuine artefacts multiplied. Dr Watkins joined them as they both looked at the plastic model of what appeared to be a neoclassical building from the eighteenth century.

'One of the Lord Manor's houses, built by the Earl of Spencer.' commented the curator in answer to a silent question. 'Demolished a long time ago, but we have so many sketches and drawings we have a feeling of how it looked inside and outside.'

'Do you have anything on the place where the festival is taking place? What was the name?'

'Cannizaro Park.' answered Viviane.

'That's the one. Such an odd name…'

'You are right in saying so, Enrico. It is Italian.' said Dr Watkins.

Enrico frowned. The pronunciation was throwing him off. It sounded Italian but somehow misspelt.

'Follow me.' added Dr Watkins.

Dr Watkins took them to one side of the museum where another plastic model was laid out and protected by a glass case from both sides. It had a white building in the centre and then a rectangular green space beyond it, all built to scale. The caption to the right, half-way up the glass panel, gave a brief history and it had the words 'Cannizaro House' and 'Cannizaro Park' in upper case as the header. Enrico could now see the name written down and smiled to himself how the name was missing an 'z'.

'Surely the name is not exactly British. Cannizzaro is a surname from Southern Italy, but I think you missed a "z" there.' the baker pointed out.

'Well done, Mr LoTrova. You are not far off.' complimented Dr Watkins, a satisfied look on his face. 'The name is linked to a story of unrequited love between a young Scottish noble woman and a Sicilian of aristocrat origin. Her name was Sophia Johnstone and she met Francisco Platamone, Duke of Cannizzaro, who had moved to England to represent the Sicilian monarchy in some role. They were soon married, but more out of convenience and they were often in and out of love. They moved in together in what was then called Warren House, near Wimbledon, and lived there as tenants for twenty years or more. Apparently, she was fond of the arts and in particular music. She held many parties and musical festivities at the house, which to this day are still celebrated with festivals at the park. Unfortunately, Francisco ran away to a mistress in Italy and broke Sophia's heart who lived alone in Warren House until her death. However, by that time she had inherited the title of "Duchess of Cannizzaro" through marriage. After her death, when the surveyors were recording house owners and tenants for the census, someone started using the label "Cannizzaro House" or "Cannazerro House" which over the years has changed spelling many times until the form we see today.'.

Enrico listened. That story fascinated him.

'Is this where The Duchess Hotel is?' he asked.

'Yes. Cannizaro House is the Duchess Hotel.' said Viviane pointing at the white building on the plastic model.

'So, the house has been around for quite some time.' added Enrico. 'What's its story? Does it have a ghost like English and Scottish castles?'

'I only stick to historical facts, Enrico.' pledged Dr Watkins with a raise of hands. 'I don't delve into folklore and legends that much, if not for amusement. Cannizaro House was built in 1710 by William Browne and had many owners and tenants for hundreds of years before it became The Duchess Hotel. It was built on the eastern edge of what used to be the Old Park.'

'Is that the green park behind it?' asked Viviane.

'That is Cannizaro Park and it is only a fraction of the size of the Old Park which extended from the golf course down to Copse Hill. The Old Park used to be the hunting grounds for the Lord of the Manor, back in the 1500s, until they started selling the land off to owners like William Browne, who built grand houses still around today, like Cannizaro House and Westside House. Both land and houses were leased as a source of income. By the early twentieth century, the Old Park had disappeared and most of it had been sold off bit by bit for house development. Cannizaro Park and the Royal Wimbledon Golf Course is what we have left of it today.'

Enrico was impressed. The curator knew his subject matter more than he thought, or probably what surprised Enrico the most was the depth of information on a small place like Wimbledon Village. The cluttered attic room around him was the proof.

They carried on chatting and walked around the space surrounding the plastic model. Viviane and Dr Watkins discussed a few details of the fair. Enrico kept to himself, taking in more of Wimbledon's history. One picture caught his interest at first sight. It was a black and white picture of a girl and a dog standing on a well-kept lawn in front of a classical statue with a beautiful mansion in the background although not in full view. A small caption read again 'Cannizaro House seen from the park'. The caption traced the picture back to the 1920s. Enrico looked at the picture from another time and dimension.

'Ah, the last private owner of Cannizaro House!' came Dr Watkins's voice boisterous from behind.

'Mr and Mrs Wilson, that is?'

'Yes.'

'Is Mrs Wilson the one in the picture?'

'No, no, Enrico. That's their only daughter, Hilary, with her dog Adele. She spent every day in the park before her marriage. She loved being there with the dog running around. I think she said more than once it was the most beautiful thing she had ever seen.'

'The statue?' prompted Enrico again pointing at the classical statue.

'No, no. The dog. Adele was like a friend to her, keeping her company in a park so vast you could get lost.'

'What about the statue?'

'That's Diana and The Fawn. It has been in the park ground since the mid-nineteenth century. The Wilsons owned Cannizaro House and Cannizaro Park from 1920 until the late Forties. After their death, Cannizaro House was inherited by their only child. She sold it to the Council and then later it was turned into a hotel. The Wilson family were the last people who actually lived in it.'

'They made Cannizaro House and its park the gem it is today.' added Viviane. 'They were both keen horticulturists, especially Mr Wilson.'

Dr Watkins moved closer to Enrico and pulled his reading glasses from his right breast pocket to get a better look at the picture.

'Mr Wilson, if my memory does not fail me, was a member of the Rhododendron Society and also key contributor to the Royal Horticultural Society.' he explained holding the glasses up and then looking away at Enrico. 'He and Mrs Wilson planted most of the oak trees and exotic plants you see blossoming in spring and summer. For example, take

43

rhododendrons and azaleas. Although they existed in Great Britain at the times of the Ice Age, they disappeared from this country until they were brought back in from China and replanted here in great numbers.'

'…And Cannizaro Park has the perfect soil for this. Acid gravel soil at the top over a layer of clay. Am I right?' commented Viviane rhetorically.

A fact she knew well and did not need confirmation.

'Yes, my dear Viviane, and you probably know best.' confirmed Dr Watkins.

'*Boh*! My knowledge sticks to flour and yeast.' added Enrico humorously.

'Rhododendrons can be invasive but are great for landscaping.' carried on Viviane. 'Azaleas too, being part of the same family. Mr Wilson, being a keen gardener, probably wanted to turn Cannizaro Park into something more beautiful.'

'Absolutely true!' confirmed Dr Watkins with a sense of excitement in his voice. 'He added a series of "gardens" where he planted all kinds of flowers, plants and trees. However, between the sale and the opening of the hotel, after succumbing to all kinds of weather and in some cases neglect, some species were lost or damaged. The management of the hotel is trying to salvage what they can.'

'Sad story!' echoed Viviane to remind everyone of her green finger.

'No need to feel saddened about it.' replied Enrico in awe to the expertise in the room. 'I am sure it is still worth seeing. I will definitely go.'

'And you will!' laughed Viviane. 'I will get the paperwork to you tomorrow and you can then officially enrol for the Cannizaro Festival. You can then start selling your bread there. Make a name for yourself. Earn your first income and open that bakery!'

Enrico smiled. She made it sound so easy and simple.

'Marvellous!' cheered Dr Watkins. 'How about some tea and chocolate digestives to celebrate?'

Eric Quercer liked his meat cooked rare and at the right temperature. He carefully pricked the thick steak on his plate to check that pinkish and bluish colour he had been wetting his lips for. He then picked up his knife and fork and skilfully cut a triangle off one end. The waiter felt under pressure and almost trembled when the Canadian looked up with a malicious expression. His mouth was still for a few seconds and then the waiter noticed him chewing slowly, savouring the moment as the piece of steak melted in his mouth.

'Excellent!' said the Canadian with a changed face, brighter. 'Compliments to the chef!'

The waiter sighed in relief and withdrew with a bow of his head.

The Canadian resumed his tasting, picking some of the vegetables and dipping them into the port-reduced, peppery sauce. He felt the vegetables were a little bit overcooked. He took a few bites and then put his cutlery aside to drink some of the Malbec on the table. Wine was at the right temperature. Food and drink were acceptable. His biggest criticism was the flower decoration at the centre of the table. The daisies were wilting and the heather was on the verge of drying up. The whole green finger approach at the Duchess Hotel was not to his taste. He also thought Cannizaro Park could be kept better than it was. Thinning rose bushes, messy round hedges and empty patches that deserved some colour. He still did not understand how books rated the horticultural history of this park as something to remember. Everywhere he looked he felt something needed fixing, and he even thought of getting hold of someone from the Friends of Cannizaro, if they were the people in charge. Probably amateurs, he thought, like the staff at this hotel, or the visitors coming to this park pretending to spot the differences between oaks and chestnuts, rhododendrons and sycamores. He cut another morsel of his steak and gnawed at it before gulping it down quickly.

All around him, the orangery was flooded with a suffused candlelight, flickering on the tangerine faces of the few guests down for a late dinner. The darkness coming from the glass panels of the veranda shrouded the venue with a church-like atmosphere, accompanied by the low murmur of voices, the distant sound of plates and glasses, feeble but omnipresent. Eric looked outside into the darkness of the park and he could only make out the bluish aura of the sky as it started to darken further into the late night. The candle on his table trembled gently and reflected its light against the opaque glass, highlighting Eric's neck and chin and the contents of the table. He had a notepad and a smartphone next to his plate. The former was open roughly in the middle, with scribbles and sketches of a map. It covered one and a half pages and it showed a large irregular rectangular shape. A header in capital letters read 'Cannizaro Park'. The smartphone vibrated against the tablecloth, almost slipping away like a snake in the desert. Eric read the caller's name and hesitated before answering. He put his fork down and glanced around to check nobody was looking. He picked the smartphone up and took a large gulp of his red wine before sliding the green 'Answer' icon on the screen.

'Hello?' he said.

'Eric!' said the voice on the other end of the line.

'Hello.' replied Eric with indifference towards the caller.

'Are you in London town?' continued the voice. 'Preparing for the walk of shame when you return?'

'Very funny!' was Eric's dry response. 'Why are you calling?'

'I am here at the club with a few of our fellow members. We thought of you at our after-lunch drink, thought how crazy of you to prove yourself wrong.'

'We've had this discussion already. You really called me about this?'

'Well, partly yes. We also wanted to check your progress, if any. Although asking how you are getting along in your ghost hunt sounds ridiculous to me. But the guys here pressed me to make the call.'

'Progressing nicely. I am close to reviewing a few specimens and about to show you how things really stand.'

'Oooo…sounds scary. We are all scared here!'

Some voices in the background echoed 'ooh' sounds of horror and panic. Eric could not stand the mockery. It felt worse than that day at the club when his claims were publicly derided, scorned.

'Have you finished? What do you want?'

'Wow, you sound like a mean Raging Bull. Or should I say, Green Giant.'

The voice laughed at its own joke. Eric kept quiet.

'No, honestly, you do sound mean and committed.' resumed the voice drowning down his laughs. 'Progressing nicely, eh? I look forward to what you will dare to bring back.'

The voice was changing tone gradually. More serious, more provocative.

'Your absurd claim could, actually will, bring shame to your forefathers, especially your distant relative and his contribution to all gardeners in the world. You know better than me. The flower you are looking for does not exist in nature. It is one of those big hoaxes people easily believe in.'

'You simply don't believe a word Edward K. Wilson wrote? He who spent more time collecting rhododendrons and similar from the Far East than the two of us put together. How could you dismiss a claim coming from someone respected within the Royal Horticulture Society, here in the United Kingdom? How could you be so certain?'

'Listen to yourself. You are so convinced you had to bet all of your family fortune and fly across the Atlantic Ocean to prove your point. I am asking you now. Withdraw before it is too late, before you do anything stupid, and make a fool of yourself.'

'It won't happen like that. Not now that I am so close to being right.'

'Is that what your piece of paper says? Your thousand documents and papyruses from another century? Eric, you will never find something that does not exist in nature. Maybe drawn on paper. But not in any garden on this planet.'

'We'll see…'

Eric hung up annoyed. He slammed the phone down on the table and nervously drank some more wine. The thickness of the red liquid punched his throat and left an acidic taste in his mouth. He coughed, scared it went down the wrong way. He placed his napkin over his mouth and closed his eyes. What a nuisance call that was. Even here, thousands of miles away, they bragged of how righteous they were and how he would be a failure. How dare they challenge him every step of the way, Eric thought. He was seeking in nature what man had not discovered yet. The digital world may have photographed the whole world, but flowers and plants blossomed and died and blossomed and ultimately evolved. If nothing was in favour or against the claims of Edward K. Wilson, then he could be the one to ascertain the truth.

Eric pulled a letter from his back pocket. He put another piece of meat into his mouth and washed it down with the Malbec while he read for the hundredth time one of the many letters he had received from the mysterious sender here in England. This sender was the one who had tipped him off about this rare flower hidden away somewhere around Cannizaro Park. He knew Edward K. Wilson had never stated such a thing. There was no such written evidence. Eric had to fabricate this little white lie to dismiss his horticultural club back home and get some breathing space. The sender though was reassuring about its existence and he knew Eric, because of his fame, would be able to put his claws on it. The letter told him about Sergej Vernikoff, a lyrical opera singer, invited to sing at the yearly Cannizaro Festival. Eric vaguely remembered the name. To his surprise, the opera singer was in possession of a paper that belonged to the Wilson family. The sender did not give much background details on himself or how he knew this, but Eric could not miss such an opportunity. He had planned his trip in less than a couple of months and he was now here in Wimbledon planning how to steal this valuable piece of paper. One which apparently proved the existence of a black azalea.

Two weeks after the WAIS meeting, Enrico had a badge and a stall number for the fair to be held at Cannizaro Park. He had received a welcome leaflet and a schedule, and so had Viviane. Enrico was impressed by the organisation, apparently all due to the good business skills of the Duchess Hotel's owner. She called herself 'Lady of Cannizaro', which Enrico thought was an apt name to value the history of the place. One more week passed, and the time came to finally visit the famous park to set up his own stall.

Cannizaro House was on the opposite side of Rushmere Green, a far and wide patch of green that separated it from the village. Anyone not local would think it was no longer Wimbledon territory. Even once they crossed Rushmere Green to the other side, they would still miss Cannizaro House. The building was part of one of the oldest rows of buildings in Wimbledon, flanking a paved road now called Westside Common. However, it was oddly set further back than the other Regency-like houses, giving enough space for a modern car park and a U-shaped driveway leading from a low-level barrier to the main entrance and back. The big dark green welcome sign, erected on a low wall, is what Enrico saw first.

The Duchess Hotel

Beyond it, the cream walls and large windows of Cannizaro House stood silently against the light blue sky. Enrico tried to remember Dr Watkins's old pictures in the museum. The architecture looked more modern and a little more sombre without those infinite details and embellishments typical of old villas. The building had become functional in order to work as a hotel, and to comply with safety rules and regulations, it probably had to shed some of the layers of architecture from previous centuries. Enrico tried to imagine Cannizaro House at the time of the Belle Époque or even the Victorian era. The size was still impressive today. It stretched wide to the size of three large houses joined together. The windows followed a delicate neoclassical symmetry on both ground and first floor except for the northern wing which seemed to have gone through a makeover in more recent times. Here and there Enrico thought he could spot the little modern signs that had made Cannizaro House a living quarter and not a forgotten mansion. A fire exit sign here, a small satellite dish there. Even the glass door as main entrance did not hold the same charm as a thick oak door from Edwardian times.

The reception and cloakroom were one small foyer to the right, off the short wood-panelled corridor. Enrico walked past the open door and the receptionist did not take any notice of him while busy working on her nails. The Italian baker was starting to feel let down by the high expectations he had built until he came out of the corridor and to his surprise set foot into a large open space, the main hall of the Duchess Hotel. High and low armchairs were scattered across the cavernous hall and they danced around the cast iron statue of a bird, a goose perhaps. Its beak seemed to point upwards to the high ceiling above. A bar made in Art Nouveau style stood to the left with its more vivid colours. The barman, with his white apron and black pin-striped shirt, nodded at Enrico with a polite smile while drying a glass. The smile faded there and then once the barman had a better look at the baker. Enrico pulled his white chef jacket straight to show the pride in his craft. He would not be confused with hotel staff. He walked across the hall and past the wide marble staircase to the right leading to the upper floor. The handrail ran up a smooth curve to a mezzanine overlooking the hall; a man and a woman were leaning on its balustrade in an idle chat. The rest of the hall was quiet, and Enrico spotted only a few hotel guests sunk into the armchairs drinking, chatting or reading. In front of him, the natural light channelled through an open French door leading to another room where the large window panels of a conservatory or an orangery came into view. Enrico looked beyond. Through the glass, the large expanse of Cannizaro Park stretched down a light slope of green grass, away from the viewer. The whole horizon was a thick backstage of trees of all sizes and a low crowning of flowerbeds and neatly cropped bushes. Enrico stepped through the French door, his eyes fixed ahead, mesmerised by the magical view brightened by the colours of spring.

'Sir, the kitchens are over there!'

A female voice came from somewhere in the room. Enrico woke up from his reverie and looked around adjusting to the bright light. A young waitress approached him. She waved her hand softly to a point behind Enrico's shoulder while she crossed the layout of dining tables which filled the full length of the room from left to right. She seemed to be waiting impatiently for Enrico to leave.

'Excuse me…I am here for…the fair?' explained Enrico timidly.

The waitress squared him, puzzled.

'Are you cooking something for the fair?'

Enrico thought he did not understand the joke.

'I am the owner of *La Pagnotta*. Viviane Leighwood, the florist of Wimbledon Village, is expecting me.'

The name clicked something, and the woman's face lit for a moment showing she understood but her puzzled look would not go away.

'What's with the chef jacket?'

'It is my uniform.'

'Right.' dismissed the waitress not fully understanding. 'Follow me!'

She spun around and started walking towards the northern entrance of what he realised to be the hotel dining room. Enrico followed suit glancing at the fine tables laid out for the forthcoming lunch and the lavish buffet being prepared to one side on a long marble counter. The room had been built recently as an extension of something that existed before. A veranda, perhaps. The large window panels run from floor to ceiling, equipped with modern double glazing and electric blinds. The ceiling was made of concrete and a thick colonnade broke the glass pattern into regular sections through which guests could sit and enjoy the view. The columns had a vague classical look, something to help merge the modern looks with the creamy neoclassical replica the hotel tried to maintain.

The waitress led them through the northern exit. She opened it and Enrico felt again the fresh air blowing against his cheeks after being tricked into a false sense of warm outdoors inside the dining room. As they stepped out into the park, they took a paved footpath bordering the dining room from the outside. A hedge of heather kept them at a distance from the large glass panels through which Enrico now only saw his reflection and the clear skies behind him. The footpath forked to the right about half-way and cut the slope of green grass right in the middle, leading down towards the horizon of trees.

Cannizaro Park was not the typical flat, green park. It thrived on rolling hills and oddly shaped slopes whose horizon was covered in every direction by a thick vegetation, giving the idea of infinity in all directions. Enrico struggled to quantify how big it was and to him it looked as if the park had no end. The footpath they were on took them down between a small pond with a couple of ducks and a high brick wall enclosing a different area of the park. Enrico glanced back and from the bottom of the slope he could now only see the roof of the Duchess Hotel. He then looked at the ducks in the pond and tried to follow the small river upstream. It disappeared through a small cleft in between two bulky, irregular slopes. A small flower bed of yellow daffodils blossomed on the opposite side of the pond. Enrico wondered whether the flowers grew wild as if by magic or by a colourful caprice of nature. Even the most skilled gardener would struggle to grow and maintain such an orderly symmetry across the wild, irregular terrain. He looked once more at the bright yellow flowers. The colour stood out against the nuances of green shrubbery in every corner of the park, somehow self-contained but deliberately overgrown.

'Through there, please.' said the waitress.

She pointed at the old brick wall and an iron gate in the middle. The waitress did not add anything else and left in a hurry to return to her duties. Enrico thanked her and focused his attention on the first sign of a man-made structure in the immensity of the park. The age of the wall could be guessed by the discoloured red-brown patterns or the mossy patches here and there. The iron gate, instead, was freshly painted in black, almost gleaming in the daylight. Enrico thought it to be another clash of old and new, of order and chaos. He wondered if the hotel was torn between innovation and preservation.

Once through the gate, the extent of the area beyond was more than Enrico had imagined. A whole new section of the park ran further west down a slightly inclined stretch of grass void of trees or shrubbery. The brick wall ran both ways in length and joined up at the very far end. It formed a neat rectangular courtyard where rose bushes and decorative stone vases on plinths hinted at a garden enclosure of some sort. A park within a park. Enrico looked beyond and over the brick wall only to see more tree lines breaking up the view of the sky and no other sign of what laid on the horizon. From the Duchess Hotel, the whole of Cannizaro Park seemed to be built on a never-ending descent. Whoever built such a park within a park wanted to somehow keep the wild nature of the park out and recreate the symmetry of classical architecture. The courtyard was split into three levelled sections to adjust to the inclination of the grounds. Each section was linked by a short flight of stone steps, lined to the side by a decorative stone balustrade over a plinth course. The presence of stone vases on short ionic columns and the well-round relief of the balusters made the courtyard resemble more a house garden from Ancient Rome or eighteenth-century

Northern Italy. Enrico somehow felt at home. He gazed at the opposite end of the courtyard. A stone archway with another iron gate led out of the enclosure and back into the wild of Cannizaro Park. To Enrico's disbelief, the park continued beyond and for a minute he felt the nausea from a mild form of labyrinthitis.

'Welcome to the Italian Garden!' exclaimed a cheerful voice.

Viviane was leaning against a vineyard pergola partially covered by healthy green climbing leaves. Enrico waved at Viviane, and while shortening the distance from her, he could see other people were under the pergola hurrying to setup stalls and hang handmade signs. He recognised some faces from the WAIS meeting and he was sure this was the spot chosen for the fair.'

'This place is big!' exclaimed Enrico still spinning around to take it all in. 'How old did Dr Watkins say this place was?'

'Centuries old, I believe.'

'I saw trees, plants, flowers, you name it, on the way here. You must be in your environment.'

'I run a flower shop, Enrico. It is not the same as handling a park this size.'

'I am a baker and I can still feed the whole of Wimbledon.' replied Enrico with a smug.

'We'll see about that.' smirked Viviane. 'Have you seen the size of the fair? There are more stalls down there. And we still have to turn people away!'

She pointed at the next two sections in line. Enrico gulped.

'The fair starts tomorrow. We will be sharing this stall here, so you can start setting up your things when you are ready.'

Enrico looked at the long plastic table with a white tablecloth over it. One half had plenty of colour already after Viviane had made a good head start in her preparations. She placed her best flowers in nice handy bouquets. She had some business cards spread in the centre and a sign in capital letters shouting website address, social page and other things Enrico did not understand. He realised he had none of that. He hardly browsed the internet, let alone setup a web or social page. His plan was to chat with people instead and make them taste his food. It worked back home. He could add the fact that you cannot eat a screen and savour it.

'What do we have here?' came another cheerful voice.

The voice had a sophisticated ring to it. Enrico looked up from the stall. A middle-aged woman in a long flowery dress approached them with a big smile stamped on her face from ear to ear. She had rosy cheeks and soft face, smoothing whatever signs of age she bore. Her figure was curvy and prosperous but well-proportioned and still looking healthy and fit as a fiddle.

'How do you do? My name is Lady of Cannizaro.' she introduced herself shaking Enrico's hand and nodding at Viviane.

'Like the Duchess?' wondered Enrico.

The woman gave a vivacious laugh. She held her hand on her bosom to contain her excitement. Her manners were delicate.

'Glad to see you have done a crash course in Wimbledon history. I wish. No noble blood, I am afraid. A stage name for my business. I am the owner of the Duchess Hotel and your host for the fair.'

Enrico was waiting for her real name, but it never came.

'How are you, Viviane?' continued Lady of Cannizaro with her pleasantries. 'Nice to see you here again this year.'

'Always a pleasure.' replied the florist. 'And this is…'

'LoTrova. Enrico LoTrova.' interrupted the baker upon realising he forgot to introduce himself. 'You can call me Enrico.'

'I hear an accent here. Spanish?' said Lady of Cannizaro.

'Italian!' smiled Enrico nervously. 'I own the new bakery to open soon opposite Viviane's flower shop.'

'Oh, I will have to try your bread then. We have not had a decent bakery in years. Looking forward to tomorrow's tasting sessions.'

'*Assolutamente, sì*'

'Will there be any nice spread with your bread? I don't know. Pesto, perhaps?'

Enrico's eyes widened. More for the disgusting combination than surprise. He was about to protest when Viviane interrupted.

'Enrico is a more traditional baker. You will be even more impressed.'

The florist smiled and then winked secretly at Enrico.

'Wonderful!' exclaimed Lady of Cannizaro. 'We want to remind people how traditional Wimbledon is. Oh, my goodness. I am so excited, and I am so looking forward to it.'

She paused and took a deep breath to recompose herself.

'Now, all suppliers like yourselves are arriving today to set up their stalls. We also have some guests from abroad coming to see the fair and they are staying at the Duchess Hotel. Let me remind you we have the great opera singer Sergej Vernikoff as the guest of honour for the fair. Please make sure to be ready for nine a.m. tomorrow.'

She gave them her wide smile again and bid farewell. Her handshake was powerful, and in making eye contact, Enrico could feel her self-confidence surge up to his arm like an electrical storm. Her style showed self-confidence and strong vibes in everything she said or did. Enrico was impressed, and he was pretty sure her last statement to both was a polite warning not to make mistakes if you wanted to do business again with her.

'Keep comments to yourself, Enrico!' commented Viviane when they were both alone again and Lady of Cannizaro had moved on to see another stall.

'What?'

'Pesto…' she hinted vaguely.

'Yeah…I mean…pesto as a spread. *Che orrore!*' protested Enrico with a grimace. 'Anyway, why did you stop me? You were scared I would insult the organiser?'

'No!' replied Viviane rolling her eyes. 'She is more than just the organiser. She owns the hotel and the park, and she is an influential person in Wimbledon.'

Enrico thought of adding something to that, but he thought best to accept the facts. He needed to make the right friends and find customers for his bakery. The fair was a good start. The earlier people started buying his bread and pastries, the earlier he could pay off his bills.

The workers were almost done setting up when a little ray of sunshine hit their sweaty faces. Their hands ached from the morning labour but now the remaining stalls, the ramps, the poles to support the platform stage, everything was almost ready, and they were just making the final touches. Lady of Cannizaro had come around earlier to check the progress and it was a shame she was not there to see the accomplishment. The workers decided it was time for a break and moved en masse to a spot they quietly agreed as the place for lunch. They sat on a few chairs under the vineyard pergola, lulled by the grapevine leaves shivering in the breeze. The Italian Garden lay out in front of them begging to be filled with the joy of people. Towards the bottom end of the garden, a few onlookers walked up and down the entrance staircase to the west to see the work in progress. They leaned on the stone baluster, some taking pictures, others chatting on how the stage looked.

One of them stood on his own at the back, against the stone archway leading out to the rest of the park. His eyes were hidden behind the black frames of sunglasses, gazing into the distance. He could not see the whole of the Italian Garden from there, but it was enough for him to know the stage would be up soon. He did not want to be seen or recognised. He looked at his watch, as a reminder of time passing. He had to move fast. His enemy could have been here already, maybe he or she was behind him right now. In the meantime, his hands were empty. He did not know exactly where to find what he was looking for. All he knew was that everything lay within the greater wall boundaries of Cannizaro Park. Of this he was sure, despite the criticisms. Yet, the last flowers had blossomed, and there would be nothing to wait for soon. He cursed himself for how he still could not find or even see it against a sea of green. He put his hat on feeling defeated and took a step out of the Italian Garden to clear his thoughts. He wandered down a narrowing path of grass where a nearby stream set the boundary between the park and the royal golf course. The sounds of the park here were subtler than closer to the hotel building. They became more intense as he crossed the tiny Japanese-like wooden bridge covered in foliage and entered a natural arch of trees and plants. From here onwards, the thick forest of Lady Jane's Wood stretched as far as the eastern tip of the park, hanging low enough to block the sky and the light but open enough to feel like the inside of a vast cave.

The man in the hat walked further, lost in his thoughts. He heard the laughter of children as they played hide and seek up and down the natural steps on the hilly side of the woods, rushing under the tunnels of colourful azaleas. He took his sunglasses off and glanced at his watch again, for no reason. He would find that precious thing. He suddenly stopped in his tracks and realised he was now fully immersed in high vegetation, on a footpath hardly beaten. High ferns, thick low pine trees and holly bushes popped up all around him. Echoes of laughter were still in the air. He recalled the laughs at his age-ridden claims. How he would only chase fairy tales. How he would not find any proof. The man took his hat off and looked at the mysterious vegetation, possibly hiding elves and fairies staring back at him. He looked further and could see the Belvedere terrace, with its orphan pillars. He had been down this neck of the woods a few times already without success. He walked up the sloping path behind it. His feet pushed against the dry mud, throwing speckles of dirt onto the hem of his trousers.

Once up, he went to the stone baluster, leaning again to admire the green void of the Heather Garden. He had been up there, goodness knows how many times already, questioning his convictions.

There was not much time left. He would search again all over the place before the fair started. It would be harder then and it was already hard now with the ghost of his enemies haunting him day and night. He was not crazy. What he was looking for, really existed.

The Cannizaro Festival was a bigger event than Enrico had imagined. It was a little after 9 a.m. and masses of visitors camped outside the hotel's car park and spread onto Rushmere Green, waiting to join the queue. More people were on their way from the village as if almost all of Wimbledon and its surrounding area was ready to flood the park and invade every single corner made public by the hotel for the great occasion.

Enrico had had to push his way through the crowds ever since leaving his bakery; he closely followed the signs to the main entrance to avoid being any later than he already was. Access to the fair was arranged through the direct entrance to Cannizaro Park, a paved road parallel to the hotel's car park which ran around the hotel building. It was accessible to pedestrians through a majestic black iron gate. Enrico glanced up at it as he passed through in haste and noticed letters forged into it at the top.

E K W

Enrico recalled the initials. Edward K. Wilson. His name was immortalised in the park's history. He looked around at the visitors' faces flowing in and the late arrivals, like himself, dashing through the gates to reach their stall. He wondered if they knew about that small everyday detail stamped on the gate. He then toyed with the idea he should be immortalised too in the town's history. Wimbledon's most famous baker. He laughed to himself and pulled up his large sack over his shoulder as he picked up his pace and entered the park. He could now see the sloped grass running off the hotel's orangery where he had walked the day before. Something, however, was different. The calm of yesterday was gone. Crowd patches filled pockets of the vast space with children running between them. The fresh air mingled with the echo of laughs and chatter, in front of the orangery, by the duck's pond, and through the tree lines, deep into the woodland of the park. The newly arrived public was everywhere and Enrico saw Cannizaro Park come to life. He rushed on with excitement and overtook the flow of visitors on its way to the Italian Garden where the main event was. The long courtyard was jam-packed with people and an orderly queue had formed just outside the tiny iron gate. Enrico showed his badge and was let through, admiring the professionalism of the British queuing system. He tipped on his toes to glace over the pergola and caught a glimpse of Viviane nervously walking back and forth in front of their stall.

'You are late!' she hissed at him.

'*Calma, calma...*' said Enrico. 'How was I supposed to know this place would be filled in ten minutes as if it were a rock concert?'

'I don't know...be ready for 9 a.m.?'

'You mean 9 a.m. sharp? I thought around 9 a.m., minute more, minute less.'

Viviane shook her head and let it go. She showed him her half of the stall, half-ready after yesterday's preparation. Enrico smiled and unloaded his large sack on it, ready for the action. Viviane watched him warily as he pulled out bread of all shapes and sizes from his sack, long and thin, round and soft. She peeked over and saw Enrico bundling his breadsticks into a sheaf similar to her bouquets. He laid out cardboard plates and some cutlery with one giant sign in capital block letters.

'A bit of an overstatement?' teased Viviane.

'You said I have bread to sell.' he said. 'Let's do it!'

Viviane pursed her lips in a mute smile and looked at the crowd. They did not talk further and instead focused their attention on the visitors as their numbers multiplied every ten minutes. Families, elderly couples, younger couples, some of them locals knowing each other and stopping in the middle of the busy space to exchange greetings. It was as if the whole town could fit in that rectangular enclosure, and this was the only place where they could gather and chat.

The morning soldiered on under a fresh, rejuvenating sunshine. Viviane was taking flower orders one after the next, engaging in gossip every now and then with one of her frequent buyers. Enrico on the other hand was a little bored after only three visits to his stall, one of which was just a mistake when a man with bad glasses misread 'the best meds of Wimbledon'. For most of that morning, he stood there simply observing Wimbledonians inspecting his fresh bread from afar and keeping a safe distance as they walked. Enrico yelped a few cries over the low murmur of the crowds in an effort to catch their attention and attract customers. He was not very convincing however, and met a few frowns here and there.

'We are not at the market, Enrico.' commented Viviane.

'How many days of this I have to do?' asked Enrico.

Enrico knew the fair was a five-day event. He wished Viviane would say otherwise.

'Do you want people to come to your bakery and buy bread?' replied Viviane. 'The more convincing you are now, the sooner you can be sure of when your opening day will be.'

Enrico did not want to hear what the obvious reasons for signing up to this fair were. He needed it, but he expected it to be easier. He expected to see people rushing to his stall. Everyone needs bread, especially freshly baked bread from very early in the morning. He then remembered Mr Wyczenski and his comment about bread being available daily in supermarkets and food chains. He realised there was one thing he was underestimating and that was competition. He glanced at his bread, neatly displayed, still looking fresh and close to getting stale by end of day if it stood there in the open for too long. Enrico wondered if he should have made pastries or something sweet.

'What is with the long face? Cheer up!' added Viviane. 'It is just the first day. Anything can happen.'

Enrico nodded vaguely and looked ahead. He then stepped out from behind the stall and moved out of the pergola to take a view of the Italian Garden. On the opposite wall, the whole space had been reserved for a stage placed towards the middle. To one side, rows of foldable chairs were stacked against the naked brick wall ready to recreate an auditorium at any time. He looked back at the stage and Lady of Cannizaro was standing on it talking to a team of helpers on how to lay out the music stands. The first evening, if Enrico recalled the programme correctly, was dedicated to Sergej Vernikoff, the opera singer, and the Italian baker could only assume a celebrity was the best choice for a grand opening although he had to say he had never heard of him. The good weather also meant the special event would go ahead. Enrico watched Lady of Cannizaro taking one music stand and explaining something. He could only grasp a few words. A small orchestra was probably expected to accompany lyrical successes like Turandot or Rigoletto. Enrico was not much into opera and he had the feeling some people thought he was, being from Italy.

'Do you like opera?' asked Enrico turning towards Viviane, still behind her stall.

'Sometimes. It can be soothing and relaxing.'

She cut him short while helping an old lady on how they could order flowers for pick-up. Enrico was about to carry on with the conversation, but the florist gave him a sardonic smile to remind him he may not be busy, or may not want to be, but she was. Enrico hunched his shoulders and turned back towards the stage. He wanted to have a bite of bread to refresh his thoughts. What he had there was not working but he had to make it work in the next five days. He left a hand-written note by the stall promising to return in five minutes and jumped into the crowd. Viviane watched him leave and felt sorry for him. She even felt sorrier for her when she realised what Enrico's note really said.

Back in five minutes. Ask the florist next door for details.

Enrico jumped into the crowd with his white chef jacket shining in the late morning sun. He exchanged a few looks with passers-by who could not tell if he were hotel staff or an entertainer for the fair in fancy dress. He took no notice and went browsing the other stalls. They offered quite a variety of things to do or eat or buy, from equestrian lessons to local produce and hairstyle demonstrations. The people behind the stalls were all from local shops or business in Wimbledon, and Enrico recognised a few faces from the WAIS meeting. He also spotted stalls from a few chain shops on the high street. Plastic coffee bars, overrated clothes retailers, cheap house décor. You could tell the difference, but he knew they had the right to promote their business just as Lady of Cannizaro and the organisers behind the fair wanted to maximise contributions and sponsorship.

The Italian baker glanced up at the stage again, now only a few metres away, and Lady of Cannizaro was now orchestrating the layout of a wide banner. The helpers, mostly volunteers or hotel staff, were running around and climbing stepping stools to meet the precise instructions of a lady who knew her taste, who knew what she wanted and when she wanted it. The banner took a full fifteen minutes to go up in style, despite the last few tweaks to meet Lady of Cannizaro's perfect symmetry. Enrico wondered if that was how she spoke to the gardener when he had to lay out the flower beds in the park. A flashing announcement gave out the details of this evening show and for the upcoming days.

Tonight @ 7pm - The great Sergej Vernikoff
Brought to you by the Cannizaro Festival and Alberyx Enterprises

There you go, thought Enrico. Sponsors. He would probably need to find one for this bakery.

'Mr LoTrova!' exclaimed Lady of Cannizaro with packed enthusiasm.

She had turned away from the finished work and had dismissed the team to work on the next task. She looked immaculate for the opening day. A long flowery dress and a necklace with emerald and maroon beads hung down her bare neck. Her cheeks were a little reddened, maybe from barking orders or exposing her skin to the mild sun. She held a beige floppy hat in her hand and she was quick enough to put it on when Enrico approached her by the stage, perhaps to hide her rosy skin or other imperfections. The Italian baker knew she was a lot older than him and Viviane, but it did not show.

'Good morning, Lady of Cannizaro!'

'Good afternoon!' she pointed out glancing at her watch. 'Past noon.'

'Ah yes!' Enrico corrected himself. 'Time flies by and it is already lunchtime.'

'Everything going well at your stand?'

'All perfect. Just took a quick break to wander around.'

'I don't blame you, Mr LoTrova. It is very hectic to see this enclosure of the park teeming with people. The rest of the year it is mostly deserted. Normally, a fifth of this crowd passes through it on any normal day. And that's if there is no rain.'

'This park is so big. I still have not had the chance to see it all. How far does it go beyond the Western exit of the Italian Garden?'

'It carries on a few yards until you come across the undergrowth and a little stream. They form a natural border with the Royal Wimbledon Golf Course and you don't really notice until you stumble across a subtle green mesh acting as a symbolic fence. I like to keep a natural aspect of the park. As you may or may not know, the park is just a small fraction of the Old Park from the 1500s. The park extends north and south from here too but if you follow the border you will notice it curves slightly and to your surprise you will return back to where you came from, whether this point or the hotel. Cannizaro Park is an odd shape. Perhaps I can give you and Miss Leighwood a tour. Always delighted to show the secrets of this park.'

'I'd love to.' replied Enrico.

Enrico was about to add something else when someone bumped into him. He saw a man in a brown felt hat and a light cricket sweater walking on without turning. The Italian baker thought not to bother. He returned the gaze to Lady of Cannizaro who was in the midst of listening to one of his staff.

'Mr LoTrova!' she resumed shortly after, turning back to him. 'Sorry to interrupt our chat but I have a few things to take back to the hotel. Just extra bunting and decorations we may use at the hotel. Would you and Miss Leighwood care to join me for lunch?'

'Yes, we'd love to.' blurted out Viviane anticipating Enrico's answer.

The Italian baker felt Viviane grabbing him by the elbow and letting herself into the conversation to Enrico's surprise. She gave him again one of her winks and he wondered for a moment if the florist was jealous or purely curious.

'Sure…why not…' muttered Enrico not sure if he should be worried about Viviane's presence or about who on earth was looking after the stand.

'Don't worry!' said Viviane to Enrico. 'I have a sign saying "Lunch Break". It also says to ask the stand next door for details.'

She let the joke hang in the air and dismissed in a flash to ease Lady of Cannizaro's puzzled look.

'Is it now ok for you, Lady of Cannizaro?' she added.

'Of course, it is. Brilliant. Now, do you want to meet me at the hotel?'

'Oh, I am sure we can come with you and Enrico will be more than happy to bring some of the boxes with you.'

Enrico felt lost for words again as if he were a mere spectator of the two women's chat.

'That is so kind. There they are!'

The four boxes were of medium size and easy to lift until the staff member decided to stack two on top in Enrico's arms. Viviane and Lady of Cannizaro grabbed one box each and quickly moved through the crowd. Enrico struggled to look ahead and from the side he could see Viviane turning her face to him with a silent giggle. He groaned and followed her slowly as Lady of Cannizaro took them behind the stage. To his surprise, there was another archway leading out of the courtyard which was being used as a stage entrance. The man in charge of security let them out and they were suddenly back in the wilderness of the park, with only the echo of the crowds' murmur hanging in the air. A few steps away from the walls of the Italian Garden and the party was welcomed by a thick undergrowth whose pathways and large natural steps were the only hint to some form of order. Enrico realised they were in a different part of the park. There were no open, grassy spaces. Here, the trees had grown tall around an intricate web of dirt tracks, some cleared or tidied up for ease of access. Lady of Cannizaro knew the park well as if she had been living on these grounds for centuries. She explained this wild area of the park, where the sun hardly shone through. A cool air made Enrico shiver and he suddenly missed the rays of sunshine in the open Italian Garden. At one point, the whole ground they were walking on became steep and they had to climb wide stone blocks put there as steps. Enrico recognised the sloped surface of the park he still could not grasp. Then Lady of Cannizaro led them onto one final step and up onto a perpendicular path cutting across the slope. They took a second to catch their breaths.

'This is called the Azalea Dell.' introduced Lady of Cannizaro with half a spin in her dress.

Enrico and Viviane could not miss the rows of azaleas and rhododendrons blossoming on each side of the path, bringing colour to the dull bark and the dark shadows of the high trees.

'There used to be more azaleas than now, and they used to form a natural arch, a pergola, but over time the plants have struggled. This feature of the park is older than you think. The whole décor was an idea of Henry Dundas, First Viscount of Melville, one of the many residents of Cannizaro House. Centuries before it became a hotel. He planted azaleas all along this path and surrounded it with beeches as a wedding present to his third wife, Lady Jane Hope. Third wife, eh? Other plants have been introduced here over the last three hundred years. Azaleas have therefore receded a little. Shame!'

'Are you planning to plant more?' asked Viviane with curiosity, edging the border of the path where she could admire the flowery shrubs abundant in red, white, purple, and various shades of pink.

'Not at the moment. There are other parts of the park that need attention.'

'Did you know azaleas and rhododendrons are highly toxic?' added Viviane, dropping an element of trivia she was not expecting an answer to.

Enrico looked around, trying to follow, but for him the vegetation was all the same. A constant pattern of light and dark colours. He watched Viviane, hopping from shrub to shrub to admire the flowers. As they progressed upwards, the florist listened to Lady of Cannizaro's explanations and each time a particular tree or a flower's name was mentioned she knew where to turn. Enrico thought perhaps he could ask them to visit the hotel's kitchen and talk about the fine ingredients available to make all kinds of bread.

The walk took the three up the path until it levelled out and they emerged into a wide, green bay, dotted with oaks and cherry trees. A few benches were placed all around in no particular order for the occasional passer-by to rest and enjoy the blissful nature. Enrico peeked underneath and he could no longer see a footpath to follow. Ahead of them, though, the south-west side of the Duchess Hotel was clearly visible in full view. Enrico remembered Lady of Cannizaro's words. The moment you followed the borders, just turn left or right, and you were bound to trace your footsteps back to the hotel or the Italian Garden.

'Is this the southern extremity of the park?' asked Enrico.

'Well, Lady Jane Wood is over there.' she pointed to their right where the woodland rose again, hiding once more what laid beyond. 'There you have the Heather Garden and the Belvedere.'

'The Belvedere?'

'A sort of temple-like pedestal with columns. A little abandoned as it is off the main pathways.'

'*Questo posto è magico...* There is a surprise at every corner!'

To Enrico, Cannizaro Park was a self-contained universe whose imaginary spherical space made sure any location could take you to another without you realising. Viviane smiled to herself when she saw Enrico and his child-like eyes staring at the large green space.

The return to the hotel was a return to civilisation. They had hardly met a soul along the Azalea Dell and gradually they now met more visitors as they approached the hotel building. The three walked up to the southern side, where a few small groups had formed. Lady of Cannizaro looked excited or perhaps she was preparing to show herself to the public. Enrico noticed a change in her stance and the way she walked and carried the boxes.

'Viviane, dear, do you mind holding my box please?' she said turning to the florist unannounced.

Viviane almost stumbled and before realising she took on the second box. Enrico chuckled but quickly turned serious when he caught Viviane's glare.

'This way!' said Lady of Cannizaro.

The two followed. Lady of Cannizaro had chosen a specific path to show off some of the treasures of Cannizaro Park, maybe to impress Enrico as the new arrival, or maybe to impress the many people enjoying the great outdoors around the hotel. She showed pride and elegance as she walked over a colourful space. It was a lower recess into the ground framed by a thick carpet of flowers, from geraniums to daffodils. The recess was accessible through two wide but simple staircases leading down to a smaller, inner rectangle. Here, another crowded flower bed stood in the centre, and anyone walking around it, would be engulfed by colours and perfumes, almost fearing they would crush the flowers with their barbaric feet. But Lady of Cannizaro did not fear that. She had grace as she descended into the recess. There, she stopped and spoke aloud to introduce her next and last stop. A few visitors nearby turned their heads, and even some hotel staff members from inside the southern tip of the orangery did so too. Enrico knew her speech was no longer for them but for a wider audience.

'This is the Dutch Sunken Garden, built by the late Edward Wilson. One of the most recent beautiful additions to the park, we try hard here at the Duchess Hotel to keep to its original splendour. And where the small wooden gate is, that is the Herbal Garden. Don't miss the opportunity to see the many types of herbs we hold there. Our chef picks some from it to flavour the dishes served in our restaurant!'

Enrico followed her hand, to see a tiny courtyard not far from where they were. It was probably one fifth of the Italian Garden or less and a tiny wooden gate led into it. The Italian baker could finally see the roofs of houses that did not belong to the hotel. He suddenly realised the park's borders were very close to the surrounding residential areas.

'Please enjoy the rest of your day,' continued Lady of Cannizaro with a resonant voice. 'and please tell your friends and families to come and see the fair. Don't forget tonight Sergej Vernikoff will sing in the Italian Garden. Thank you!'

Lady of Cannizaro was welcomed with a short clap of hands by near standbys. Enrico and Viviane pulled an awkward smile, standing there with boxes in their hands. To avoid embarrassment, they had taken a few steps back to avoid stealing Lady of Cannizaro's centre of attention.

'Is she always this theatrical?' whispered Enrico.

'I am afraid so.' sighed Viviane.

'Now you wish we were both at the stand, don't you!' joked Enrico.

Viviane's deep brown eyes stared back at him.

'Consider this exposure as a contribution to your rise to fame!' she commented.

'Touché!'

The show Lady of Cannizaro had put on quickly dissolved and the scene returned back to normal. They watched her leave the Dutch Sunken Garden from the other side, taking her time to shake hands or hug friends and co-workers. Enrico and Viviane hesitated until she gave them a nod from afar to follow her. Lady of Cannizaro did not wait and they quickened their pace behind her balancing the boxes uneasily. They walked in front of the orangery and Enrico recognised they were coming near the northern wing of the hotel, not far from the public entrance to the park. The flow of guests coming to the fair had slightly reduced but still they could hear the faint echo of voices and clamour rising from the park, especially from inside the walls of the Italian Garden somewhere down the slope.

'If you could leave the boxes outside here, that would be fab.' said Lady of Cannizaro, pointing at an open service door where staff was busy coming in and out. 'Thank you so much! I shall repay you with a nice lunch. Let me check with the chef. He makes some fantastic sandwiches. In the meantime, why don't you take a seat inside the orangery, our dining room?'

She thanked them a second time and then nodded to the waiter who had just opened for her the door to the dining room. She crossed the orangery and disappeared inside the hotel. Enrico and Viviane stepped inside to follow and the waiter took them to a table on the opposite corner from where Enrico could see the Dutch Sunken Garden. Viviane sat across him.

'Sandwiches for lunch? Is that it?' blurted out Enrico, disappointed.

'She is a good host, Enrico. She must run this hotel like a tight ship.'

'*Va bene, va bene...*' grumbled Enrico hearing his stomach starting to growl in protest. 'You must have been in your world back there, no? Flowers, trees, plants. You seemed very interested!'

'I am a florist, Enrico. It is my partly my job. But I am an amateur in comparison to what they accomplish here. I should come to this park more often.'

'You don't?'

'Well, when you live near a beautiful place, you hardly go and visit, and instead you dream of faraway places. Have you ever experienced this back home?'

'I did. We can take the opportunity of this five-day fair and go for walks around this place. I am sure by then we would have covered every single corner and know it by heart. It may even feel smaller!'

They both laughed. Enrico looked away through the glass of the orangery and enjoyed the view. The sun felt warmer. The dining room had a few clients, but it was not busy, and a low murmur bubbled evenly across the room. He then glanced over Viviane's shoulder while she casually checked the menu out. He could see the colourful patterns of the glorified Dutch Sunken Garden. Beyond it, behind where before they had stood with the boxes like sitting ducks, there was a row of trees hanging over a shelter of brick and stone with a wooden bench inside. For a moment, he thought he saw a man leaning against the shelter. He wore a brown felt-tip hat and kept glancing at his watch. Enrico frowned, thinking he recognised the man from before, but his face was hidden under the hat. The man looked up at some point. Enrico thought he was looking straight at him inside the orangery. Yet, the man's sight hovered above his head and Enrico realised the man was looking at the upper floor above. Enrico saw a pointy chin and a big, straight nose. He thought he saw something out of the ordinary. Before he could make it out, the man looked back down, his face hidden again, and the Italian baker looked away. Someone then passed in front of Enrico's field of vision, and in an instant the man was gone.

71

That is when the loud bang came, followed by a deep single tremor. The building shook briefly to Enrico and Viviane's shock who immediately stood up from the table on alert. They exchanged glances mixed with confusion and horror. The whole dining room turned into a loud scream. Enrico looked outside in the direction of the Dutch Sunken Garden and where the man in the hat had been. He could no longer see anything. A cloud of smoke had descended upon it and pieces of brickwork and other debris had fallen off from somewhere above. Viviane held her hand on her mouth, incredulous. Enrico grabbed her by the arm without hesitation and pulled her toward him. They both dashed out of the orangery and ran away from the hotel, fearing the whole building would collapse. As the dining guests flooded out into the park in fear and panic, Enrico took Viviane to a safe distance and looked carefully at the southern side of the hotel. The whole building seemed intact and it did not shake further. What they witnessed though was something they never thought would happen in such a peaceful, quiet place like Cannizaro Park. The corner room on the first floor of the hotel had literally blown up, sending the two window frames and large parts of the southern-facing wall into the air, scattering them all over the place and crushing innocent tulips. A big hole in the wall was now in its place, filled with smoke and flames. The hotel staff and Lady of Cannizaro came rushing out, terrorised looks on their faces. Enrico could tell from their looks this was no ordinary event in Wimbledon. He glanced around to see if there was anyone hurt on the ground. A few people were being led to safety. They were showing bruises and blood stains on their arms and faces. He then looked up again and he squinted to see through the thick black smoke. He thought he saw a hand, waving. Someone was hurt.

'Stay here. Make sure they've called the emergency services!' cried out Enrico.

'Where are you going?' shouted Viviane still in shock.

The Italian baker, good-natured, sprinted off past the stranded crowds and ran back towards the hotel. Some of the staff tried to stop him, shouting at him. He dodged them and cried out someone was hurt upstairs, not caring if they heard him or not. He dashed back into the hotel, past the orangery and up the stairs. More guests and staff were on their way out and Enrico struggled to push through in the opposite direction. As he reached the landing, the smell of burning coming from the southern end of the corridor hit him hard. He looked down and the corridor slowly disappeared to a cloud of thick black smoke. Some doors to other rooms had been left wide open but light failed to penetrate the thick cloud. Enrico put the lapel of his chef jacket over his mouth and pushed through, determined to help anyone who was in danger. His eyes burnt a little and became watery as he moved deeper into the smoke. He slowed down the pace until he heard a moan ahead of him. He shouted to catch attention. The moans increased. It rang like a cry for help Enrico could not ignore. He stepped forward. The heat on his skin became uncomfortable and the smoke now scratched his throat, making it harder to breathe. He looked ahead with his burning eyes and then he finally saw a body lying on the floor of the corridor with his arms stretched upwards to alert his position. Enrico kneeled by his side.

'Are you ok?'

The man nodded feebly. Enrico noticed cuts and bruises across his face, mixed with streaks of blood trickling down to his chin. He made no sounds of groans of pain as Enrico pulled up the man's arm over his shoulder.

'Are you able to walk?' shouted Enrico realising time was not on their side.

The man nodded. Enrico started to walk out of the smoke. He wanted to run but he was aware of the man's condition. For a second, he felt stupid about the risk he had taken until he heard a siren wailing in the far distance. The emergency services. Enrico lengthened their stride as much as he could. Before the smoke started to fade away and they could breathe purer air, the man grabbed his wrist. The Italian baker thought he would lose grip on his lapel and breathe in that awful smoke. Instead the man wanted to look at him and say something.

'The azalea…It was not there…' he whispered. 'The black azalea…was not there…'

Enrico frowned. He was not sure what it meant. Another hand came out of nowhere to grab him, startling Enrico. A fourth one came out to pick up the injured man until it became clear the fire brigade had arrived to lead them to safety.

Inspector Baynard kept his icy stare on the sparse crowd gathering around the yellow police line his men were busy setting up around the most complicated perimeter he had ever faced in his investigations. As per the inspector's instructions, all access to the hotel and the park was off limits until he had all the facts checked. He stood by the hotel entrance stroking his silver goatee. His pale grey eyes flickered with the intense blue lights of the police cars stationed in the hotel's car park along the ambulances and fire engines. The car park was being used to look after those with minor injuries. Paramedics and policemen were in groups attending the unfortunates who had been hit or scratched by flying debris. No deaths, fortunately. He gave a stern nod to a few of his men, checking they had what they needed or approving of their work.

Baynard glanced up to his right. The thick cloud of black smoke was still rising and towering above the Duchess Hotel like an ominous vulture in the serene sky. The smoke was now visible from afar, all around Wimbledon. He could not miss it the moment his car took the first roundabout on Wimbledon Village High Street. He remembered the look on people's faces, eyes petrified, mouths twisted in cries of shock and disbelief. An explosion of such proportion was unheard of in the time he had been in the service, but Baynard felt it could have been worse. He put a gum in his mouth and started chewing savagely. It helped him think and keep calm. While gathering his thoughts, he wondered what could have been the cause. Perhaps a gas leak or bad wiring. He then made a mental list in his head of the next steps. First of all, it was better to clear the mess, remove any false leads, get the report from the firemen loud and clear. He remembered it was the first day of the awaited Cannizaro Festival. It complicated things for two reasons. One, he regretted he had to cancel his plans to bring his two young daughters. Two, he knew the organisers and anyone involved would be behind the corner to ask him how soon they could lift the police block and re-open the hotel and the park. The explosion had shaken everyday life in Wimbledon and cancelling the yearly event would have been a double trauma. Baynard looked at the crowds of people spreading on Rushmere Green as they were being escorted off the park or outside the hotel. What a logistics nightmare, he thought. The gum in his mouth had become tasteless but he carried on. He had over-chewed the gum as he always did when he was overthinking.

Baynard grabbed his little notebook and made his way into the hotel past reception. He then crossed the empty hall to enter the orangery. The first person to call his name with an expression of desperation was Lady of Cannizaro.

'Inspector Baynard!' she almost cried leaving the police constable with her. 'Thank God you are here. This incident is a real disgrace! Such an ignoble act!'

Baynard's stare did not change. His icy stare lingered on unabashed by the woman's emotional response. He looked around carefully, wondering who could have heard. His pale grey eyes were void of any colourful reflection, and his face became sterner and more inquisitive. He did not like the fact Lady of Cannizaro spoke as if the incidence was someone's fault.

'Good afternoon, Lady of Cannizaro. I came as soon as I heard the call. My presence here is simply to check and confirm what happened after I heard from the fire department. I hear they are still upstairs working on it. I don't think we can say this explosion was done on purpose. There may be a culprit but probably this is down to bad maintenance.'

Lady of Cannizaro sneered at the insinuation that her hotel was not kept to health and safety standards.

'Inspector,' she said, annoyed. 'I run my hotel like clockwork. My staff tell me immediately when our standards are compromised. I would have known if there was a fire hazard in the room.'

'So, you think it is the most logical conclusion to think a culprit is behind all this?'

Lady of Cannizaro smirked. Baynard glared back not keen to make a scene.

'How long before we can re-open the fair?' she added in a hurry to get the conversation over.

'Too early to tell. I would assume up to seventy-two hours but until I see the firemen's report, no comment. In the meantime, seeing you are so eager to find out who did this, would you be able to tell me what happened, what you remember, and your movements before the explosion?'

Lady of Cannizaro's face darkened with disdain.

'How dare you suspect me?' she said, her voice a little raised.

'I am not. Nobody is. You are a witness, though, and anything I can put in the report will help speed things up with your insurance.'

The woman wet her lips, caught off guard by the inspector's canny comment. He looked at her without flinching.

'We are all shaken by this event.' resumed Baynard. 'If you have done your job well, let me do mine.'

Lady of Cannizaro snorted, still flustered and disappointed by Baynard's unapologetic tone. This is how the inspector was. Direct and abrupt, within the boundaries of politeness.

'Before the explosion, I was in the kitchen, talking with the chef about preparing a quick lunch for two people who have a stall at the fair.'

She went on about how the walls shook as if an earthquake had hit Wimbledon. She then described how they dashed out of the kitchen, through the orangery, and into the open park, grabbing hotel staff and guests stranded along the way. When she thought it was safe, she and some of the staff approached the Dutch Sunken Garden to help the injured walk away from the scene. Inspector Baynard scribbled line after line.

'Would you say you were first on the scene?' he interrupted.

'Sort of. The first to arrive was Enrico LoTrova. I was the first to assist the injured.'

'Henry who?'

'Enrico LoTrova. Baker.'

Baynard wrote down the word 'baker'. No time to spell names.

'How about the first floor? Was it you or a member of your staff who realised someone was injured where the explosion had taken place?'

'No. Enrico went to save that man from asphyxiation.'

'Henry who?'

'The baker.'

'Again? Does he work here?'

'No. He was here because of the fair. He is the owner of a new bakery opening in Wimbledon Village. I was meant to have lunch with him, and the other person to join was Viviane Leighwood, the florist.'

Baynard grumbled something of a nod. He did not know much about this new bakery. He did know though this man popped up in every aspect of the story as if he were a hero. He over-chewed his gum, which had now become an indistinguishable blob in his mouth. He may want to ask this baker a few things, just to be sure there was nothing that could hinder insurance claims.

He quickly finished with Lady of Cannizaro and thanked her for her co-operation. By the time the questioning was over, she was back to her charming self, resolute and smiling. Re-telling the story somehow helped her calm down. The inspector reassured her they would do whatever was necessary. He knew well Lady of Cannizaro was influential enough to stir

77

things in high places. The last thing he wanted was for the explosion to become a storm in a tea cup. The Chief Superintendent would not have liked that, even if the explosion was down to a faulty toaster.

Next thing to do on the inspector's little notebook was visit the site of the explosion. He made his way back into the hall, glancing sideways at the bird-like statue in its centre. Before making the short walk upstairs, he asked one of his men to find this Enrico to get his statement. He would deal with it personally. When he reached the first-floor landing, a second barrier had been set up by the fire brigade and the whole upper floor was off limits to gather evidence. The young police constable on guard told Baynard the firemen had just confirmed the building was safe from collapse or a further explosion, and the blaze had been tamed. The inspector kept his icy stare but deep inside he sighed in relief. This building was an old treasure of Wimbledon that had to be safeguarded.

He was let in and moved deep down the southern corridor until he came across a red line cordon. Firemen walked backwards and forwards, their yellow helmets deep over their heads, faces blackened by smoke and sweat. Some carried burnt items. Others were in the room where the explosion had taken place, or what was left of it, taking measurements and knocking down parts of the wall deemed unsafe. One saw Baynard and immediately called out to their chief.

'Hello, inspector!' said a man in his late forties with a uniform of a different colour to reflect the rank.

'Afternoon.' replied the inspector curtly. 'What do we have here?'

'What a mess!' confessed the chief firefighter. 'We are gathering all the items ready to take to your forensic team at the station.'

He stopped and widened his eyes at the end of his sentence. Baynard did not flinch but hammered his teeth on the gum. There was no need to send items or any other evidence to his forensic team unless foul play had been found. The chief firefighter called him out to the room opposite, whose door

78

had been blown off its hinges and lay flat on the floor. He checked nobody was listening, even though he knew only his men were about.

'Nothing complex. Home-made explosive. This was no terrorist attack. Something on a smaller scale which was meant to have an impact in a very small radius. It still caused an awful amount of damage, but I think whoever planted it in the room was not exactly sure of the consequences.

'Are you sure about this?'

'Pretty sure.'

'What have you sent to forensics?'

'Some wirings, and bits and pieces from the low cabinet and the small safe inside it.'

'When can I have a look inside?'

'A couple of days. Mind you, the hotel will want to fix this all up fast. It is the Duchess Hotel after all, and the Cannizaro Festival is also on. I can allow access first thing tomorrow morning. It will get complicated, inspector.'

The chief firefighter spoke in vague tones. He knew Baynard would understand. There was no need to cause panic now, there was already enough in the air. The bombing of a private building was technically arson and voluntary manslaughter. It would require a full investigation that could take weeks or months, but the Council, the local news, the hotel, Wimbledonians themselves, would demand an explanation the moment he confirmed the cause of the explosion. Not to mention the impact to the hotel and local business, once they learned the hotel had to be closed off indefinitely, or until the investigation was complete. Baynard's mind raced already to understand why someone would do such a thing. He had to move quickly before it became all too complicated.

'I heard a man was in the room or nearby at the time of the explosion.' the inspector asked.

'Yes. He is in the car park with the paramedics. Lucky fellow. He must have been far enough to avoid any lethal injuries, but the scars and burns tell me he was in the room.'

'Do you know the name?'

'No, I am afraid.'

'Was it his room? The one that blew up.'

'I don't know, inspector. Perhaps he was playing with more than just a little chemistry set. Or worse, the explosion was a way to scare him or someone else. Not to mention…you know…'

Baynard ignored the word 'kill'. He had to for the moment. Words needed to be chosen carefully in the next two or three days, or even less than that. Time was of the essence. It was time to check guest lists, rooms, the whole crime investigation package. The note about the baker popped in his head. Better check his version of the story while fresh in his mind. He could then talk to his sergeant and think how to best communicate this to the outer world. People out there on Rushmere Green probably wanted answers and maybe social media was already buzzing with the craziest conspiracy theories.

The inspector thanked the chief firefighter for his time and reminded him to call him or his sergeant once everything was handed over to forensics at Wimbledon Police Station. They both understood the urgency. Baynard walked out into the corridor and back down to the hall. He grabbed one of his men asking if this Enrico LoTrova was available and he was told he was waiting for him by the Dutch Sunken Garden outside.

The park outside was teeming with policemen and firemen, and the stranded guests still being escorted off the premises. Some were crying out in protest, not knowing what had happened to their room or where they would stay for the night having come from afar. Baynard knew they were stuck in limbo as much as he was. He walked towards the Dutch Sunken Garden and observed his men struggling to cover the perimeter. Cannizaro Park was large. It would be a challenge to block any access or ensure there was no leak of evidence. He then thought of all people stranded on Rushmere Green. What if the bomber was one of them and he or she had just got out, the inspector thought. Baynard had a finite number of resources. He could not justify back-up or put the entire guest list of the fair under suspicion without stirring suspicions. He brushed the thoughts to the back of his mind to keep it clear and moved on with a casual air about him not to raise concerns.

As he reached the Dutch Sunken Garden, he scanned the area for details. The blast was as bad as they said, even if only the work of a small bomb. He could see the layers of bricks from different eras that made up the solid exterior wall of Cannizaro House. He knew there were roughly four hundred years now scattered across the flower bed of tulips in heaps and rubbles. Baynard felt a little anger but did not show it. He joined a group of his men and they pointed at his next witness. To his surprise, the man was wearing a white chef jacket. The colour had lost its splendour with stains of cinder all over. The man's hair was tangled and clomped together. He was drying the sweat off his forehead, sitting at a wooden bench under a stone shelter. Baynard approached him with one of his stern nods. Enrico looked up, puzzled.

'Enrico Lariva?' Baynard asked.

Enrico frowned.

'Excuse me?'

'Enrico Latriva?'

'LoTrova!' corrected Enrico.

'Right!' nodded Baynard not paying attention. 'I am Inspector Baynard, from Wimbledon Police. I have a couple of questions for you.'

'About time. I have been waiting here for a while.'

Baynard sat impassively, not taking notice of the comment.

'I am here to ask you a few questions about the explosion.'

'*Grazie a Dio*, inspector! Did you find who did this?' You have to get him.'

81

Enrico talked in a rush, overlapping words or mispronouncing them with a thick Italian accent. Baynard already found his over-zealous excitement annoying.

'Easy, Mr Lartiva.'

'LoTrova!'

'Yes, yes. We are already working on this terrible tragedy…'

'Did you ask the man I saved if he knew who did this? You should send someone to search the park, the hotel, the whole area.'

Enrico rambled on, not sure if under shock or if a terrible sense of revenge had crawled under his skin. Maybe because of the wounds he had seen on the injured man he had saved, or because he had seen a seventeenth century house losing part of its soul, like when Italian churches are hit by earthquakes. He knew though his chances to sell bread and make an impression had been thwarted by whoever had the crazy idea to blow up the Duchess Hotel. He realised the inspector was looking at him with an inquisitive stare, his eyes intrusive without being a threat, as if reading every single shimmer of his anxious soul. He did not seem moved or touched by the hellish scene around them. Enrico wondered if he cared too much. Perhaps because he wanted Wimbledon to be his home.

'Slow down, sir. We are doing all of that.' spoke Baynard with a plain tone. 'What makes you think there is someone behind all this?'

Enrico cursed his tongue and did not answer, not knowing what to say. Baynard eyed him suspiciously.

'Why don't you tell me your movements before the explosion and what you remember after it? This is standard procedure.'

Baynard did not let any of his worries filter through. Yet, he found it odd to meet, after Lady of Cannizaro, another witness fanatical about murder mysteries. Either the fire brigade was worse at keeping secrets than he thought, or both this baker and Lady of Cannizaro had a very fervent imagination. Unless they knew something he did not. He listened on.

'I was with Lady of Cannizaro and Viviane…'

'Is that Viviane Leighwood?'

'Yes.' confirmed Enrico, confused. 'We walked from the Italian Garden, where the fair is, to the orangery here. Lady of Cannizaro went to get lunch when…'

Enrico paused a second. He quickly recalled the man in the hat looking up. He thought he could see him standing there next to them as he relived those few instants before the explosion. Enrico realised he had a perfect view of the room window, now smashed into tiny pieces. He disappeared right as the explosion shook Cannizaro House. There was something Enrico thought he saw but could not put his finger on it. The strange coincidence scratched the back of his head.

'Must have been a very long lunch…' asked Baynard to make Enrico snap out of his reverie.

'Erm…sorry… She went to get lunch when the whole building shook and I realised debris and smoke were literally pouring out of the building. I ran outside to witness the aftermath.'

The inspector made a note while checking out the Italian baker's hands and arms as they gestured frenetically between them. He pointed out where he had been and where the debris had fallen as if he were a painter raving mad on his unfinished canvas. He also noticed the little pauses Enrico made. Baynard wondered whether he was just having difficulty in finding the words, or if he missed out something from his version of the story voluntarily. Inspector Baynard could be a very suspicious man. It came with the job.

'And how come you sprinted to the first floor? Didn't you know of the danger?' he continued.

'*Ma sei matto?* I glimpse his hand through the smoke and I do nothing? Someone needed help. I could not just stand there.'

'Very heroic, Mr Lerteva.' commented Baynard, unclear to Enrico if sarcastic or thankful.

'LoTrova!'

'Right. Couldn't you have waited for the firemen and leave it to the experts? You could have been killed.'

Baynard put on a condescending tone to test the baker's temper.

'And what? Wait to fill in a form while the man maybe caught fire…'

Enrico looked away, trailing off after his sarcastic comment, unable to hide his drama. He glanced at the Dutch Sunken Garden, at the last few people being interviewed by police, at the hotel. He knew he had done the right thing. Baynard kept looking at him.

'I understand you are new to Wimbledon and to this country. We have processes in place here, Mr Latriva.'

'LoTrova!'

'Right. I suggest you get accustomed to them so that we avoid a misunderstanding. Are you around in the next few days if we have questions?'

Enrico nodded, signing the truce. There was more to be said but he saw no point in arguing now. He then spotted Viviane in the orangery through the glass talking to one of the police constables. Enrico realised she would have stopped him there and then or maybe even a little earlier in his conversation with Inspector Baynard. He could feel her grab his arm, giving him a reproachful eye. He kept nodding and let it be.

'One last question: did you know the man you saved?'

'I have never seen him before.' replied Enrico.

'Do you know if he was staying at the hotel?'

Enrico shook his head.

'I hope he is ok.' he added. 'He was mumbling something about flowers.'

'Flowers you say?'

'He could not find an azalea or something like that.'

Baynard wrote it down in haste, not paying attention.

'Probably the shock. You will be pleased to know he is and will pull through. Thank you!'

Baynard did not wish to stick around further. He had other pressing matters to address and time was running out. He wished the Italian baker goodbye and dismissed him. Baynard watched him leave, a little disoriented, as one of the police constables escorted him out. The inspector kept looking at the top floor of the hotel and back at the Italian baker. What gnawed at him was how the Italian baker had been quick at advocating for a culprit, just like Lady of Cannizaro did. Baynard wondered where all these rushed assumptions came from. It annoyed him even more, now that he knew this was not an involuntarily explosion. An evil or careless man was behind such ghastly act and he was a step ahead. The inspector chewed his gum to the core, now insipid and flavourless. He knew there was a hard truth to face but nobody was ready to hear that and it was time to give a statement to the hotel management and to the press.

Baynard walked back into the orangery to look for his sergeant and close assistant, Jeremy. He was leaning on one of the buffet counters, now filled with notepads and tablets. His bright ginger hair and freckled face could not go unnoticed. He was a smart young man and took his job seriously. He was also very brave for he had been the only policeman to apply for the job of sergeant, which meant reporting directly to Inspector Baynard himself. Not everyone at the station felt ready to deal with a man tough to read and very suspicious. The inspector in return had liked him ever since his very first day for the way he handled police paperwork was something extraordinary.

'What a mess!' he commented, announcing his arrival.

Sergeant Jeremy looked up.

'So I heard.' he added knowingly. 'I have just had the fire brigade's report secretly handed over to me, as if we are in a film of spies. They've finished upstairs and are wrapping up. The ambulances also confirmed they have been able to release many injured already. Where do we go from here?'

Baynard looked around the dining area in the orangery. The afternoon sun shone through and reflected against the topped wine glasses and the stranded cutlery on the empty tables. He looked out onto the park. The day was coming to an end. Less time for him and Jeremy to play with.

'Let's start by letting people go home. Check first that we have both the list of attendees for the fair from today and the hotel guest list. Name, address. We can then track the people we need for questioning.'

'How about the hotel and the park? Unofficially, they are now a crime scene.'

'I want the hotel and the park closed for at least forty-eight hours, maybe seventy-two. I do not want anyone in or out.'

'How about the guests staying here? Lady of Cannizaro will have a heart attack when she will hear the hotel needs to be closed.'

Tough call, thought Baynard. He knew he could get a two- or three-day break to carry out the investigation away from prying eyes. They would easily relocate hotel guests across Wimbledon and Putney. Any period beyond that would be impossible without exposing the bombing to the public or getting pressure from Lady of Cannizaro to reopen the hotel.

'Let's close the southern section of the first floor of the Duchess Hotel and block access to the whole of Cannizaro Park. It is the best we can do. Lady of Cannizaro will be able to use the ground floor and half of the rooms upstairs. I want a patrol in the hotel and one in the park at all times for the next three days, so we keep an eye on things around here. If the hotel staff asks, tell them preservation of evidence while the causes of the explosion are confirmed. In the meantime, get the Rose and Crown and the Dog and Fox on the phone. These pub hotels will have rooms to accommodate the hotel guests who don't have a room. Lady of Cannizaro can arrange to relocate them temporarily.'

Baynard looked away for a second, thinking it through once more. He then returned Sergeant Jeremy's gaze.

'Noted.' confirmed Jeremy. 'What's next then?'

'Don't we have two leads already?'

'We have?'

'Start by telling me the name of the man caught in the explosion. Do you have it?'

Jeremy gulped and scrambled for his notes.

'Yes!' he sighed in relief, close to cause Baynard some disappointment. 'His name is Eric Quercer. A Canadian horticulturist.'

'Bizarre...' the inspector murmured. 'And was that his room?'

Jeremy ran through the notes again, looking for the hotel guest list.

'Let's see. Room 54 is the one that blew up. And the room belongs to...'

'Faster, Jeremy! I can already feel the Chief Superintendent's breath on my neck.'

Jeremy scrolled through the list of names and room.

'Here it is! Room 54. It belongs to Sergej Vernikoff, the opera singer.'

Baynard gulped and he realised he had swallowed his gum.

The Rose and Crown pub had been subject to an invasion of guests for centuries. Ever since opening as an inn as far back as 1651, it was the key meeting place for the local vestry and any other local society. Later on, it also became a key stop for the regular stagecoach service into London via Putney, used by noblemen and politicians who lived in Wimbledon or further afield. Fast-forward to modern times, the Rose and Crown was always jam-packed during those two busy weeks in June when the Wimbledon Open called tennis fanatics from all over the world. This time round the Rose and Crown was subject to an invasion of stranded guests from the Duchess Hotel and until teatime the flow of people came and went, carrying their suitcases across Rushmere Green or grabbing a taxi for the 1-minute car journey from Cannizaro Park. For a couple of solid hours in the late afternoon, the tiny pub area and the car park next to it looked like an overcrowded refugee camp. Wimbledon Village was built on a small scale and the presence of large masses of people made any corner of it look like a Glastonbury concert or a protest march towards Westminster.

The exodus from the Duchess Hotel and Cannizaro Park had been as smooth as it could be. Wimbledon Police co-ordinated the output of people onto Rushmere Green on one end, and the staff of the Duchess Hotel on the other handled the grumbles and cries of protest from the guests who had to be relocated. The Rose and Crown had more rooms available at such short notice and it was the simplest choice to make for Lady of Cannizaro after hearing Inspector Baynard's public statement. Apparently, the causes of the explosion were more complex than the police thought and therefore the parts of the hotel and the whole park had to be quarantined to guarantee a thorough and impartial inspection. Lady of Cannizaro had initially complained but subdued to the fact she had to guarantee the safety of her guests.

Enrico and Viviane stuck around to listen to Baynard's statement until the end, just as the sun was setting beyond the Duchess Hotel. They then followed the direction of the crowd returning to their homes or to their new temporary accommodation. They, like everyone else, were both busy talking about what had happened and were still dazed in disbelief. It came as a natural decision to stop by at the Rose and Crown and calm each other's nerves over a drink. By the time they finished their second, the tiny pub started to look normal and no longer teeming with disoriented visitors from another hotel looking for shelter. The inside was cosy and authentic, with its dark wood and an old stone fireplace to one side. The twilight outside started to spread the darkness indoors creating shadows of heads and pints against the walls and pockets of light lit up to fight back and keep the atmosphere alive. Enrico stared at the windows from their table towards the back, mesmerised by the lighting effect or perhaps the strong ale which made him talk without inhibitions.

'Causes of the fire yet unknown?' he blurted out half-paraphrasing Baynard's statement. 'How can they not know yet? I thought there were processes...and forms to fill in... *Idiota*!'

'Easy, Enrico. It has been a full day and I see you are still in shock. I know because I am too!'

Enrico shrugged, rolling the pint glass in his hands.

'Hey, at least a man was saved!' he cheered raising his glass.

Viviane chinked his glass with hers and returned a half-smile to put the troubled day behind.

'What did you say the wounded man told you when you pulled him out?' asked Viviane with a gulp of her gin and tonic.

'Something about a black azalea and it was not there. The black azalea was not there, that's it!'

'The flower, you mean?'

'Is it? You are the florist, Viviane. You tell me.'

'Azaleas are common in Cannizaro Park. You have seen the whole footpath where apparently there used to be a tunnel made out of them, the Azalea Dell. You can find azaleas easily everywhere though. Your theory of a bombing is ridiculous. I don't think bombing a hotel is a means to finding a flower.'

Enrico shrugged. He had shared with Viviane his suspicions about someone being responsible for it all. She had laughed at him and challenged his deductions. He did not have much to go on to prove it, except the image of the man in the hat kept popping into his head, together with the echo of the explosion. He was not sure what to make of it and he had not spoken to Viviane about it yet.

'But...' continued Viviane thoughtful. 'A black azalea per se does not exist. Or at least I have never seen one. It is not one of the colours found in nature.'

'What do you mean?'

'It means any plant only grows with specific ranges of colour. Black is not one of them for an azalea. That man, whoever he was, was probably hallucinating. He did look in terrible shape, the way you described him.'

'He probably confused colours...'

'Or he is cleverer than we thought.'

'What are you trying to say?'

Viviane chuckled.

'Don't get over-excited, Enrico. All I am saying is that a black azalea would be a rarity, a horticulturist's own El Dorado. Such a unique piece would be worth millions.'

'Millions?' echoed Enrico with a hint of greed.

'Anyway, is that man ok?'

'He'll pull through.' said Enrico vaguely, his thoughts stuck to azaleas and millions. 'I saw paramedics looking after him and then taking him somewhere. Not sure if he was staying at the Duchess Hotel.'

Enrico saw again a flash of the man with the arm around his neck, pulling himself close to him to share his secret or his hallucination. He thought perhaps the man was raving mad, speaking out without thinking, or in his words perhaps there were half-truths.

'I see inspector Baynard grilled you a little.' carried on Viviane moving swiftly on. 'Not sure what you were used to back home, but you should probably comply with the police and don't let your temper get in the way.'

'My temper?'

Viviane nodded with a sip of her drink. Enrico had his reasons. She did not see what he saw. The man in the hat may have not been a bomber but there were too many coincidences in the way he was acting, minutes before the explosion, as if he knew something would happen. Because of this, he could not forget the whole thing or let it go. Something was odd. Maybe he was not hot-tempered as Viviane implied but he had to admit he was a curious man. A very curious man. Enrico swirled the empty pint in his hands and let the flat foam at the bottom draw circles and waves. The pub had regained its cheering attitude, the loud noise slowly rising in time for late evening drinks. The Italian baker was toying with the idea of telling Viviane about the man in the hat. He had felt the burden ever since entering the Rose and Crown. Somehow his mood was a little lifted and realised he had nothing to lose if he confided in one of the people closest to him, here in Wimbledon.

'There is another thing…' he started.

'Wait!' interrupted Viviane. 'Do you want to get food here? I am a little peckish.'

'It can wait!' Enrico dismissed.

Viviane pulled a wry face, not following. He smiled to brush off the abrupt manners.

'I mean, we can get food in a minute. I wanted to tell you I saw a man.'

'What man?'

'I saw a man. At the park.'

'Yes?' queried Viviane, still not following.

'OK, listen. Right before the explosion, there was a man in a hat by the Dutch Sunken Garden. I saw him from the orangery. He stood out there alone looking at the upper floor. Then minutes later he disappeared and…'

Enrico moved his hands upward to mimic an explosion.

'Did you tell the police?' asked Viviane, concerned.

'Well…no' said Enrico, embarrassed.

'What?'

Enrico could feel Viviane's disappointment. He quickly added something to justify himself.

'It was so quick. I thought it was a coincidence or my memory was playing tricks on me. But now, the more I think about it, the more it looks strange.'

'Did you see him or not?'

'Yes, I did.'

'Did you recognise him?'

'No, he had a hat and it covered his face in shadow. I did see his nose and chin. Their proportions would not go unnoticed if I saw him again. There was also something else, but I can't remember.'

'The police can still help. Why don't you go and tell them?'

'Maybe. That's not the point.'

Viviane listened.

'It is no coincidence that man stood there, as if waiting for the explosion, and then he left right after it happened. What if he is the bomber responsible for what happened today? What if the explosion was no accident?'

'And?' challenged Viviane playing along.

'The police did not mention anything of the sort. Do they really believe it was an accident?'

Viviane tried to recall the inspector's public statement and the policemen she talked to. They looked a little on edge when wrapping up the questioning, but it could have been simply down to shock. Enrico's theory seemed far-fetched.

'Ok. Let's play along.' she blurted out in defiance. 'Why would someone want to blow the Duchess Hotel, Enrico?'

'Keep your voice down!' Enrico hushed her.

A man stopped by their table, stumbling against the round edge and catching their attention. His red eyes and off-balanced position clearly told them he had been drinking for a while and he was tipsy enough not to mind interrupting their conversation.'

'The D-Duchess…Ho…Hotel?' he shouted with alcohol-scented breath you could smell in every direction. 'Did you see that today? Ka-boom!'

He grinned and made the gesture of the explosion without looking at them or acknowledging their reaction. A few people sitting nearby scowled, finding the explosion no laughing matter.

'*Ubriaco fradicio!* Excuse me…' Enrico said. 'We were talking!'

'I know.' said the drunk ignoring him and talking almost to himself. 'That bloody explosion took away my opportunity to finally see Sergej Vernikoff. Here, in Wimbledon frickin' Village.'

The man's face was red, and he was out of breath. Viviane rolled her eyes to Enrico.

'Sorry to hear…' added Viviane desperate to find a peaceful way to dismiss him.

'You are not sorry. You…you don't understand. I have been wa…waiting years for this. I paid for my ticket in advance, booked my front row seat, and now…and now they won't bother telling me when Mr Vernikoff will now play. All because someone left the gas on or burned their toast. I am so dis…disappointed…'

The drunk ranted on with no intention of stopping and grabbed an evening copy of the Wimbledon Guardian from the bar. He slammed it on their table. Enrico had had enough, and he was ready to stand up and leave when his eyes fell on the front page of the newspaper. The headline announced in shocking capital letters today's explosion but to the right there were two inset photos. One of the Duchess Hotel with its column of black smoke seen from Rushmere Green. The other a group picture of Lady of Cannizaro and a man, both surrounded by an orchestra. The man wore a hat he could not have mistaken anywhere in the world. He could see his face in full front. It was thin, with high cheekbones and a hard, pointy chin. His nose struck Enrico. It was big and straight, making him look far from good looking if it wasn't for the white smile and slick tuxedo he wore. The photo description did not list the names, but Enrico recognised the stage in the Italian Garden. The article mentioned the music events at Cannizaro Festival were cancelled until further notice.

'Who is that?' yelped Enrico as if he had seen a ghost.

He put his finger below the face of the man in the hat and tapped it furiously to get the drunk's attention. Viviane looked up not sure what the

Italian baker was getting at. He kept his gaze on the drunk as he repeated the question to her.

'I have seen this man before. Who is he?'

Viviane quickly made the connection and mouthed something in stupor. Enrico started shaking the drunk by the shoulder to get an answer, and a few heads in the pub turned. The drunk man was confused. He freed himself from Enrico's senseless grip and started grinning, almost laughing to himself, before replying in a somehow coherent slur.

'You are an ignorant…in music! You…you don't even recognise famous singers? That man is the great Sergej Vernikoff, the opera singer.'

Baynard had been sitting at his desk for more than two hours. His hips ached, locked forever into the same position. He rubbed his eyes and pulled away from his desk to take a break from the computer screen and the stack of statements Sergeant Jeremy and his men had been collecting all afternoon. Outside, the streets disappeared into the night and all he could see were the soft spotlights of the lamp posts alongside Alexandra Road. The street was not dead silent. Noise from the junction a few feet up the road could be heard as the only sound of something still alive and well. The traffic crossing through Wimbledon town never went to sleep.

The inspector had lost track of time. He sipped the cup of black coffee Jeremy had brought him earlier. It was now disgustingly cold, but he needed the caffeine. He could not let his guard down until he had all the facts checked out. He stood up and moved by the window. His icy stare saw its reflection in the glass pane. Baynard stared at it and ran again through what he knew.

Room 54 blew up at around one thirty p.m. Room 54 was Sergej Vernikoff's room, but he was not there at the time of the explosion. Sergeant

94

Jeremy was now trying to track the opera singer down after Lady of Cannizaro confirmed he had been in London for a few weeks. The inspector found it odd he was absent when he was meant to sing that same evening. Nevertheless, whatever the reasons, whatever suspicions he was brewing, the opera singer was urgently needed for questioning.

Then there was the wounded man. Eric Quercer. Canadian horticulturist visiting the UK. Baynard had never heard of him until today but a few searches brought up some of his world-wide fame in the sector and he came across a few unfounded references to his ill reputation in the trade of plants and flowers. Even though Eric Quercer did not suffer serious injuries, paramedics told Baynard he was badly shaken and needed some rest before he could answer any questions. Sergeant Jeremy had been able to book him for questioning at the Duchess Hotel for the following morning. They found out Eric Quercer was now staying at the Rose and Crown and Inspector Baynard did not hesitate to look up where his room had been at the Duchess Hotel. It was only a few doors from Vernikoff's but far enough from the blast. His injuries meant he was closer to the source of the explosion and it only meant he was near the room when everything happened. Baynard had to ascertain his movements as soon as possible.

He then thought of the Italian baker. He had come across as frantic, a little nervous, too over-excited for Baynard's taste. Something about him did not fit in and he was not sure what it was. Through his searches, he could not find much about who he was. He had no website for his business and there was nothing on him back in Italy. When he checked the Interpol database for criminal records, it came back with no results. He looked clean. Fortunately, he knew his whereabouts and could easily drop in at his bakery at any time for a chat. Perhaps someone at the WAIS could help too.

Baynard sipped his coffee, and then gagged at the cold, dull taste. He put it back on the desk and took one last view of the street outside. Time was already running out and he had to shortlist some suspects without forcing his hand. He was sure of one thing: a bomber was out there on the loose and it was better for Baynard he or she did not strike twice.

'Chief, still here?' came in Sergeant Jeremy's voice, strangely chirpy at that time of night.

'Your voice is too happy for a late date stuck at the office.' commented Baynard dryly. 'I hope you are not on cocaine. Do you need me to give you more work to do? Or are you the bearer of some news, good or bad?'

Jeremy escaped Baynard's stare, ignoring his usual sarcasm. He was used to it. The sergeant quickly drew the attention to a bunch of files he placed on the little space left on Baynard's desk.

'I'd rather be at the pub to drink this over. I found some more bedtime reading for you.'

'Oh, so it's alcohol and not drugs. Good for you. And thanks for the gift. Why don't you join me?'

The two exchanged glances, each drawing energy from that short banter. Sergeant Jeremy had worked for Inspector Baynard long enough to know what he expected, and he was now more or less prepared for Baynard's short bursts of sarcasm, which only came about when it was only the two of them or when they were at the police station. Otherwise, to those who did not know him, Baynard was a stern hawk with fine eyesight for detective work and immune to any form of distraction.

The only difference this time was the seriousness of the case. Wimbledon Police had seen anti-social behaviour, low-scale robberies, a few cases of fraud or domestic violence. Although nobody was saying it, the explosion at the Duchess Hotel was a first they were not prepared for. Both Baynard and Jeremy knew the stakes were high and there would be more heavy-lifting needed towards the case.

'This is the preliminary report from the fire department.' started Sergeant Jeremy. 'I also sent you a digital copy.'

'Care to give me the gist of it? I am not good at reading tomes as high as War and Peace or Lord of the Rings.'

'It is confirmed, inspector. A small bomb was placed in Vernikoff's room.'

Baynard listened carefully, giving Jeremy his full attention.

'The odd bit is that the remote detonation was programmed.'

'Programmed?'

'Someone activated the bomb remotely, at short range, but the explosion was triggered automatically.'

'A booby trap?'

'Sort of.'

'How?'

'The explosion was triggered when one of the bedroom cabinets was opened.'

'Which one?'

'It does not say. Perhaps the one holding the room's safe.'

Baynard did not comment further. His inquisitive stare was now focused on the paperwork scattered on the desk. He was thinking.

'Do you have Mr Vernikoff and Mr Quercer pinned down for tomorrow?'

'Mr Quercer made himself available for tomorrow first thing in the morning. Lady of Cannizaro said you can use the orangery or any of the rooms on the ground floor.'

'It will be an informal questioning. To them, we are simply getting their statement. How about Vernikoff?'

'I contacted his agent and we are struggling to get hold of him. Does it look suspicious to you?'

Baynard snorted.

'He is a celebrity, so I will give him the benefit of the doubt for a few more hours. Then unleash the hounds.'

'Do you think he is a suspect?'

'Too early to tell but don't let things slip out of our hands. Is Cannizaro Park off limits as I instructed?'

'Yes, patrols at the gate and at the doors leading to it from the hotel. Our mandate covers us for seventy-two hours this evening.'

'Good. Let's adjourn to tomorrow.'

'What should we tell the Chief Superintendent? We have not briefed him yet on the explosion.'

'And we won't. Not yet. First, I want to hear Mr Vernikoff and Mr Quercer's version of the story. Then check out Room 54.'

'He may not be happy about the fact we are hiding this.'

'What do you prefer? Town-wide panic?'

Jeremy hoped Baynard knew what he was doing. He could not ignore the faint tingling of panic under his skin. The hotel and the park were off limits for three days. That was all the time they had to secretly find out who planted a bomb in one of Wimbledon's historic buildings.

Lady of Cannizaro could not sleep. The cries and the panic tormented her dreams and she kept staring up at the ceiling. She lit the bedside table and reached for the glass of water she had filled only one hour or so before. The bedroom was quiet. There was no sound outside. The whole building was dead silent, now half-empty and void of the joy and thrill which had filled the days until this morning. Cannizaro House had never been so silent. It made her feel lonelier in the small bedroom next to her office and she suddenly regretted she had decided to stay for the night rather than go home. She was worried, that's all. Worried about her hotel. Worried about the fair and the community. She was also worried about something else.

She glanced at the alarm clock and could not believe time did not move at all. She thought it best to get up again and look for some sleeping pills. She put her slippers on and walked into her office. Light from the hotel's car park filtered through the drawn curtain, creating a pale blue haze inside the room. The silence pervaded with only the ticking of a clock to accompany her. Lady of Cannizaro moved to her desk. She opened one of the drawers and took out the aluminium foil containing six capsules. Her intention was not to swallow them. Sleeping was only delaying uncertainty till tomorrow. She was more interested in the note scribbled on the white side, in between the bumps containing the sleeping pills. A phone number, in case of emergency. Like medicines. She looked at her mobile and then preferred to use the landline. The phone rang forever on the other end of the line.

'Hello?' answered a voice.

'Were you sleeping?' asked Lady of Cannizaro.

'No. Why are you calling?'

'They are looking for him.'

The voice sighed.

'I know. He made himself available to the authorities. I told them he will be available at the hotel tomorrow morning and he will fully cooperate.'

'Isn't that risky? He could have died today. What makes you think someone, you know who, will not try again tomorrow?'

'We can't give the wrong impressions.'

Lady of Cannizaro paused for a second, worried she heard something outside or a funny noise down the phone line.

'You do speak like an agent. Is the sheet safe?'

This time the voice paused.

'Today was meant to be a big day.' carried on Lady of Cannizaro, wishing to let a burden off her chest. 'We were going to announce something of great historical importance. We can't lose that sheet!'

'We can still make the announcement. We simply need to wait it out patiently. The sheet is safe and you should stay out of it. The less you know, the better. We can manage it without you or the Trust being involved directly.'

'What is he going to tell the police?'

The voice hung up. Silence returned to the office and for a moment the woman held the phone to her ear, expecting to hear a crackling noise or maybe a gusty sound. Cannizaro House would soon be haunted by the ghosts of history.

Eric Quercer tried to keep his eyes open, fighting each of his winces while he dabbed the sore, dried injuries on his face and arms with some ice. Nothing major, paramedics told him, but it hurt like hell. Eric felt humiliated. From the moment he was dismissed from Parkside Hospital, he did not waste a single minute cursing at Sergej Vernikoff. The opera singer turned out to be a clever fox. His hidden explosive was something Eric did not expect when he broke into Room 54. Vernikoff knew someone was coming after him and he had come to the hotel prepared. Eric wondered if surviving the aftermath was part of Vernikoff's plan too, or if the bomb was meant to kill. Still, he could not withstand the humiliation he had suffered, and what made it worse was the fact he had come out of it empty-handed. The paper was not there, nor was any other sign of the black azalea.

Eric clenched his teeth in anger. The police also knew about him after he was saved from the blaze and they wished to speak to him the following morning. He seriously hoped his face was not all over the news. Apart from putting his plan into jeopardy, he could not stand further mocking by the club if the news reached across the Atlantic. His thoughts then turned to the mysterious man who had tipped him off about the whole affair. Eric wondered for a moment if the man's tips were genuine, or if he had been a victim of misinformation and he, like him, had underestimated Vernikoff's determination. The Trust seemed very adamant not to sell their secrets to the highest bidder.

He now sat uncomfortably in a tiny chair examining his wounds. The room given to him at the Rose and Crown was comfortable but a lot smaller than the one he had at the Duchess Hotel. Although it did not suffer any damage during the explosion, it fell within the radius deemed unsafe by the authorities and Eric had to be relocated. Upon returning late that evening, half-drugged and half-covered in plasters, he found his belongings had been safely transferred across but piled up in one corner without care. To make things worse, the plants in the room had lost all their lush green and were dying together with what he thought was an outdated décor. Another humiliation.

A knock came to the door. Eric froze, ice pack sweating in his hand. He wished it was not a nuisance call of any kind. It was the end of a very bad day and he was not in the mood.

'Who is it?' Eric called out.

'Message for you, sir.'

Eric looked around the room for something to defend himself with. The revolver was in his suitcase. He thought twice whether to take it out or not. Too noisy. Instead, he picked a deodorant spray and kept it hidden to his side. He had to take extra care from now on. His cover may not be blown but he could not be sure it was not Vernikoff waiting on the other side of the door.

A second knock came and Eric half-opened the door showing his face. The man at the door wore a fine suit, close to a uniform, and had a black cap under his arm. Eric thought he looked like a chauffeur or an airline pilot.

'Eric Quercer?'

'Who is asking?'

'Message for you.' said the man in uniform.

He handed him an envelope, without checking he was really Eric Quercer, and gave a brief bow with his head before walking away down the small corridor. Eric was speechless. He closed the door and opened the envelope without hesitation. It contained a printed one-page letter. It was from the mysterious man. He had never met him and had only exchanged information through correspondence of all sorts. Eric wondered whether the man in uniform worked for him or if he were just a messenger. Regardless, it was obvious the mysterious man was aware of his movements and current whereabouts. Eric read on.

Apart from a polite apology for the unfortunate series of events, the sender was tipping him off again about Vernikoff's movements. The police had been looking for him after the disaster and he finally made contact for an interview the following day at the Duchess Hotel. Eric saw an opportunity dawning on him. In the letter, the mysterious man reminded him to proceed with caution and confirmed there was a high probability Vernikoff was carrying the valuable piece of paper with him. The one showing where the black azalea was hidden. The letter ended reassuring Eric that his identity had not been exposed to the Trust and Vernikoff would not know who he really was if they met. Yet, the mysterious man could not guarantee this would last and the only way to get hold of the piece of paper was to get rid of the opera singer.

That was the end of it. No means of contact apart from how they had agreed to meet once Eric was in possession of the black azalea. Until then, and this is how it had been ever since he had made first contact, the mysterious man would only get in touch personally if plans changed. Eric found it unsettling how this man was able to trace him wherever he was. Eric had tried changing clothes, cars and phone, fearing a bug or radio transmitter of some kind, without avail. The mysterious man was all-seeing, all-knowing.

Eric re-read the letter. He paused at the section where he was reminded how he would hand over the black azalea to the mysterious man. This part, present in almost all communications, left Eric suspicious. He always kept the rare plants he discovered, no matter the means used or the rewards promised by avid collectors. For the first time, though, someone had asked him to find something for them. Yet, the mysterious man's intentions had never been clear. Surely, a black azalea would be worth millions, if not billions. A rare species never seen before. A hint of malice crossed his tired face. The black azalea could be his and his alone.

He crumpled the letter and then struck a match to burn it. He then dumped it in the bin and threw a book on top to kill off the smoke. He covered the fire alarm with a wet plastic bag to be sure no more sirens went off for today. He stretched his muscles, still aching. He needed time to rest before tomorrow but first he would have a shower to shake off the tension. As he took off his clothes slowly, through winces and pains, he thought of what the police may ask him and how he should eliminate Vernikoff. He glanced at the open suitcase for some ideas. He checked a small box full of vials filled with liquids of different colours. He then checked the status of the revolver and how many bullets he had. He was not sure about using such a barbaric tool, but he knew that if he had to fire it, it would be only when he had the black azalea in his hands and he was ready to get out of the country. He closed the suitcase, and before going into the bathroom, Eric Quercer checked one of the dying plants in his room. Yellow leaves, too much water. He snorted at the merciless act.

Viviane had been clear. Headstrong clear. Enrico was not a vigilante. He was a baker who had to focus on getting his business up and running. He nodded on hearing all of this, his eyes on Viviane, his mind on the explosion, the wounded man, and Sergej Vernikoff watching it all happen from afar.

Enrico knew he would disappoint his friend the moment she left to attend her flowers. He could not bear not knowing. He had to find out. Yet, he did not rush out of the bakery straight away. His hands had been pricking throughout the conversation with Viviane, and the moment he woke up in the early hours of the morning, he spent a good hour kneading a fresh batch of bread. Rolling, pressing, rolling, pressing. His hands moulded a round bloomer loaf while his thoughts moved onto the opera singer and the black azalea. The massaging of the dough made him relax and made him think clearly. He tried to remember what he had seen from the orangery. The hat, the cricket sweater, the nose. He remembered that outfit. He then recalled a man that bumped into him when chatting with Lady of Cannizaro in the Italian Garden. Same outfit. Why was Vernikoff hanging around incognito at the fair? Enrico's thoughts went back to the image of the opera singer out there by the Dutch Sunken Garden. Then, as a magic dusting of flour was sprinkled on the final bread work, Enrico remembered the one detail of Vernikoff he had completely forgotten. Something in his hand. A small phone perhaps. No, he touched it with his thumb without looking. A joystick or a small remote controller maybe. Enrico paused for a second. What if Vernikoff himself blew up the hotel room, he thought. He could not believe what he was thinking. It did not make sense. Enrico carried on dusting the large oven tray and lined up his batch of bread for baking. He wanted to be known for his bread and instead he would be known by the police for his overexcited curiosity into a case of arson. He feared his whole business would fall apart, without any money to pay bills and licenses. Perhaps Viviane was right in letting it all go. Then again Viviane herself told him the black azalea was a rarity worth a lot of money. Millions, as Viviane put it. Enrico knew that, if it really existed, someone would profit from it at the expenses of Wimbledon. The Italian baker stared at the line of perfectly identical bloomers, ready to have a crispy crust and soft crumb inside. He had nothing to lose. He had to go back to the Duchess Hotel and make sense of it all. If he were wrong, he could at least be sure he had just got the wrong end of the stick.

A little before eight a.m. Enrico slipped out of the bakery with his chef jacket wrapped round his body. Viviane's shop was not yet open and the last thing Enrico wanted was feeling Viviane's suspicious eyes on him while sprinting up the street. He crossed Wimbledon High Street from south to north, passing the yawning shopkeepers and the rattling shutters, as Wimbledon Village welcomed a new morning after the chaotic events of the previous day. The air was fresh and breezy, but once off the high street and onto Rushmere Green, outside the protection of the three-hundred-year-old buildings, the gusts of wind spreading on top of the hill from the north hit Enrico with their full magnitude. It felt colder than usual and the sun was in the mood of playing hide and seek with a swarm of fluffy clouds plotted against a pale blue sky. Enrico wrapped himself in his chef jacket and kept his head down, his wavy hair flung about. He could see the short grass at his feet trembling and across the pond light ripples creased the surface of the water. The trees lining around the southern edge of Rushmere Green shook against the wind and held firm with their thick, secular trunks. Enrico looked north of the small triangular patch of green, beyond Cannizaro House, where a dense cluster of trees hid from view what lay beyond. They swayed from left to right like choir singers, dancing to some mysterious but playful rhythm.

Enrico walked up to the hotel car park and found his path blocked by a police cordon line. He walked alongside it, up to the black iron gates leading directly into the park. Three policemen stood behind the cordon and patrolled the area up and down. One of them saw Enrico passing by. He eyed him suspiciously and nodded politely without smiling. The Italian baker returned the favour and tried hard to act normal, to show he was merely passing by. His mind in the meantime raced on, thinking what he should do next or why he had come all the way there. The whole park and part of the hotel had been closed off by the police and the sight of patrols only fuelled Enrico's theories and imagination. Trying to break into what was now a police-guarded area was probably dangerous, and one more reason for Viviane to be angry at him. Even the chances of bumping into the inspector and raise his concerns about Enrico multiplied as well. Despite all this, the Italian baker needed to check out the explosion. A quick check would not hurt anyone, he kept repeating to himself. Deep inside, though, he did know what to look for.

Dr Watkins said the park used to be part of a bigger one and most of Wimbledon evolved around it. He was sure its enclosure was easier to climb at some point. The Italian baker carried on walking, coasting the exterior of small private mansions which stood between him and the actual high walls of the park. He reached a bend and turned into Camp Road. The road was quiet. The row of small private mansions ended and to his left he could see the high wall of Cannizaro Park, with ivy crawling up to redecorate the ageing bricks. It did not look strong enough to hold him and there was nothing easy to grab. Enrico thought again if he was being reckless. He carried on until the road diverged from the wall. A tiny bright red door to the left, in the middle of the dark grey high wall, cut out an entrance into the park worthy of Alice in Wonderland. It looked even smaller when Enrico moved closer to it. Locked. Of course, it would be. Enrico then spotted a small cottage ahead of him, built right next to the wall where the road bent up north. The odd location was an indication of the erratic expansion and partitioning of Cannizaro Park over the centuries. The high wall of the park was probably the most recent enclosure, built by Edward K. Wilson, the last private owner, to protect what was then his large private garden. The cottage on the other hand had a charming, authentic look, but its appearance was more recent, probably restored to keep up with the times.

Enrico looked at the high wall and the cottage and calculated the distance. It was wide enough for a jump. He moved into the gap, on the side of the cottage, and checked the downspout. Solid enough, Enrico hoped. He took a first step and slipped. He then heard a car passing by and walked further into the gap to stay out of view. Once clear, he tried again and was able to get a good grip this time round. He climbed up to the gutter and looked back. Not high enough. He had to climb over the roof. The tiles rattled a little and the wind was blowing in his face. The Italian baker balanced himself and calculated the distance once more. He knew he had to be quick before anyone saw him, but he also did not want to break a leg. He paused, and before he came close to chickening out, Enrico sprinted along the roof edge towards the narrowest point. He waited until the last minute before leaping forward, arms stretch into the void. His hands did grab the edge, but his face fell flat against the bricks, almost crushing his nose. The pain he felt was nothing compared to the strain on his hands and fingers as the weight pulled him down. For an instant, Enrico regretted his course of action. Yet, he could not let go and he pulled himself up as hard as he could. He kept his groans to a minimum, so as not to be heard. In his ears he thought people were yelling at him from the streets. The policemen rushing down accusing him of trespassing, the owner of the cottage coming to check what the noise was. Enrico pulled himself up out of fear until he was able to swing his leg over the wall. Feeling relieved to have made it, he released his grip on the edge but did it too soon. He rolled over to the other side and fell down on a mass of high bushes and low trees. He felt his body crashing against the web of branches until he hit the hard ground. Enrico coughed and laid still where he landed, deep in the undergrowth. He winced at his sore fingers and checked his bruised body. Nothing seemed to hurt. He could move without any blinding pain. He was lucky the branches had slowed down his unplanned descent.

Enrico laid there for a few minutes. He held his ear out, listening to the sounds in the park. Nobody seemed to be out there, and hopefully nobody heard him fall. A few minutes passed before Enrico stood up and tip-toed out of the thick foliage into an open space. Enrico did not recognise where he was. It was a section of Cannizaro Park he had not been to, which looked completely different from what he had seen so far. To the left, a small cottage built into the wall stood up almost as high as the wall itself. Enrico realised the tiny red door outside probably led into it. The cottage guarded a beautiful rose garden, laid out in a circle where the first signs of colour were on the verge of blossoming. To the right, the park continued along the wall, and ahead of him trees of maples filled the view without revealing anything beyond. Enrico felt he needed a map. He did not know which way to go for the Duchess Hotel, or to be more precise, a way which would not involve bumping into the police. He jumped onto the path and decided to go right. If Lady of Cannizaro's statement held true, by following the borders he would get to the hotel eventually. He walked briskly ahead, keeping low. He quickly came across a classical statue whose white was long gone and the moss had turned it into a grey, dark figure. It depicted a woman and an animal. Enrico was quick in recognising the statue from the old picture in the Wimbledon Museum. This was the statue of Diana and the Fawn, standing behind Hilary Wilson, right outside Cannizaro House. He wondered why they had moved it here, almost abandoned. Enrico moved on, turning left and down a gentle slope. He followed a wide footpath lined with maple trees on each side until he realised the downward direction was taking him to more familiar places. He could now see the northern outer wall of the Italian Garden. The pond was to his left and directly across the steps leading up to the hotel. He could still not understand the shape of the park and Enrico promised to himself he would ask Dr Watkins or Lady of Cannizaro to share a map with him.

He reached the end of the slope and ahead of him the tree line ended opening up onto another open space following in parallel the outer wall of the Italian Garden. Enrico wondered which way was the safest. Following the borders of the park would probably help him avoid meeting the police or hotel staff on the way. He was still making up his mind when he heard voices coming towards him. Opposite him, coming down from the hotel, Lady of Cannizaro was being escorted down towards the pond by two police constables. She was talking energetically but he could not distinguish what she was talking about. The Italian baker hid behind the walls of the Italian Garden until the words became clearer.

'This is my hotel, you know? I don't need this kind of treatment.' she complained.

'Our apologies, Lady of Cannizaro,' said one of the policemen in condescending tone. 'but the inspector's orders have been very clear. We do not want people wandering in the park without police permission until the situation has been cleared.'

'It is the room upstairs that needs to be cleared. How long before I can re-open half of my hotel? Surely, the firemen have found out the cause of the explosion.'

Lady of Cannizaro rambled on as Enrico heard them approaching and stepping into the Italian Garden. She did not show signs of relenting or even let the policemen speak, her voice was loud and clear. Enrico was lucky enough to understand everything she was saying.

'We had a fair to run and we have left it all here half-done.' she said.

'No need to shout, ma'am. We are standing right here.' complained the other policeman. 'It will be quick. We just have to check the status of the fairgrounds.'

'Baynard's orders, I presume?'

Enrico followed her voice and walked along the outer wall. He could not see where they were going. He came across a long modern shed placed against the wall and thought it was low enough to climb onto. Without making any noise, he lay flat on the roof and crawled to the edge of the wall looking over the Italian Garden. Lady of Cannizaro was standing on the steps joining the first two terraced sections. She kept her graceful posture while crossing her arms and bearing a disgruntled face at the two policemen wandering around the empty stage and the empty stalls. Enrico wondered if his bread was still out there, probably no longer fresh to eat. Lady of Cannizaro kept talking and the two policemen were clearly bothered by her presence. Enrico watched carefully. She was tapping her foot, impatiently. Nerves, probably. It was no ordinary situation. Yet, her voice became louder as the policemen came closer to the stage and the seats she had arranged nicely the day before. Something was not right, Enrico thought. After less than thirty minutes, the policemen gave up their inspection and said they would come back when Baynard arrived.

'Not sure what you plan to find here.' snorted Lady of Cannizaro. 'Can we go now?'

'Yes, yes.' repeated the policemen, annoyed.

Enrico had to admire Lady of Cannizaro's power of persuasion. He watched them leave from the iron gate of the Italian Garden, going back up to the hotel, and gradually slid forward to jump off into the fairgrounds. They were empty, abandoned. Almost a ghost town. He did not make a sound and looked at the eerie emptiness of it all. He walked over to his stall and touched his bread almost hard as stone. Too bad, he thought. He then walked near the platform stage and he remembered he could take the stage exit through the Azalea Dell to reach the hotel unseen, or at least for a good part of it. Then a sound alerted him. He froze and crouched behind a stack of loudspeakers nearby. He looked ahead, to where the sound was coming from. Backstage he saw a man kneeling over a small trap door leading into the raised flooring. He was taping something and then reached underneath the floor to fix it. Enrico could not believe his eyes. The man was wearing the same clothes as yesterday. A hat. A cricket sweater. Sergej Vernikoff.

Baynard's car screeched as he swerved fast into the car park. His men saw him coming and lifted the police line to let him through. He gave them a stern nod, as per usual, and lined himself up to the few vehicles parked neatly in front of the Duchess Hotel.

The inspector did not get out of the car immediately. He mulled over his thoughts and theories scattered across his little notebook in the form of doodles, shapes and half-legible words. He had done the same before going to bed the night before, but they still did not come together to make sense of it all. Less than three days, now. That is all he had before the hotel and park could be re-opened in full. According to an early call of the Chief Superintendent, the fair could not be delayed further or rescheduled. He appreciated Baynard's rigorous process, but it was already too long to investigate a fire hazard. According to the organisers, they had already lost Sergej Vernikoff's opening night and the whole event was at risk of making no revenue or profit. Baynard understood all that and for a minute he was willing to spill the beans, tell him what had really happened. His love for Wimbledon stopped him in his tracks. He could not let panic spread wide. He told himself to wait until he had spoken to the two men on his list. If this was something bigger than he could handle, he would raise the alarm.

In the meantime, he asked his men to search the park, especially the fairgrounds, and he would look at the room or what was left of it. He did not know what he would find and Sergeant Jeremy thought it was a waste of time, to which Baynard gave him a derogatory note with his icy, inquisitive stare. The idea stuck in the inspector's head was that, if Vernikoff had planted a booby trap in his own room, then he was protecting himself against someone. He would have to find out what it was. He was glad to know the opera singer had come forward in the end and was happy to give his statement later that morning, before lunch.

Baynard finally stepped out of the car after a full five minutes and checked out the vehicles around him. Nothing suspicious. He then walked through the main door and once again he was inside the majestic entrance hall. It was rather quiet and not many guests or staff around. A lady followed him up from reception and welcomed him warmly, quick to recognise who he was.

'Good morning Inspector Baynard.' she said. 'Lady of Cannizaro went with two of your men to the Italian Garden, as requested. She told me to let you in and ,make you comfortable as soon as you arrived.'

He looked at the woman from the corner of his eye, wondering if she had the slightest idea why he was here. Jeremy had been careful enough to convince Lady of Cannizaro that additional witness statements would have helped putting a timeline against the explosion. Something vital for the court and the insurance companies to address, or something along those lines. She believed it. Yet, the inspector did not want to raise a single suspicion. It took very little to let people's imagination run wild.

'Thank you. Where can I stay for the day?' asked Baynard.

'We arranged a corner table for you in the orangery. No breakfast will be served there so you will have all the privacy you need. We offered room service on the house for the few guests staying in the northern wing. Tea, coffee?'

'Coffee, please. Black, no sugar. Is Mr Quercer here?'

'He is waiting for you.'

Baynard thanked the receptionist while trying to hide his surprise. Eric Quercer was already here. The man had suffered an explosion first hand and in less than twenty-four hours he was already up and about, ready for questioning. Perhaps he had something to say. Or perhaps something to hide.

The receptionist took him across the central hall, past the bird statue. Baynard noticed a few guests still hanging around, reading a newspaper or having a hot beverage at the bar. He was led into the orangery which he was surprised to find empty.

'I hope this is ok with you, sir.' said the receptionist pointing out the far table.

Eric Quercer looked up from the bacon and egg on his plate upon hearing voices. He saw the police inspector standing there and squaring him off with an inquisitive stare across his face that could have meant many things. His expression hardly changed when he thanked the receptionist and walked over to the table. Baynard held his hand forward and Eric shook it, trying to read those eyes and their hard stare. The Canadian played it cool with no intention of feeling threatened.

'Good morning, Mr Quercer.'

'Morning, inspector…'

'Baynard. Thank you for making yourself available at such short notice. I see you recovered pretty quickly.'

'Yes. The paramedics did wonders.'

Baynard could now have a better look at him. He had a mop haircut with a lock of hair slightly hiding his blue eyes. He had a bright coloured shirt with some tropical theme splattered around. Despite the scars and bruises on his face and his hands, his stylish look made Baynard forget the image he had of a boring horticulturist.

'Please take a seat.' added Eric Quercer. 'As you can see, the paramedics restored my hunger as well. I hope you did not mind me asking for something to eat.'

'Not at all.'

The receptionist came with the inspector's black coffee, and when she asked him about breakfast, he simply said 'no'. He then made himself comfortable in his seat and grabbed his notebook while Eric Quercer finished his plate without a rush.

'I hear an accent. American?' lied Baynard.

A casual chat to start with always helped warm things up for questioning.

'Canadian. I know the accent may be difficult to spot for you Europeans.'

'How long have you been here in Wimbledon?'

'Around a month. I had a few meetings with the Royal Horticultural Society here in London, and was planning also to attend the Cannizaro Festival until, you know…'

Baynard nodded slowly in agreement. Eric did not look straight at him all the time. He knew he had to stay cool. The police could have checked all kinds of information on him. Even if they were investigating the blaze, he had done nothing wrong.

'My colleagues told me you are a horticulturist. Interesting line of business?'

113

'It can be rewarding. It runs in the family. Did you know my great-great-grandfather knew Edward K. Wilson? They worked together on some of the flower collections used here in Cannizaro Park. The Royal Horticultural Society contacted me for, let's call it, a "cultural exchange" or something like that.'

Eric Quercer paused for a moment. The inspector kept nodding. His stare hardly flinched. The Canadian knew what he had said so far was true and it was indeed his cover. If Baynard wanted to call the Royal Horticultural Society now, they would confirm everything. And in terms of illicit activities, it was all hearsay. Nothing more.

'But I don't want to waste your time, inspector. I was told you wanted to get my statement.'

'Yes, indeed. Please allow me to re-iterate that this is a standard procedure when a blaze of this proportion happens. We need to check out the facts so the inquiry, which may be against manufacturers or whatever started the fire, has the information to know who will pay for damages. I have to say this before we start, so we are clear this is no questioning and no legal counsel is required.'

'Understood.'

Baynard found Eric Quercer very compliant. His forced smile soldiered on against the signs of trauma visible on his skin.

'Could you confirm your room here at the Duchess Hotel, on the first floor?'

Baynard gave him the number and even stated the distance from Room 54.

'Correct.'

'What were you doing at the time of the explosion? What did you see?'

'Not much. I was just coming out of my room. I heard a sound and I turned towards the end of the corridor. I made a few steps forward and before I knew it, a huge smoke spread over me and I felt the wave of the explosion as it hit me hard.'

'Sorry to hear that. I hear you owe your life to the man who saved you.'

'Yes, so I have been told. I will need to thank him. I did not catch his name.'

Baynard read his notes and then Jeremy's correct spelling next to it.

'Enrico...LoTrova. Did you know him?'

'Not at all.'

'What kind of sound did you hear in the corridor?'

'A ticking or clacking sound. Hard to tell. It was very faint.'

'Don't worry, Mr Quercer. All this can be helpful. What were your movements before the explosion?'

Eric Quercer stood in silence, pretending he was recalling the events of the day. Instead, he was moving his own pieces on the chessboard. This was no ordinary witness statement. The police knew someone was behind the explosion. Things were about to move quickly.

'I was here at the hotel mostly. I spent some time at the fair and that's about it.'

'Noticed anything strange?'

Eric Quercer shook his head. Baynard took a moment to scribble a few words and flip back to old pages, looking for anything to refresh his memory. Something caught his eye. Something he had written.

'One last thing, Mr Quercer.'

'Please, Eric.'

His smile was starting to become nauseating for Baynard. However, he could not turn him into a suspect just because he was annoying.

'The man who saved you. Enrico...Lor...Lot...whatever. He said he heard you mumbling something when he found you. Something about a flower you could not find. An azalea or something.'

Eric Quercer froze and held Baynard's gaze. He kept his smile, but his mind raced in panic as the chessboard pieces were suddenly caught in a deadly move. He did not recall saying that. Maybe he said it while half-conscious. He cursed his tongue. He had to stay calm. It did not expose him in any way.

'I…I…I don't know. I must have been talking gibberish.'

'Probably.'

Baynard had done this job for a long time and one thing he was good at was spotting when people were hiding something, whether for better or for worse. It was that subtle change in expression, the way the eyes flinched, the skin creased. Eric Quercer knew something that could help the inspector in the investigation, but the Canadian was not going to share it. Still, there was no motive for him to be behind the explosion. Unless he had been the target of Vernikoff's booby trap. Baynard hit the brakes to his thought process for a second and quickly concluded the conversation.

'Thank you, Mr Quercer. That'll be all.' Are you around for longer? Or will you be returning home soon?'

'Around a week, inspector.'

'Good. We'll be in touch.'

Baynard stood up and shook hands as if they had been good acquaintances for a very long time. Eric Quercer watched him leave and he realised he had to find the black azalea and leave the country before this damn park re-opened.

Enrico stayed put, crouched behind the loudspeaker. He kept one eye to the left, hoping Lady of Cannizaro or the two policemen were not on their way back. With the other, he followed Sergej Vernikoff's movements. The opera singer first checked whatever he had fixed under the platform stage. He then closed the trap door and pushed a heavy trunk on top of it. He stood there for a minute to catch his breath and looked around the empty backstage.

When his gaze turned towards the loudspeaker, Enrico slid deeper into his hiding place and prayed Sergej Vernikoff was not planning to leave via where he was. He held his breath again. A few seconds passed, and Enrico did not hear noises or footsteps. He peeked around the corner and he realised Vernikoff was gone. He wondered what on earth he was up to. Setting another trap perhaps. Another bomb under the stage. Enrico told himself to calm down and keep going. He came out of his hiding place and walked up to the heavy trunk. He then traced the only other way out from there: the stage exit. The same he had walked through the previous day. On the other side of the wall, Lady Jane's Wood's overgrowing forest stood like a cliff over the Italian Garden and the rest of the park behind him. Enrico listened for voices and footsteps. He swallowed hard, fearing Vernikoff could be looking at him from behind the bushes, and then stepped out of the Italian Garden to disappear in the deep green of Lady Jane's Wood.

Once inside, Enrico felt even more under threat and kept glancing sideways, watching out for anyone approaching. It dawned on him how reckless he had been by trespassing the police line and how he was getting into more trouble by following a suspicious man who was probably more dangerous than he thought. Enrico cast his thoughts aside convinced he could still get to the bottom of this.

Enrico walked across the Azalea Dell, scanning the azaleas as he passed through, to see if Viviane was right. She was. No black azaleas. He stepped out of the pathway and made a few other twists and turns in what he thought was a northerly direction. He wondered why the walk with Lady of Cannizaro had appeared shorter. The rich damp smell of the undergrowth and the resin-imbued scent of the old thick trees was pungent and inebriating. The footpath Enrico thought he was on started to fade, swallowed by wild herbs, high ferns, a more anarchic undergrowth that made it impossible to know which direction to go in. Enrico stopped walking after a while. The sun struggled to push through the tall pine trees and those few rays reaching the ground were like magical beams casting a

117

spell of blissful silence. Enrico looked to his right to see a green wooden fence, and house roofs on the other side. He had no idea where he was. He could not have asked for more: trespassing and getting lost. He spun around a few times and decided to keep the fence in sight on his right. Sooner or later, the Duchess Hotel would appear.

A new sound made him stop. It was not the birds chirping or the wind making the treetops sway back and forth. It was more like branches creaking, followed by stones clattering. The Italian baker looked behind him. Nothing. He half-crouched and moved in the direction of the sound. He stayed as low as he could although there was nowhere to hide even if he wanted to.

The sound was intermittent. Sometimes there was a pause and then it resumed. It was as if someone nearby was walking in circles or was hitting the same spot over and over. Persistent, nervous. Enrico stepped forward, careful not to make a single noise and watching his feet for soft ground, free of dried twigs or branches. He reached a thick pine tree and knew the sound came from behind it. He peeked round it to finally see what it was.

Beyond the pine trees, the wild shrubs and mossy ground, there was a dusty dirt track. It bent around a thick, square stone wall structure almost twice as high as Enrico. At the top of the structure, he could see a stone balustrade evenly spaced around the perimeter, and in the middle of what was a raised stone platform, there were four high Doric columns arranged in a perfect square. The temple-like architecture showed reminisces of what the Italian Garden used to be like, but the stone used was pale yellow and looked less afflicted by the passing of time.

The sound came from the base of the wall structure where Sergej Vernikoff walked up and down, knocking at each individual stone in the wall and repeating it all over again. Sometimes he stopped, thought it over, and reached out with his fingers into the thin cracks in between the stones. Dangerous and mad, thought Enrico. Whatever he was searching for, it was out of an act of desperation. His breath sounded heavy, tired. Enrico hedged for a few more minutes. Sergej did not seem armed at all. He was busy looking for something and for the Italian baker there was only one item he felt confident enough to gamble on.

'Looking for the black azalea?' he shouted out from his hiding spot.

Sergej spun around and fell back against the stone wall. Enrico saw the scared look on his face as if he had heard a ghost's voice. His eyes opened as wide and big as his nose, and it made him look like a rabbit in the headlights.

'Who's there? Don't shoot!' cried out Sergej.

He raised his hands in surrender, his eyes lost in the silence of the woods.

'S-s-sh!' pleaded Enrico. 'I am not going to shoot you.'

He reduced his voice to a raspy whisper. He did not want anyone to hear them. Vernikoff shut his mouth and kept nodding to show full compliance.

'Stop nodding!' blurted out Enrico when Sergej's widened eyes started to freak him out.

The Italian baker could not believe this was the man he had deemed dangerous and capable enough to handle explosives. He watched Sergej from behind the tree. He had to be sure the opera singer was not bluffing but the more he looked, the more he seemed more innocuous than a lamb.

'Ok, I am coming out.' Enrico warned.

'Stay back!' said Sergej terrorised.

Enrico stepped out slowly and walked towards him until he was at a safe distance. He had his hands forwards to calm down the neurotic opera singer.

'Don't come near me, you thief!' shouted Sergej.

He had his fists half-raised at Enrico. The Italian baker saw the white knuckles trembling and considered the possibility this man may have never picked a fight.

'S-s-sh! What? Thief?' echoed Enrico baffled. 'You are the one bombing houses.'

'I say stay away.' protested Sergej. 'Whatever you want to steal from me, I don't have it!'

Enrico did not follow.

'I don't want anything from you. I am not even sure what you want. I want to know who blew up the room at the Duchess Hotel. I saw you from the orangery. Was it you?'

Enrico laid his suspicions out in the open. Sergej paused but did not lower his guard. He was observing Enrico with scepticism.

'Who are you? Do you work at the hotel?' he stammered.

Sergej hinted at Enrico's chef jacket.

'Sort of. I am Enrico, baker. Are you Sergej Vernikoff?'

'Yes.' confirmed Sergej, still hesitant. 'What are you doing here? The park is off limits.'

'Then that makes us two trespassers. I am here to help.'

Enrico changed his tone. Anything to make Sergej believe he was not the enemy.

'You called me a thief.' he continued. 'We had no robberies at the hotel. Just a dangerous explosion with, I am sorry to say, your name on it.'

Enrico dropped it there once again, hoping Sergej would take the bait. He still could not believe this scared man with a faltering voice was the great Sergej Vernikoff.

'It was not me. Well, it was me, but it was in self-defence.'

Enrico scratched his head. It was getting complicated.

'Did you or did you not blow the room?'

'It was my room!'

'What? Your room? Why on earth would you…'

'It was a trap. A dangerous man is after me. I had to stop him… I had to… You are not him, right?'

Enrico found Sergej a little unprepared and somehow naive. He did not come across as the man who could pull what he claimed he did and keep quiet about it. He rushed with his words and fear flashed on his face as he tried to prove his innocence. Sergej was either too astute or too stupid.

'Ok, Mr Vernikoff. Please calm down. What were you doing here?'

'How do you know about the black azalea?' answered Vernikoff with another question.

'Second time I hear this.'

'You do?'

Sergej looked intrigued, not sure what to make of this man in a chef jacket appearing out of the woods, whether friend or foe.

'Yes. A man at the hotel mentioned it.'

'Be careful of that man.' pointed out Sergej raising his finger at Enrico. 'We need to find the black azalea before he does.'

'Who's we?'

'It doesn't matter. The problem is, I don't have the black azalea. I have information, though, that could lead me to it. Information worth millions.'

Until then Enrico had found the situation absurd but in the last few minutes it had become even more so. Sergej talked about this flower like something special, out of this world. Viviane said black azaleas did not exist in nature. He had now found two men looking for it and he was more and more convinced such a rare item was not a fragment of someone's imagination but something real worth more than he could ever imagine.

A phone rang. Sergej froze and let his phone ring out into the dead silence of the woods for a while.

'You'd better take that.' said Enrico.

Sergej answered his phone.

'Yes?' he said. 'I am still in the park. Yes. I am coming up now. What's the time? Christ, I am on it!'

He hung up and pulled himself together.

'I need to leave now, Mr…'

'LoTrova.'

'LoTrova! I need to…erm…go… Stay out of it! It is for your own good!'

He quickly scrambled and ran round the corner without saying anything else or waiting for Enrico to reply. The Italian baker realised he had not asked him about what he had hidden under the platform stage. He had to

121

quickly decide whether to run after the crazy opera singer or trace back his steps to the mysterious hidden item. There was no third option.

The bar at the Duchess Hotel was becoming a little more alive. A few hotel guests opted in for taking a seat in the main hall while others ventured out into Wimbledon to kill time or put their minds to something else other than yesterday's events.

Eric Quercer was taking his time. He had ordered another coffee at the bar and was looking around idly. Anyone passing by would have thought he was another stranded hotel guest deciding what to do. Eric Quercer though had only one thing in mind. Sergej Vernikoff. The man himself would be showing up this morning to meet Inspector Baynard. He had to be ready to put his plan into action and grab that valuable piece of paper.

Ever since the mysterious contact had written to him about the black azalea, he had never stopped dreaming about it. At first, he doubted it. His family had been living and breathing the world of flowers, trees and plants for generations and hearing now about a black azalea was something out of mythical legends. Then each letter, bit by bit, hinted at more and more facts that he could no longer deny. Photos from old manuscripts and ancient hand-drawn drawings. None showed how the black azalea looked. Then, when his mysterious contact mentioned someone else was looking for it, the greed blinded Eric. The challenge was on for him to take. The mysterious sender claimed a so-called 'Trust' in England had recently found old papers that revealed the true location of the black azalea and there was a high probability it was here at Cannizaro Park, in Wimbledon. Eric Quercer knew at this point he could not arrive second. He accepted the job, regardless of whether the only evidence he had on his employer were just printed words on fine paper. One night, at his horticulturists' club back home, he boasted about the black azalea while drunk. Everyone mocked him for his fantasies and Eric Quercer could not tolerate his fame being put into questioning. The bet was on, and he fabricated a whole story to convince them all he would go to England and return with the rarest of flowers: a black azalea.

The Canadian checked his watch and glanced around. He was sitting on the far end of the bar, out of view, and his eyes were fixed on the entrance from the reception hallway. Sergej Vernikoff would be coming through that door, and the paper would surely be in his pocket. He did not know what the paper contained, very likely a map. He had attempted to buy it from the Trust at first, approaching them several times as an unknown collector. He had been unsuccessful. He then began threatening them, but they would not relent, and now he would need to steal it from them by force. They had been warned he would stop at nothing. Then six months ago, the mysterious contact tipped him of a conversation between the owner of the Duchess Hotel and a famous member of the Trust about an exciting discovery in the history of Cannizaro House soon to be announced. Eric Quercer would never have thought Sergej Vernikoff was a member of the Trust. He realised then he could win his bet.

The Canadian sipped his coffee, slowly, patiently. Sergej Vernikoff would be expecting him but he did not know what he looked like. Eric had the tactical advantage. He checked the waiters bringing drinks and snacks to a few tables around the hall. He then reached for his pocket and touched the sachet inside. Old herbal recipes always work, he thought.

Baynard sat at the corner table in the orangery. He asked the receptionist when Sergej Vernikoff would be arriving and she told him Lady of Cannizaro knew the exact time. She would come over soon. The inspector thanked her and sat there waiting, alone in the deserted orangery. He could hear a low murmur coming from the main hall. He was surprised to hear guests still hanging around. He did not mind except he felt it was a distraction to him and his men. Yet, he was not here on an official crime investigation. Lady of Cannizaro would be the first to try calling his bluff, or at least complain one way or the other about the current state of affairs.

'Inspector Baynard!' rang her voice from afar.

He looked behind him and there she was, wearing more casual clothes. A white blouse and a pair of jeans. Her hair fell over her shoulders, a little wilder and voluminous.

'Nice to see you again.' she continued while approaching the inspector.

Baynard stood up half-way but Lady of Cannizaro motioned him not to worry.

'Morning, Lady of Cannizaro!' he replied softly.

'I believe you are here for your questioning. Do you have everything you need?'

'Your receptionist has been very kind. And it is just a talk, ma'am.' he shrugged aloof.

'Of course! We don't want to create unnecessary panic.'

The subtle condescending tone did not go unnoticed for Baynard and fuelled his fears. The image of the hotel was dear to Lady of Cannizaro. If not already tarnished by safety hazards, it was at risk of getting a bad reputation, and in a way Wimbledon Police was too, if the story broke out of a bomber on the loose.

'It is a precaution, as I told Mr Quercer, so that we can advise you in case anyone sues you for damage. There may be details that could help any surveyor sent by your insurance.

'Be careful not to put frivolous conjectures into Mr Vernikoff's head. We want him to return, if possible. He is our special guest.'

'Do you know when he will be arriving?'

'I called him and he is on his way. Less than half an hour I suppose.'

'How are the guests?'

Baynard decided to fill in the time with some pleasantries. After all, Lady of Cannizaro was going through great lengths to accommodate him and the police. He gave her a deferring look. Lady of Cannizaro kept a radiant smile, full of positivity, as she talked about the general attitude and about her plans to restore the rooms upstairs to their original splendour. She was ready, the moment the police gave clearance. She was not one to waste time.

'Excuse me, Lady of Cannizaro.' asked the inspector. 'Would it be possible for me to inspect Room 54 now while we wait for Mr Vernikoff? It could be an efficient use of police time.'

Baynard thought it best to get on with the investigation and have the feeling he was doing something.

'Please do, but keep a low profile.' answered Lady of Cannizaro, in need of reassurance. 'We do not want to scare off the people staying here. I will send someone to call you when Mr Vernikoff is here.'

Baynard showed a vague sign of agreement. He then finished his coffee in one last gulp and followed Lady of Cannizaro out of the orangery. He did not need anyone's permission to go upstairs, but Lady of Cannizaro insisted on informing one of her hotel staff. She spoke with calm as if she wanted to infuse normality back into the place, making Baynard an ordinary official just doing a routine check.

The inspector did not wait for the end of that spiel and took the stairs up to the first floor and down the blackened corridor, beyond the cordon put up by the fire brigade. He then pulled out a pair of white plastic gloves and slowly made his way to the end of the corridor. The path had been cleared in the most efficient way. Some of the wallpaper was torn or burnt. The air tasted smoky in Baynard's throat, despite the constant swirl of wind from the open window. He pulled his purple handkerchief to this nose and mouth. The walk through to the corridor took him to Room 54.

The door had been broken through and taken away. A wide space run across the room to the first window on the south-facing wall. The fuzzy shape in the floor hinted at where furniture had been. All had become a jaggy, shapeless mass of blackened walls and furniture. Baynard tiptoed around heaps of smashed glass and half-burnt chunks of compressed wood. Some untouched patches of carpet still bore traces of the colour and texture before the fire had taken place and were now mixed with dust and footprints and scratches. A large black blotch spread across the southern wall where the blue colour of the tarpaulin sheet covered the hole in the wall. The light outside filtered feebly through it and made it all look as if Baynard was under water recovering sunken artefacts. The inspector scouted the room and took a few steps inside carefully stepping off the plank placed by the firemen. The crunch and creaking of debris made a chilling sound in the dead silence of the burnt room. He could hear his feet crushing on the tiny fragments of glass the firemen had forgotten to sweep up. He walked across to the opposite corner, by the hole in the wall, where the source of the explosion had been. To the right, he could see a second blotch of burnt wallpaper, smaller and more contained. It did not look natural or spontaneous but rather targeted. A couple of labels could be visible on the floor around what was left of a low cabinet. Only the base was left and splinter-shaped chunks stood out like spikes. He turned around. The wardrobe next to the entrance was gone but a white shape against the wallpaper was proof of its sheer size against the high ceiling. He walked to the bathroom, where the ceramic was still intact and lathered in a wet ash-colour paste. The white had faded to a sickly yellow and it was plain to see that again not much was left. Baynard returned to the bedroom. The floor was intact, robust enough to resist whatever had blown up in here. He tried to remember details of the report from the fire brigade and the forensic team.

This was the epicentre of the explosion where traces of home-made explosives had been found in great quantity. Not much was left but forensics had found wires, supposedly linking the mains with a remotely controlled explosive equipment. Baynard could see a wall plug and traced an imaginary line of black ash. The explosion was loud but its impact limited. He wanted to know whom Sergej Vernikoff was trying to scare off and what he had been hiding here of such great importance. Forensics claimed the safe, to which the explosive was connected to, was empty. No money or jewellery vaporised except the few belongings Sergej Vernikoff had in the room, which was close to nothing. Baynard found it strange, as if the opera singer was not staying here officially. Celebrities, he thought. They had extravagant lives and they also had enemies from time to time.

The inspector sighed. He wondered what he could come across here, if anything. Then an electronic, beep sound arranged in an 8-bit tune filled the room. It came from outside. The sound was then cut short. Baynard stepped around the debris to reach the broken wall and lifted the tarpaulin to peer outside over the Dutch Sunken Garden, into the bright morning daylight. In a flash, the inspector saw something disappear in the distance, behind one of the park walls to the east. He blinked. He thought he saw something sparkling white reflect against the sun. A white shirt perhaps. Baynard stood there, watching outside, waiting. His inquisitive stare almost cast a spell on the nature outside, trying to squeeze the truth out of it and confirm to him what he thought he had seen.

'Inspector Baynard?'

The receptionist's voice called out from the corridor, calling Baynard's attention.

'Inspector Baynard,' repeated the receptionist. 'Sergej Vernikoff is here!'

The inspector took a deep breath and gathered his thoughts for the next round of questioning, or in this delicate case, witness statements. He then made a mental note to contact a third person for questioning. A man who liked to wear white, white chef jackets to be precise. He wanted to ask him if he liked to use decade-old mobile ringtones, and whether he always loved being in the wrong place at the wrong time. Baynard was convinced he had caught a glimpse of Enrico LoTrova.

Enrico was standing over the trap door. He had pushed the heavy trunk aside. He was ready to open the trap door and find out what was under it. Back from where he had met Sergej Vernikoff, he felt as if he was being pulled further down the rabbit hole. His curiosity was leading him down a path he did not know the end of, but if he had clearly understood what the opera singer had told him, there was something of value to retrieve. He was no criminal; he had never hurt anyone. Yet, a thorn of guilt still worried him as he opened the trap door and stuck his head inside. A folded sheet of paper was taped a few inches from the opening, underneath the floorboards. He pulled it off slowly, so as not to rip it apart. It was folded inside a plastic freezer bag. The sheet of paper was old and yellowish from oxidation. Enrico was not sure whether to open it and read it. It seemed fragile. He thought of Dr Watkins. He may have the tools or the skills to handle this. He was not a historian, but this paper was something from the past that Sergej Vernikoff was trying to hide. He then recalled what the opera singer said. He had information leading to the black azalea. Worth millions. Was this it? This old piece of paper?

Enrico looked up. The stillness and silence of the backstage made him feel alone and in danger. The abandoned fairgrounds were the only witness to his discovery but he knew others would soon be on his tail. He had to talk to Sergej Vernikoff once more and find out more about the man after him. Without thinking twice, he slid the plastic bag into the back of his trousers and closed the trap door, putting everything back as it was. The walk back through Lady Jane's Wood took him through new twists and turns, and to his surprise he did not take the same route as before and ended up a few inches away from the wide green space from which he could see the Duchess Hotel. Enrico looked back and thought the strange temple-like stone structure was somewhere to his right, deep into the woods, or so he thought. He did not know if he could find his way back to it unless he had map.

The Italian baker bordered the trees until he came to the clear spacious green extending towards the front of the Duchess Hotel. He was under the impression Sergej Vernikoff had to go somewhere or meet someone, and unless there was another exit he did not know about, he was sure he must have gone back to the hotel for one reason or the other. Neither were supposed to be in the park, so he too had found a way to sneak in and out of the park unseen. Enrico kept moving forward until he was next to the Dutch Sunken Garden. Ahead, on the first floor, a large sheet of tarpaulin fluttered in the breeze to cover the gaping hole cut out of the Duchess Hotel. Right below, Enrico recognised the orangery where he had been sitting. As far as he could see, it was completely empty inside. Nobody was around.

Enrico hesitated on what to do next. The chances of catching up with Sergej Vernikoff were slim and the more he stayed in the park, the more chances he had of getting caught. He had played with fire enough for today. Best option was to give the paper to Dr Watkins. He checked it was still in its place and then looked around him. He remembered there was a small garden nearby, with all the herbs. Quickly, he snuck out of the bushes, and ran past the Dutch Sunken Garden, up to the small wooden gate which opened up to a tiny courtyard where strong fragrances of rosemary, sage and lavender filled the air. A gravel path led straight across to a thick oak door under a pergola. Bushes of herbs from all over the world filled the lanes to each side, and overwhelmed Enrico's nose who for a moment dreamed of rosemary he used in one of his sea-salted focaccias. He stopped for a minute, breathing in the scent, until the quietness was interrupted by his Nokia 3310 ringing loud between the four walls of the Herbs Garden.

Enrico freaked out and pressed hard on the red button to end the call. It was Viviane. She was probably wondering where he was. Enrico could already imagine Viviane's angry face as he explained how his morning had been. He glanced around and started running, worried in case hotel staff or police would be jumping out of the bushes to get him. He ran as fast as he could and jumped up the wall next to the thick oak door. He climbed as fast as he could, scratching his arms and legs. The fear gave him the strength and adrenaline he did not have earlier and, in a flash, he pulled himself over onto unknown territory.

The fall was not as long as before and he fell on soft, short grass. Enrico easily fell on his feet and checked his new surroundings. A garden. A private one at the back of a house that looked older than anything else he had seen in Wimbledon. He heard the sound of cars passing by. The Italian baker realised he was out of the park and probably near the road circling around Rushmere Green. The house looked empty and dark inside despite the bright day. He did not wait any longer there and walked around the outside of the house. There was a locked gate to one side of the house. He climbed it again, eager to get out of there as soon as he could, before anyone saw him. Enrico could see Westside Common Road and Rushmere Green extending beyond towards Wimbledon Village. He was a few houses down from the entrance to the Duchess Hotel car park. Almost there.

'Enrico?'

The mellow voice sounded puzzled and filled with marvel. The Italian baker stopped in his tracks, a few inches away from the short outer fence of the house. He turned to his right and the flamboyant curator, that was Dr Watkins, was observing him astonished. He was standing by the narrow gate leading into the front garden. He was either on his way out or he had just arrived.

'He...hello...' blabbered Enrico, stupefied.

'What brings you to my house?'

Sergej Vernikoff arrived late at the Duchess Hotel. He was welcomed by Lady of Cannizaro with open arms and let through to reception. His sombre entrance into the hall, accompanied by a bodyguard, was met by a low commotion among the few guests who dared look up to see who came in and out of the hotel. A man at the bar gave a brief clap of hands and a cheeky young lady sitting nearby dared lean forward to shake his hands. The opera singer gave a gentle wave of his hand to thank the crowd. He had slick hair, freshly gelled, and a white radiant complexion on his face. His cheekbones and lips were highlighted with a warmer hue of colour. Overall, it looked like the celebrity was wearing stage make-up as if he had never left the theatre lights.

Baynard leaned on the handrail of the staircase. He took a good look at Mr Vernikoff and he thought he could see the reflection of a thin line of sweat across his forehead. He guessed the opera singer had probably rushed all the way here to comply with the police. Although he appeared calm, the inspector sensed he was agitated.

'Inspector,' said Lady of Cannizaro, approaching Baynard. 'We thought of holding the interview, or whatever you want to call it, elsewhere rather than the orangery. Mr Vernikoff would feel more comfortable behind closed doors due to his status. I am sure you agree.'

'Fine by me.' confirmed Baynard not caring that much as long as he spent the time he needed with his second suspect.

Lady of Cannizaro nodded and she asked the receptionist to take the inspector to one of the business suites in the northern wing. She then walked back to attend to Sergej Vernikoff pulling one of her big smiles. Eric Quercer had watched the whole scene from the far corner of the bar where he had been sitting. He was surprised to see a different location for questioning had been chosen and ran through the plan once again to check if he could still go ahead with it. He watched Baynard disappear behind a double door at the beginning of the corridor on the ground floor of the northern wing. Lady of Cannizaro and Sergej Vernikoff followed, accompanied by one last applause from the hotel guests. The bodyguard stood outside the closed door and spoke with the waiter who was waiting to take any drinks orders. Eric Quercer told himself not to lose sight of that waiter.

Baynard was the first to enter in what he thought was too big for the occasion. There was a long table in the middle of a light purple room with a tapestry-like carpet. Ten empty wooden chairs were neatly laid out around a long mahogany table except two pulled away to form a separate small circle of trust.

'Sergej, please allow me to introduce you to Chief Inspector Baynard of Wimbledon Police.' announced Lady of Cannizaro once all three were in the room.

'Good morning, Mr Vernikoff. Pleasure to meet you.'

'Nice to meet you, inspector. Please call me Sergej.'

The inspector did not feel intimidated by the pompous modesty Sergej Vernikoff showed. He still managed to pull a thin smile out of politeness and in respect of Lady of Cannizaro's special guest.

'Please take a seat. I hope you are fine with the arrangements made by Lady of Cannizaro. Your statement is a pure formality since your room was the source of the explosion here at the Duchess Hotel. Anything you may know or remember will help authorities to clarify what happened.'

Sergej nodded. He took a handkerchief and wiped small beads of sweat from his forehead.

'Could I have a glass of water, please?' he asked turning to Lady of Cannizaro.

'Of course. Anything else?' she replied.

Baynard was fine with another black coffee and Sergej opted for a cup of tea without milk. She confirmed the orders and left the room for the conversation to start between the two.

Sergej sat upright and rubbed his hands before placing them on his knees, palms down. He looked at Baynard, but his eyes escaped the inspector's inquisitive stare. The opera singer shifted in his seat, not feeling at ease, and looked around the room. Baynard shifted his gaze to his little notebook.

'Could you please confirm your movements from yesterday?' he said at some point without looking up.

'Am I a suspect, inspector?' he said.

Baynard found the opera singer's accent odd when he heard him speak. A weird concoction of English, American and his native Russian accent.

'A formality, as I said, Sergej.'

Baynard analysed the man in front of him. Famous. Educated. Special guest in Wimbledon for the first time. His manners seemed impeccable, but his looks did not fit the bill. The trousers and the cricket sweater were a little untidy and Baynard thought he saw dirt at the hems. He could not resist to ask him why there was an explosive device in his room and what he wanted to keep out that his bodyguard could not.

'I had a few meetings in London. When I heard about the accident, I decided to stay in the city centre since the Duchess Hotel would be out of bounds for a few days.'

'Where are you staying?'

'My agent has a few apartments available for me to use across London.'

'Are you aware it is your room that blew up?'

'Of course, inspector.'

'And did you notice anything malfunctioning in your room since your arrival? Any detail, big or small, is welcome.'

'Normally, it is not something I would check.' replied Sergej. 'but as far as I recall the room was fine and in perfect condition. My security confirmed that too.'

'Was your bodyguard outside the room at all times?'

'Only when I was in.'

'You are lucky you weren't yesterday. Also, you probably know already not many of your belongings were destroyed. You travel pretty light.'

'Well, it makes it easier to move around.'

Vernikoff forced a smile that broke into a smirk. He shifted in his seat again and joined his hands on his lap, tapping his opposite thumbs. Baynard carried on in search of an inconsistency that would catch Sergej out. He recalled for a second the chef jacket he thought he had seen disappearing beyond the park walls. Unlikely to be a coincidence, he could not understand how the baker fitted into the picture.

'Did you know the man injured in the explosion? Does he work for you?'

'No, inspector.'

'Eric Quercer. Does it ring a bell?'

'No, I am afraid. Who is he?'

'Horticulturist. Specialises in flowers and plants and green stuff.'

Sergej frowned. His hands parted for a brief moment, as if he had realised something.

'I am afraid not, inspector…' answered Sergej uncertain. 'Is he ok?'

'He is. Just a few bruises.'

'Was he near the blast?'

Baynard noticed Sergej was suddenly asking him questions. Perhaps he could use the answers to drop the bait.

'Very close. You could say he was not far from your room… In any case, the blast must have had an impact on him. When they found him, he was babbling about flowers and azaleas…'

Baynard's quoting of the Italian baker came to his mind at the right time. Eric Quercer's raving mad sentence was puzzling. It would have been interesting to see Sergej's reaction too.

Sergej nodded nervously. He dabbed once again the sweat on his forehead. He rubbed his hands again and escaped Baynard's icy stare. He was no longer asking questions or engaging in conversation, and Baynard conjectured from his silence something was pressing him. Either he cared for an injured man or something else bothered him. It did not hurt playing his wild card.

'Is everything ok with you?' the inspector asked.

'What do you mean?'

'I don't know. Do you feel in danger? Do you have enemies at the moment?'

Sergej glared. It dawned on him the inspector could have known something and was dotting the lines. His agent had warned him. He expected questions like this, but he was not prepared. He considered letting it all go for a second.

'What do you mean?'

'Or were you trying to injure someone?'

'I beg your pardon?' said Sergej showing disdain to the accusation.

'You heard.' kept on going Baynard, impassively.

There was no change in his tone of voice. He had his eyes glued on Sergej as he spoke those provocative questions.

'This is preposterous…' complained Sergej, standing up in protest.

Baynard saw the opera singer was easily losing his temper, writhing in suppressed fury.

'Calm down, Sergej.'

Baynard paused to ensure he had his attention.

'We know about the booby trap.' he added straight after.

There was silence in the room. Perhaps it was short but somehow long enough for Baynard to see Sergej's face switching between spite and despair. Baynard did not flinch.

A knock came at the door and Lady of Cannizaro opened it to let the waiter in with his tray.

'Teas and coffees, as requested!' she announced.

Both men took a deep sigh and broke off their gazing at each other. Baynard looked at his notebook and Sergej turned around from where he stood pulling his stage smile. They both tried to act normal.

Lady of Cannizaro sensed their conversation had probably taken a strange turn and she eyed Baynard to remind him about Vernikoff's importance. The inspector pretended he did not see and took his cup of coffee. Sergej drank his water fast and then took his tea. He walked to the window at the far end, cup in hand, taking his distance as if both men were boxers in between rounds.

'Inspector,' said Lady of Cannizaro. 'Sergeant Jeremy called, saying he could not reach you. He asked if you could stop by the police station later. He told me to pass on the message.'

Baynard nodded. He read Jeremy's message on his phone already, but his thoughts were elsewhere. He was close to crack Sergej Vernikoff. He knew something. He gulped his coffee in two large sips. Time was not on their side. Time was never on anyone's side.

'Thank you, Lady of Cannizaro.' he said without looking at her. 'Sergej, shall we resume?'

He did not receive an answer. He looked up and Lady of Cannizaro had her mouth open. Baynard then saw her rush past him, down the length of the long table. It all happened so fast and yet the inspector felt time had slowed down as he turned to look at the window were Sergej Vernikoff was previously standing. The opera singer was no longer there. He was gone. Baynard then stood up and he could see him on the floor, broken tea cup to one side and his body shaking rapidly and uncontrollably.

'He's having seizures. Call 999!' shouted Lady of Cannizaro kneeling down over him.

Baynard's world fell around him. The shouting seemed to multiply in thousands of echoes. Panic was about to strike Wimbledon.

'Let me get this straight… You broke into Cannizaro Park against police orders, you stalked a celebrity and stole something of his. What is wrong with you?'

Viviane's voice was soft and sweet to Enrico's ears, even when angry. They faced each other, alone in the small hall that was Wimbledon Museum. The florist's eyes shone with copper like filaments in the natural light coming from the only window built in the slope of the attic-like ceiling. Her voice resonated loud enough while Enrico played with a pencil sharpener, glancing at her occasionally. She had just arrived after Enrico texted her and her welcome was not one of the warmest. Dr Watkins thought it best to go and make some tea before they talked but Viviane could not resist to let her thoughts speak.

'*Senti, bella*... The man needs help.' Enrico kept repeating with his hands flying in the air. 'If I hadn't faced him, I wouldn't have found out the mess he is in. He is a VIP and not an ordinary man, *giusto*?'

'That is why you have the police for this.' insisted Viviane. 'You could be accused of complicity. Did that not occur to you?'

Enrico's careless attitude was upsetting her. Viviane could have let Enrico go down this route and let his business fail. Yet, something in her could not give up on him, although, if anyone asked her now, she would not be able to list one thing that made her hold onto this stranded baker from Italy turned rogue.

'Did you hear the whole story?'

137

Viviane sighed, after hearing that statement for the third or fourth time. She put a hand on her waist and gave a quick glance at her shoes and the carpeted floor. Anything to keep her cool. The Italian baker was a little hard-headed or maybe too ingenuous. She did not understand how they could help a man who tried to bomb the Duchess Hotel. She could not even grasp how Enrico tried to justify it.

'Yes, you started telling the story and it makes no sense. Bombing a room in self-defence? And if you are doing this for a reward, let me remind you black azaleas don't exist. I am just a florist, but I happen to know the subject.'

'*Aspetta aspetta aspetta...* you did not let me finish the story! What about what I found in the trap door?'

'Easy, easy, you hot-blooded youngsters!' came Dr Watkins voice.

He pushed the door to the museum, accompanied by the rattling of teapot and cups on a silver tray.

'Everyone can hear your arguing from downstairs. Thank God, the wood on this door muffles your voices and nobody can understand what you are saying. Yet, a bit of discretion, please.'

Dr Watkins's entrance came in like a judge at a divorce hearing, casting a truce to halt all quarrels, at least while tea was served.

'I think everyone knows anyway.' spoke Enrico. 'A house like the Duchess Hotel blowing up is breaking news here. I am sure I am not the only one raising my suspicions.'

'Breaking news? Not really. The original Cannizaro House, or at least what was an augmented form of the original first house over centuries, did burn down in a fire in the year 1900. It was saved but it had to be rebuilt mostly from scratch. What you see today, apart from a modern refurbishment from the last twenty odd years, is a re-interpretation of the original building although pictures are rare.'

'And the reason?'

'Don't remember. I don't even know if the reasons are recorded somewhere. In any case, your explosion is nothing compared to it. What I am interested in though is this piece of paper you found.'

'See?' whispered Enrico in scorn at Viviane. 'I am not the only keen one to know what it is.'

'Whatever piece of paper you found, it is not yours.' spoke back Viviane. 'What are you? A thief?'.

'Hey, I am trying to help. It is an act of charity. The plans for the fair are out of the window, no?'

'Do you really want to come across as a troublemaker, here in Wimbledon?'

'Enough!' said Dr Watkins firmly, slamming the plates on his desk. 'Stop going for each other's throats.'

The two stopped and sighed, hardly looking at each other now but instead pretending the glass showcases or the old maps of Wimbledon were of more interest. Enrico looked at Viviane. Her features had softened a little or so he hoped; she could be harsh and lovely at the same time. What she said made sense and he was not ignoring her advice. He simply did not break the law. True, he stepped inside Cannizaro when off-limits but that was no crime. The real criminal was out there. To Sergej Vernikoff, the criminal was the man Enrico saved. However, the Italian baker was not sure what to believe of what he heard coming from the opera singer's mouth.

'Tell me you will step away from this whole thing, once we know what we have, then maybe we should tell the police.' asked Viviane.

Enrico looked at the curator who was giving him the eye, although he did not understand what he meant. Dr Watkins had been forthcoming ever since finding him in what turned out to be his house, near West Side Common. Enrico had not explained everything on the spot but indicated he had something to show. He ranted words like 'historical', 'museum piece', or anything that would catch the curator's interest and imagination. Half an hour later they were both at the Wimbledon Museum, waiting for Viviane to arrive, who had been trying to reach Enrico hundreds of times. The Italian baker knew he had to keep them on his side.

'Ok, you win, Miss Leighwood!' he said in sweet surrender. 'We let Dr Watkins look at the paper I found and then we call the police, if not Baynard himself?'

Viviane sighed again. A deep one this time, which Enrico first thought was filled with suspicion and regret. She looked at him and then away. Then she chuckled to herself. Enrico waited but he knew a definite answer would never come. Peace is usually signed without words and it usually lasts longer than any treaty. Dr Watkins stepped in between them holding two cups of tea. A thin column of steam rose between them and above their heads. A chocolate digestive biscuit was balanced to the side of each cup, inviting them to sit back and enjoy.

'Have you two finished?' he told them, peering from above the reading glasses on his nose. 'I am not ready for marriage counselling and I think we have better things to do. Shall we? Anyone for a chocolate digestive before we start?'

Both Viviane and Enrico could have argued more if it weren't for Dr Watkins's phlegm and elegance. He had already freed his desk of all the clutter and laid out the folded paper at the edge of it under a big desk lamp. All three stood around it and they could see rows of pentagrams printed from top to bottom. Musical notes were marked across.

'What is this?' asked Enrico.

'A music sheet.' said Dr Watkins.

The music sheet was very old, probably forty or fifty years old, but the print was still legible. At the top there was a letterhead. It showed a coat of arms in black and white and underneath, a name followed by an address in West Sussex.

The Countess of Wrenbury Trust
Founded 1958

140

'Do you know the name on the header?' asked Viviane to Dr Watkins.

The curator was already reading it for a second time. He took his glasses off and pulled a small handkerchief to wipe them gently. He took his time to reflect, and then read it again before raising his eyes to Enrico and Viviane.

'Who doesn't know the Countess of Wrenbury Musical Trust?' he explained. 'I now recognise the address. A fine academy for musicians. It was actually founded by Hilary Wilson, the daughter of the Wilsons, when she was married to the 5th Earl of Wrenbury.'

'The Wilsons?' queried Viviane. 'Didn't we hear this name before?'

Enrico smiled to himself to see Viviane's interest suddenly change.

'The last private owners of Cannizaro House, of course.' replied the curator pointing at the far away black and white picture they looked at last time.

'Why would Sergej Vernikoff hold onto this so secretly?' thought out loud Enrico.

'Sentimental value perhaps.' guessed Viviane. 'Why keep it all these years and hide it under a platform stage?'

'Maybe it is more valuable than we think. How old is it, Dr Watkins?'

'Hard to say. Paper was kept in good condition. Not dented or worn out at the borders. At least forty years, I would say.'

'Sergej said this paper gave him information about the black azalea.'

Viviane laughed incredulous.

'It is just a music sheet. Can anyone read the tune?'

The two men looked at each other hopeless. Viviane rolled her eyes and read the pentagrams again with the fifth-grade school knowledge of music she had left.

'I don't know.' she concluded after a few random hums. 'It is not a famous classical piece, and when I hum it, it sounds horrible. No melody at all.'

'There is something here…' said Dr Watkins.

He carefully picked up the music sheet and placed it directly over the lamp. The paper was thin enough to see through and the back of it was blank. He squinted behind his lenses and focused to the bottom of the music sheet. Enrico watched him frown in deep thought, underlining the wrinkles on his forehead. He admired how meticulous he was.

'There's something here…' he mumbled again.

He looked away from the light and pulled open one of the narrow desk drawers filled with stationery. He took out an old magnifying glass. Enrico and Viviane followed him getting back into position with the paper against the light. They looked at him and the paper and then back at him again, puzzled about what Dr Watkins may be looking for.

'I see odd lines, almost veins, in the paper.'

The curator stared at the void for a few minutes. He then bent the sheet slightly against the light. He suddenly stopped perplexed.

'Mmm…I may know what this is.'

'What?' asked Enrico but the elderly gentleman was no longer listening, deep into his research.

Dr Watkins stopped again. He put the paper down once more and walked to the back of the small museum, out of view for a couple of minutes. Enrico and Viviane looked at each other as they heard clamour and a loud bang of utensils crashing against each other. Dr Watkins returned with a nondescript white plastic bottle that could have been mistaken for table salt. In his other hand he held a fresh rag and a spray bottle containing water or a transparent liquid of some sort. He started by laying the rag neatly on the reception desk and put the piece of paper on top. He then unscrewed the nozzle from the spray and poured the contents of the white plastic bottle into it. The white thin powder quickly dissolved, turning the clear liquid into a cloudy substance.

'Let's see…' started the curator without finishing his sentence.

142

Like a shaman performing his ritual in front of the whole tribe, an aura of mysticism drifted around him as he stood carefully in front of the sheet and prepared to spray the mixture on it. Enrico and Viviane looked at him in doubt.

'Is this safe?' asked Viviane sceptically.

'Are we sure it won't destroy the music sheet...?' added Enrico, still concerned to return what he claimed as borrowed.

Dr Watkins seemed to be in a trance and not able to hear them. He sprayed without hesitation a few drops at the bottom of the paper. Enough to make it humid and not soaking wet. He placed his tool aside in an orderly fashion. He then put the palm of his hands on the desk, to the sides of the rag, paying close attention, waiting for a magical spirit to appear and reveal the answer to their questions.

'Can't believe this... Last time I did something like this I must have been eight or nine.' said Dr Watkins after a period of silence.

The informality of his words broke the spell which had captivated Enrico and Viviane. The two blinked a few times before looking at each other. Dr Watkins smiled at their puzzled faces.

'It's invisible ink.' he explained. 'Or at least a rather sophisticated form of it. I used to do it with lemon juice and vinegar. This one seems to have been created with chemical agents. You'd better start reading. It will disappear in a few minutes.'

Enrico and Viviane were taken by surprise, not sure how to take Dr Watkins's words at first. They glanced over the music sheet. There at the bottom, one by one as if written by an invisible hand, words started to appear in a dark blue ink scattered like dotted islands on an empty ocean.

One of the most beautiful personalities I had ever known. The loveliest thing I had ever seen!

It took a few seconds for the words to settle. Not just on paper but also in the mind of the three curious readers.

'I'd better take a picture.' said Viviane pulling out her smartphone before the text was invisible again.

And gradually, as fast as they appeared, the words started to fade away, drained of their life bit by bit, until there was nothing left but an empty and aged letterhead.

'Incredible!' exclaimed Dr Watkins, breaking the silence. 'Whatever this is, I am sure the museum would love to share this piece of Wimbledon history.'

'Let's not get ahead of ourselves.' warned Viviane, clearly not ready to handle two excited schoolboys. 'All we have is an out-of-tune melody and a random sentence written with funny ink!'

'Does the sentence make any sense to you?' asked Enrico.

'No, but I know someone who can shed light on this.'

Dr Watkins was checking his mobile phone from under his glasses. Enrico and Viviane exchanged quizzical looks.

'Actually, she should be here soon.' he added.

The knock on the entrance to the museum came unexpected. The curator seemed to have more than one ace up his sleeve.

'Come in!'

The door opened and Lady of Cannizaro barged in, looking flustered and agitated. She did not seem surprised to see Enrico and Viviane; however, she was wary of her surroundings. She closed the door quickly and pushed her way forward to the desk. Enrico found her different from the bubbly, confident woman he saw back at the hotel. What happened must have had a bad hit on her.

'Is everything ok?' said Dr Watkins, sharing the same concerns as Enrico's.

'Sorry for getting you involved, Dr Watkins. Here are the keys.'

Lady of Cannizaro pulled a heavy set of keys from a small messenger bag and dropped them on the desk. Somehow it looked as if she was taking off one of the many albatrosses hung around her neck.

'Sergej Vernikoff has just been poisoned.' she added. 'He is alive but in a critical condition at Parkside Hospital. I am not sure I can stay long enough. I need to go back to sort out this whole mess. The police are all over the place and they may be looking for me.'

'Good grief! I am not sure what you got yourself into, but we have something you ought to see. Maybe we can help.'

'*Aspetta...aspetta...aspetta...* Hold on!' interjected Enrico who for one minute felt the whole reality crashing down. 'What does all this mean?'

'What?' said Dr Watkins.

'This!' repeated the Italian baker waving at him, the keys and Lady of Cannizaro.

The curator chuckled.

'This bulky set of keys opens a few historical doors in Wimbledon. I am responsible for it. One of them opens the door in my back garden, which Lady of Cannizaro knows about. You probably remember it. It is the oak door leading into the Herbal Garden. Lady of Cannizaro asked if she could borrow it for Sergej Vernikoff to use in secret. If I had known, I would have lent it to you too rather than making you climb the walls.'

Enrico was bewildered. He now understood how Sergej had managed to disappear so easily from Cannizaro Park.

'And you didn't tell us?' insisted Enrico.

'Well, you never asked.' replied Dr Watkins.

'Are you two accomplices?'

'No, Enrico.' spoke Dr Watkins on behalf of both him and Lady of Cannizaro.

He seemed amused. Enrico and Viviane could not say the same for Lady of Cannizaro.

'I know as much as you, Enrico.' explained the curator. 'I thought of calling Lady of Cannizaro yesterday without avail after I heard about the shocking events at the hotel. When today you popped out of nowhere with this music sheet, I had to get hold of her and let her know. I need an explanation as much as you do. What was Sergej Vernikoff doing in Cannizaro Park?'

He moved his gaze towards Lady of Cannizaro as he finished the question.

'I told you something was up…' Enrico whispered to Viviane.

'It does not justify any of the things you did.' she bit back.

'Cut me some slack. Can't you see they were working together?'

'They were not…'

Dr Watkins coughed to draw attention back to his question.

'Excuse me, Lady of Cannizaro.' said Dr Watkins aloud. 'These two love birds can get carried away. You have more pressing matters. Why don't you tell us what is behind all this? What do you know about Sergej Vernikoff?'

Viviane and Enrico tried to hide their embarrassment. Lady of Cannizaro sat on the chair and put a hand on her forehead to massage her temples. She had been listening without uttering one single word. Not her usual self. All three could see her now how tired she was, and an air of defeat or despair hung on her like a sword of Damocles. The colour on her face had drained, the blouse took an ignoble shape as she slouched on the chair.

'Thank you…erm…Dr Watkins.' she spoke.

She had a croaky voice. She quickly cleared it and pulled herself together.

'I think I owe you an explanation, and I appreciate both your help, Dr Watkins, and Enrico's, whose help however may have started for all the wrong reasons. Without realising, I may have put you in danger. It all started more or less six months ago when the Countess of Wrenbury Musical Trust contacted me for a special meeting.'

'Is that the same trust as the one written on the music sheet?' asked Enrico.

Dr Watkins nodded, anticipating Lady of Cannizaro.

'Correct.' she continued. 'Apparently, a year ago, they found an old rusty deposit box in their security vault, one of those only opened when a will needs to be verified against the Trust's archive or where old members' belongings have been left only to be claimed decades later by their grandchildren. Inside it, there was this music sheet.'

Lady of Cannizaro pointed at the yellowish, old paper.

'The Trust did not understand much about it, but their musical expertise came in. Just by reading it, they could tell the tune or melody written on these few pentagrams was unplayable. Awful, in the least. They told me it sounded like a cat jumping on a piano!'

Viviane gave Enrico a smug face.

'By the time the Trust contacted me, they had already found out the musical notes were just a message in code. A poem.'

'A poem?' echoed Dr Watkins becoming more and more interested.

Lady of Cannizaro nodded.

'To be honest,' continued Dr Watkins. 'it goes with Hilary Wilson's character, I suppose. She was a great supporter of the arts, especially music. She wanted to echo the feats of other patrons who lived at Cannizaro House like Sophie Johnstone, Duchess of Cannizzaro, and Adela Schuster, who called herself "Lady Wimbledon". Hilary Wilson finally founded the Trust in 1958 to help young musicians achieve their full potential as performers, and actively followed the career of its beneficiaries, whether singers or composers.'

'So, this music sheet is definitely not older than fifty or sixty years.' mentioned Enrico. 'Did the Trust ever decode the whole thing?'

'Sure!' replied Lady of Cannizaro. 'Here's the transcript Sergej Vernikoff asked me to keep in my office.'

She slipped her hand underneath the blouse and reached something a little above her breast. She took out the ripped page of a notepad, folded to a square tiny enough to stuck it in her bra strap. The most secure place she could find on her way here. Her delicate hands took time unfolding it, as if as old as the music sheet. The other three leaned over more curious than ever.

'He, nor anyone at the Trust, could make any sense of it.'

She laid the new piece of paper flat next to the music sheet, its modern white colour in big contrast with the other. A few lines were scribbled on it in handwritten black ink.

That black azalea, smooth to the touch
Father's precious gift brought from the tides
Until my heart and mind bled so much
One hot summer with books and guides
From that female beauty which remains to be seen

'Marvellous!' exclaimed Dr Watkins out of nowhere. 'A posthumous poem of some sort from Hilary Wilson herself. Whatever it means, we cannot ignore the historical value. The museum would love to exhibit it.'

'The black azalea…' muttered Enrico scratching his head.

'Is the black azalea a gift Hilary Wilson received from her father, assuming it exists?' added Viviane.

'It has to be.' concluded Dr Watkins. 'Edward K. Wilson was an outstanding gardener, member of the Royal Horticultural Society. He is the only person that would have been in a position to find and recognise such a rare species of flower.'

'In Cannizaro Park? Growing just like that?'

'Edward K. Wilson worked in transport. He was the director of both the Ellerman and Wilson Shipping Line and the Wilson North East Railway Shipping Line, from Hull. Through his connections, he brought all kinds of unusual shrubs to Cannizaro Park from North America and the Far East. Although not much is left now, back then the park was more glorious under the Wilsons than it had ever been since the eighteenth century, when Henry Dundas, First Viscount of Melville, came up first with the idea of creating a new park. What we see today carries nothing special and extraordinary about what was there yesterday. No offense, Lady of Cannizaro.'

'None taken.'

'Perhaps,' continued Dr Watkins. 'through the commercial success he made abroad, he may have indeed found this black azalea.'

'I know the botanic history of the park, Dr Watkins.' objected Viviane. 'I know about flowers, and I have doubts about what you are saying. I am telling you, like I told Enrico, azaleas in a black colour don't exist!'

Viviane had joined the debate with passion. Enrico smiled without saying anything. A few minutes before he thought he would not be able to get her florist friend involved and committed as much as he was. She was still not buying it and maybe she never would. Yet, she had no intention of hiding her scepticism about the whole matter. She was confident enough to share what she was certain of in the sea of mystery they faced.

Enrico scratched his head again and could not make much about the poem. He tried to remember the end line they revealed with the invisible ink, just below the music pentagrams. Whether the end of the poem or a note by the author, it made no sense.

'Lady of Cannizaro,' said Enrico. 'it seems to me all these clues, the music pentagram, the encoded poem, they all lead to this mythical black azalea and everything that has been happening. Is such a legendary flower worth a lot of money, if it exists?'

Enrico gave Viviane a preventive look to warn he was simply exploring possible reasons. Last thing he wanted was another green-fingered lesson.

'I don't know.' replied Lady of Cannizaro. 'The Trust does not know either, or at least they didn't back then. When the Trust contacted me, things started to get complicated.'

Dr Watkins, Enrico and Viviane suddenly stopped asking questions and listened. Lady of Cannizaro's grave expression suggested her revelations would open doors which perhaps were better kept shut.

'The Trust' continued Lady of Cannizaro. 'wanted to go public with the discovery, sharing its historical value with members of the Trust but also with Wimbledon. The plan was to announce it at the Duchess Hotel, a symbol of Cannizaro House history and the Wilsons' legacy. They were not interested in understanding the meaning of the poem. Not until they started to receive plenty of letters from a mysterious sender, offering a lot money for the music sheet. Only a very few from the Trust and the Council knew of the discovery and the planned announcement, and you can imagine the concern among them on how the information was leaked. The decision was simply to reject each offer; the item was not for sale. Each time they rejected though, another came at higher value to the point the letters became very aggressive, almost a threat.'

'Why didn't you call the police?' interjected Viviane, a voice of reason.

'Because the letters then stopped after a while. Just like that.'

Lady of Cannizaro snapped her fingers in the air.

'How does Sergej Vernikoff fit into this?' asked Enrico.

'He was the chosen ambassador for the Trust. He is an honorary member, you see. He, like many, owes his success to the Countess of Wrenbury Trust, where he studied for quite a few years to become the opera singer he is today. He contacted me at the time I was starting to plan Cannizaro Festival and I was thrilled to hear about it. The Trust planned to announce the discovery of the music sheet at yesterday evening's event, with Sergej as special guest...'

'...which of course never happened due to the explosion.' concluded Enrico.

Lady of Cannizaro nodded.

'One evening,' she continued. 'about a week ago, Sergej Vernikoff came into my office, slightly worried. He told me all the background information he had omitted when he first approached me. The offers, the threats. He thought everything had stopped, but since arriving at the Duchess Hotel he had had the feeling he was being followed. His room was found unlocked more than once and complained to the hotel. He was convinced someone was after him and the music sheet.'

'Did you know he bombed his own room?' commented Enrico.

Lady of Cannizaro widened her eyes.

'It is not a good time to joke, Mr LoTrova.' she said coldly.

'He said it himself when I met him in the park today.'

'You were in the park today? I thought you were joking earlier on the phone, Dr Watkins? The police put the whole place in lock down and I am responsible for who…'

'What can I say?' shrugged Dr Watkins. 'He's Italian.'

'Why was Sergej Vernikoff in the park too?'

This time Viviane spoke. Lady of Cannizaro's explanations were ground-breaking so far to the point she now felt she had to restore faith in Enrico. The story though was incomplete, or it was deliberately delivered with blanks.

'*Giusto!*' exclaimed Enrico, happy to see Viviane starting to come around. 'He was not allowed to be in there. You let him in by giving him Dr Watkins's keys. Why?'

Lady of Cannizaro sighed. Her back was against the wall, unable to escape Enrico and Viviane's accusatory eyes. She glanced around the room with haunted eyes. If Sergej was behind the bombing, it meant what he said was true and now he lay on a hospital bed between life and death. She then came across Dr Watkins's disappointed face, who had entrusted her with the key to the Herbal Garden and she had lied about the real motives. Everything came tumbling down.

'I am sorry…for everything…' she apologised. 'I thought it was part of the Trust's plan. The same evening Sergej shared his opinion on the whole thing, he told me he was under the impression the man after him was after

151

the black azalea mentioned in the poem. I asked him why he was so sure. He said the poem was a coded message. Something important. Otherwise why would it stay locked for such a long time hidden within the fake notes of a pentagram?'

'The black azalea?' repeated Enrico again.

'Sergej thought it really existed. That is why, whoever chased him, was after the music sheet. To find this black azalea. Perhaps one of the many lost treasures of Cannizaro Park. Somehow he did not want this flower to fall into the hands of someone other than the Trust or maybe Wimbledon Museum.'

'Do you have an idea who this man or woman could be? They could be the same person behind Sergej Vernikoff's poisoning. They could be after you and us next. Anyone know someone interested in black azaleas?'

Viviane turned to Enrico with an air mixed between terror and blame. She looked at Enrico in the eyes, and the Italian baker for a moment could read her mind. Enrico shivered in the cool air of the museum hall. He had been listening to Lady of Cannizaro's story, and while everyone talked of the mysterious blackmailer as an enemy without a face, it did not take him long time to understand the man he had saved from the explosion was the same person. A dangerous man, Sergej had said. Enrico thought hard to re-imagine how he looked but his memory failed him. He wondered what his name was. Sergej did not know. He did not know. Nobody did, and that man was now out there looking for the piece of paper lying flat on Dr Watkins's desk. While the Italian baker had gloated about being right from the start, the bitter aftertaste of glory was already forming in his mouth upon realising all four of them were now in real, life-threatening danger.

Eric watched the dramatic scene play out in the hall of the hotel. The screams, the panic. The inspector ran out of the room trying to keep everyone calm. Hopelessly. He was conscious the sight of the police and the ambulance, showing up at Cannizaro House for a second time in less than twenty-four hours, would have scared and enraged everyone. Eric knew it would create enough distraction for him to slip through the crowds, unnoticed. All he needed now was a couple of minutes and the opportunity would present itself. He was near the staircase when Inspector Baynard called for a doctor or someone who knew First Aid. Eric Quercer and one of the hotel staff made themselves known. The inspector hesitated when he recognised him, but Eric knew the inspector could not refute. A man needed urgent assistance.

They were led into the room and Eric Quercer took time to contemplate the outcome of his little plan. A silent honey-like liquid dropped in an unsupervised cup of tea, a gentle stir and the sweetness of it all made Sergej Vernikoff fall down a spiral of pain and paralysis. Granayotoxin, or more commonly 'mad honey', could be mistaken for an old grandmother's recipe by the untrained eye. Eric Quercer knew it well as all botanists do. The irony of it all was that azaleas themselves, and flowers in the same family, were great producers of this neurotoxin. He could not have chosen a better poison. Eric ensured the dosage was near fatal so that Sergej Vernikoff was out of the picture, lost to a world of hallucinations, but not dead completely. He had to pin him down to get what he wanted. He would kill him off when he was sure he no longer needed him.

Sergej Vernikoff was lying on the floor, spluttering a white foam, which Eric found peculiar for he had never come across such symptoms. They had to keep him alive while the ambulance was on his way. Sergej's body was trembling as if in epileptic seizure. Eric looked in his glass eyes. The opera singer did not know who he had in front of him, but probably by now he did not even know where he was or who he was. Without wasting precious time, Eric helped shift the body to one side, and with the excuse of unbuttoning cufflinks or loosening his belt, he checked Sergej's pockets. Bit by bit. He had enough time to try once more. The music sheet was not there. Impossible, Eric thought. For a minute, he isolated himself from the confusion in the room, from the distracted instructions to keep Sergej alive. He looked at the opera singer and he could see himself asking where on earth he had put it.

Eric was forced to stop fumbling when the paramedics arrived, and moved out of the room. Sergej was still alive but in critical condition. The horticulturist did not know what to think of it. The game had been going on for too long. He went into the car park after a while to get some fresh air. The heat and noise in the hotel were unbearable. He needed time to think. He had to trace back Sergej Vernikoff's movements but that meant the sheet could be anywhere in London, anywhere in the UK. He cursed under his breath. Another plan had gone south. For a second, his scars ached again to remind him of another failure. He stood outside the car park for most of the event, watching Sergej being hauled into the ambulance and taken away. The police were now all over the place, taking orders from Baynard one after the other. Eric thought it best to move out before anyone started asking questions.

He walked along Westside Common and then across on Southside Common, lost in thought. It was the longer route around Rushmere Green, with hardly any traffic and the occasional daily jogger. Eric planned to return to the Rose and Crown to rethink his next move. He wondered if the mystery man would get in touch that same day. Maybe he already knew what had happened, all-knowing as he appeared to be, Eric thought he could ask him if he knew where the music sheet was. That would make it a lot easier.

He crossed a few roads until he arrived at a half-moon island where Murray Road merged with Southside. A black saloon car was parked on the bend, facing away from Eric. He did not take notice and walked on. He then heard the sound of a door opening and closing.

'Mr Quercer?'

Eric turned around, nervous. Nobody knew him here in Wimbledon and someone calling him out like that was not a good sign. The voice came from the man in uniform, the one who had delivered the message to his room. He wore his black cap and stood by the black saloon car.

'You again?'

'Please jump in, Mr Quercer.'

'Not sure who you are or what you…'

'Your employer is waiting…'

Eric froze. The driver opened the door to the front passenger seat and waited, no hurry in posture and not a single hint of concern Eric would run away.

The saloon car was as black as coal. It had been polished that same morning. On its metallic surface and tinted mirrors, Eric could see the reflection of the blue skies, perhaps to cast away the death-like colour. He wanted to believe his mystery sender was inside. He could somehow trust the driver. After all, he is the one who gave him the message yesterday. He could also recognise him among the crowd if he really needed to at some point in the future.

'If you say so…' said Eric with a hint of malice.

He got into the car and the slamming of the door suddenly isolated him from the outside world. No sounds. The driver stepped in shortly after him and waited at the seat. He did not try to turn on the engine. Instead, the driver sat there without talking. He passed his hand above the dashboard to wipe what he thought could be a layer of dust. He then adjusted his cap in the rear-view. Eric followed his line of sight. Behind him, a tinted window separated them from the passenger seat.

'Is he in there…? What's with the theatricals?' commented Eric.

The driver shushed him without breaking his impeccable stance behind the wheel. A buzz came from behind them and the internal tinted window slightly parted, enough for Eric to peer through. The backseats were in the penumbra despite the sunny spells outside. Eric thought he was glancing at the lounge of an old, abandoned house, its windows barred up to keep anyone out. There was a silhouette behind the driver's seat. He could not see it in full but could feel its presence. The little light coming through the gap in the separating window showed a black suit and shiny black leather boots. The face was shrouded in the shadows, shy of the dim halo of light invading that inner sanctum Eric had no wish to enter.

'Good afternoon, Mr Quercer.'

The voice was deep and smooth.

'Are you the mystery sender?' asked Eric unprompted.

The man in black did not reply. The silence and aura around him were enough for Eric to convince him he was not the man in control of the conversation.

'Your plan did not go well.' said the man in black.

'It did. Sergej is out of the picture.'

'But something tells me he did not have the music sheet.'

'And how do you know that?'

'Driver, please take us to the bottom of Lingfield Road but you can take the long way round from where the Ridgeway starts.'

The man in black did not bother answering Eric's question and he did not speak until the driver put the car into motion and slowly left the curb to drive away towards an unknown destination. Eric felt uneasy. The negative tone in the man's voice was not at all reassuring.

'I am not sure where you are taking me, but I can tell you I can still get what you want.'

Eric looked at the road and held onto the edge of his seat, worried for his life. For a moment even considered jumping out of the car.

'Do you think so, Mr Quercer? Do you think you are worthy of finding the black azalea?'

'Let me prove it to you.'

'Third time lucky, they say?'

The man in black leered to himself. He had to admit he had chosen well. They were both eager and ambitious. The horticulturist though was malleable and easy to manipulate. He could not resist his promises of grandeur. Money, fame, the usual vices. However, any investment needs to show returns at some point and Eric Quercer was simply not getting any closer to what he needed to finally start his masterplan. Without it, there would be no beginning or no end.

'Sergej Vernikoff did not have the music sheet on him. It was not in his room, unless he had been happy to blow it to pieces. I have no idea where he could be keeping it.'

'That's because he is one step ahead of you.'

Eric gave a subtle sight to hold his nerves. He was enraged inside. Nobody spoke to him like that.

'Now,' continued the man in black. 'the spanner in the works is always Sergej Vernikoff and his celebrity's luck. When you tried to lure him out, Mr Quercer, he was clever enough to bring the matter into the open. We have the Duchess Hotel staff, the Wimbledon Police, the Council, almost anyone has his eyes on the Duchess Hotel and Cannizaro park.'

'What's your point?'

'My point is, Mr Quercer,' stressed the man in black to dampen the horticulturist's insolence. 'Sergej Vernikoff is not acting alone the same way you are.'

'I can deliver.'

'With whose help?' he said scornfully.

'Hey, mister…'

Eric turned around to look at the man in the face, when the car came to an abrupt halt. The horticulturist was pushed forward, and before he realised where he was, the driver had him pinned down with a gun.

'Easy…' said Eric, his hands half-raised in surrender.

'What now, sir?' called out the driver.

'Mr Quercer will now shut his mouth and listen. Turn it on.'

The driver turned on the radio and fiddled with the knob to change the frequency, moving through harsh buzzing noises and local radio stations, until they could distinguish a female voice speaking with the echo of a room behind her.

'…apparently, a year ago, they found something in one of the vaults…' said the voice, caught in mid-sentence.

Eric recognised the voice of Lady of Cannizaro.

'Just in time!' said the man in black.

Eric was confused. He was about to say something but held his tongue. He listened on, unsure whether curious or threatened to comply to the gun held low and aiming at his waist. The street was deserted with only a few passers-by and a few cars interrupting the view of the Ridgeway from the side streets they were parked in. Opposite he could see the end of what was Lingfield Road. There was a church to one side and on the other he saw a building that looked like a church but then the owner or the builder had changed his mind and built a gothic mansion. The post said 'Wimbledon Village Club'.

'Where are we?' asked Eric.

'Outside the Wimbledon Museum. Now listen!' ordered the man in black.

The conversation Eric heard on the radio involved four people. Two men and two women. One woman was Lady of Cannizaro and through the dialogue he realised one of them, easily recognisable from his accent, was Enrico LoTrova. The inspector had mentioned this name before. The man who saved him. He kept on listening, revelation after revelation. They all knew about the music sheet and the possible existence of the black azalea. Lady of Cannizaro was the one who helped pull some strings for Sergej Vernikoff. He then wondered if this Enrico LoTrova had been there not to save him, but to keep an eye on him. Eric Quercer felt the man in black and the driver were making fun of him. He was now caught in a web which was closing in on him.

The conversation over the radio came to an end. They agreed to stay in touch and the voice of the other man, a little older, said he would give a closer look at the poem. Lady of Cannizaro said goodbye and they heard the door close.

'Now, look to your right, Mr Quercer.' said finally the man in black.

Eric watched the building at the corner for a few minutes. Then he saw a woman coming out of a door looking onto the Ridgeway. Lady of Cannizaro.

'What is the meaning of all this?' he asked without looking at the driver or the man in black.

'You have more people looking for what you claimed you could get easily.' advised the man in black with a hint of malice. 'The older man you heard is Dr Watkins. The curator of the Wimbledon Museum.'

'What are we waiting for then?' exclaimed Eric. 'We know they have the music sheet and they already decoded the hidden poem for us. Let me get in there now and grab it. Done! We can then learn if this poem can give us any clues, and we will be more than half-way to finding the black azalea.'

'Why rush, Mr Quercer? Let them find the clues for you and keep tabs on their every move so that when the time is right, you'll know what to do.'

'How...?'

Eric did not get a response except the buzz of the separating windows sliding back into position. The driver, without further explanations, handed him over an envelope. Inside, the horticulturist found an earpiece and a bug, probably a copy of the same tracking technology they had put on Lady of Cannizaro. There was a letter that came with additional instructions. Eric chuckled. More letters, and not enough face time.

'You may leave, Mr Quercer.' said the driver, turning the car engine.

'Where am I? Where's the Rose and Crown?'

The driver did not answer and using the gun told him to scram. The horticulturist stepped out and crossed the road to walk away from there before Enrico LoTrova or anyone could see him. He toyed with the earpiece in his pocket and chose his target. Perhaps the curator, this Dr Watkins, who seemed to know a thing or two about the Cannizaro Park's history.

The driver watched Eric Quercer walk briskly up Lingfield Road until he disappeared into the distance.

'What would you like to do about this other man involved, sir?' he asked leaning his head to the left where the separating window had slid open again.

'Is this Enrico LoTrova? Who is he?'

'A baker.'

'What?' hissed the man in black. 'How does he come into all this? Someone must have got the wrong end of the stick, either the Trust when hiring manpower or the police looking for suspects. What is he going to do? Hit us with baguettes?'

The driver thought of laughing but did not hear a chuckle coming from the backseat. His boss did not laugh at his own jokes. He waited in silence unsure how to react.

'Shall we head home, Lord Awlthorp?' asked the driver after the long pause.

Lord Awlthorp's face emerged from the shadows of the backseat. He peered at his driver through the rectangular window. Two deep black eyes watched attentively, almost without blinking. They were cold and heartless, void of any feeling but a cruel expression. His short and curly corvine hair was slicked back, and only streaks of white and greyish hair running back from above his forehead broke the dark spell against his faint olive-like complexion.

'These are uncertain but exciting times.' he said, almost to himself. 'We ought to be careful if we want this test to be successful. Call Reginald and ask him to come and see me. I have a job for him. Let's go.'

The driver nodded. He sent a message and started the car.

'You think Mr Quercer is unreliable for our first test?' he asked checking for incoming traffic.

Lord Awlthorp grinned.

'Ingenious chap, I must say. Erratic, though, and therefore a liability. Recent events have brought a lot of things into the light and now we already have too many dogs on the trail of the black azalea. It could jeopardise our business agenda.'

'Do you think, sir, Wimbledon Police will extend the park closure now they have more reasons to believe something fishy is going on?'

The driver looked in his rear-view mirror. Lord Awlthorp sat back, engulfed by the penumbra and darkness of his black overcoat. He was not sure if the lord was looking at him or outside the window.

'Whether the park stays closed or re-opens,' replied Lord Awlthorp. 'we must ensure the black azalea does not leave Wimbledon. Mr Quercer needs to speed things up before tomorrow morning. That's for sure. Reginald could help us deal with some of the nuisances on his tail.'

The driver drove the sombre black saloon car through the streets behind Southside and then onto Wimbledon Village High Street. They stopped at an intersection. A few passers-by looked at the odd black car, unable to see inside, perhaps guessing there was a celebrity inside. Lord Awlthorp returned an indignant look, unseen.

'Sir!' interrupted the driver, hesitantly. 'Sorry to disturb. Reginald confirmed he will join us soon. He also said he found the chemistry boys you talked about…do you know what he means?'

'Good. Very good.' commented the lord, pleased. 'Finally, things are getting into motion. Once the black azalea is found, there will be no turning back. Everything will soon be mine. Past, present and future.'

Lord Awlthorp's eyes glinted with selfishness as the driver sped through the unsuspecting inhabitants of Wimbledon Village.

Dr Watkins shook the dusty rag after running it down the glass showcase of one of Wimbledon's relics from the Iron Age. He noticed a smudge on the side glass and quickly attended to it. A couple of fingerprints seemed to grab the corner of the showcase and Dr Watkins wiped it off, cursing the too curious adult or the child who had leant against the glass. He checked it against the ceiling light, but one wipe was enough to make the glass shine again. Being curator of a small local museum was no easy matter. He might have less space and fewer relics, but he was still a one-man team in charge of keeping it all clean and tidy, as well as running the office. Dr Watkins did not complain, although he could not deny there were moments when he wished there were more funds which would allow him to hire cleaning staff or an accountant to manage the books. His passion for the history of Wimbledon had been a long one and so was his membership at the Wimbledon Village Club, even before it had changed its name from John Evelyn Society. His mind took a little trip through time. It was remarkable how much history lay below and above the relatively modest square metre on which Wimbledon resided. It was even more baffling how much archaeologists and historians could retrieve from libraries and digging sites, sometimes found far away from Wimbledon itself. Who knows how many more secrets would be revealed. Dr Watkins smiled at the thought. He recalled his chat with Enrico and Viviane about Cannizaro House, and how that house had been around almost five centuries. Now, something new had come to light. A rare species of flower hidden in the grounds of Cannizaro Park. It could be a great moment for Wimbledon history.

Enrico glanced at him working while he sat at the desk with Viviane, both crouched over the copy of the poem left by Lady of Cannizaro and the original music sheet. They were absorbed by them and Viviane kept scribbling notes on a small post-it. Dr Watkins though did the heavy lifting, shouting out ideas and words as he carried on his spring cleaning. The Italian baker found him odd, in a clever way. He could already remember the poem and it seemed that getting lost in the relics of Wimbledon inspired him just in the same way he was inspired by kneading dough into perfect bread.

'Ok, I think the whole thing makes sense up to line three. A black azalea. Coming from far away. Present from *papà* she loves so much. What about the rest?'

'One of the most beautiful personalities I had ever known....' repeated Dr Watkins, his eyes focused on shuffling a few laminated maps from the eighteenth century. 'That could be anyone or anything. I think she is just comparing to how beautiful the black azalea is or was. For me, the key is in the fourth line. One hot summer with books and guides...'

'Why would Hilary Wilson write the last sentence in invisible ink?' asked Viviane.

'I don't know.' said Dr Watkins. 'Maybe to complicate things. The poem does not follow a metric without the written line so it can be confusing.'

'One hot summer with books and guides...' repeated Enrico. 'You said she loved art, so I assume she read a lot of books.'

'I believe so, but she was not a book worm.'

'What about guides? She wrote any?'

Dr Watkins stopped for a second.

'Enrico, remind me again, where Sergej was when you caught him searching like a madman?'

'By some sort of Greek or Roman temple. A raised stone platform with columns.'

'The Belvedere.' added the curator.

'Do you think he was searching for the black azalea there?'

'Brilliant!' mocked Viviane. 'He was looking for a mythical flower hidden behind a brick or under a boulder? Are we sure Sergej Vernikoff did not lose his marbles? I am still ready to go and talk to the authorities before anyone gets hurt.'

Enrico realised Viviane had a point. Something that unique would not be easy to find by the looks of how Hilary Wilson had decided to hide it, but it never dawned on them that basic knowledge of gardening told you a flower could not survive without light or water. He looked for Dr Watkins's reaction who had his rag at his waist and was tapping gently at his chin, looking up, lost in thought.

'I don't know…' he murmured. 'When I read that fourth line, though, it reminds of something.'

He walked up to a shelf and picked a book, from which he flicked the pages in haste. He then grabbed his smartphone and typed a few words.

'See,' said Viviane. 'He has something better than your Nokia 3310.'

'I hate that thing. It is too alive to my taste.' moaned the Italian baker.

'Ok. Here it is.' said finally Dr Watkins. 'I thought it rang a bell.'

'What? Is the Belvedere where Hilary Wilson spent her "hot summer with books and guides"?' said Enrico light-hearted, recalling his wanderings in Cannizaro Park earlier that day. 'Strange place. It was so remote from everything and there were no flowers in sight.'

'A good guess, I suppose.' resumed Dr Watkins closing the book. 'The Belvedere, with its apparent classical architecture, was actually built in the late 1970s, around the same time Hilary Wilson died. If I look at the Retreat nearby, a round green square with a weird late art deco feeling to it, it was built thirty odd years after Hilary Wilson died. She could not have spent her summers reading books in either of those places, or at least it is very unlikely she would have done so.'

Enrico was amazed in hearing Dr Watkins. The man was indeed a reliable source of local history.

'However, you should know Edward Wilson was a great supporter of girl scouts, called Guides or Brownies, and actually let them have space for them to gather in Cannizaro Park. Hilary Wilson was an active scout herself and she enjoyed it apparently. Her father turned Chapel House into a place where they could hold meetings and summer camps.'

'Chapel?' repeated Enrico.

'I remember it.' said Viviane. 'Is it that old chapel-looking building in the northern part of the park?'

'Yes, an old chapel built by a Roman Catholic priest in the nineteenth century; I think, to support the workhouses in Camp Road. It belonged to the neighbouring Keir House at one point before Edward Wilson added both house and chapel to the park, his own private estate. It is called Chapel House or Guides' Chapel.'

'So that means…' started Viviane.

'The black azalea could be in Chapel House!' exclaimed the Italian baker, enjoying the eureka moment.

Viviane did not comment. She gave Dr Watkins a disappointed look to which the curator shrugged, almost as if to say he could not help it. Enrico was getting more excited by the moment.

'What do you plan to do now, Enrico?' she asked.

Viviane was stating the obvious and she did it with her head tilted to the side, expecting Enrico to share his plan with them and a damn good reason why they should pursue this.

'We make a visit to the Chapel House tomorrow!' exclaimed Enrico with a surge of determination that was making him forget the dangers ahead.

He opened his arms Italian style and shrugged to demonstrate the simplicity of it all. His face was all lit up.

'Breaking the law again? The park is cordoned off. Well, after the attempt on Sergej Vernikoff's life, it will be sealed off for good. Poor man!'

A shadow shrouded across Enrico's face, bringing him back to reality away from treasure hunts and hero quests. He and Viviane thought of the opera singer for a moment.

'What about going to the police?' reminded Viviane.

'Think of Lady of Cannizaro. She needs help, badly. And she did not go to the police in the first place for questionable but still valid reasons. We are not murdering anyone. Just a simple visit to see if Dr Watkins's interpretation is true. He also has the keys to the place. What's the worst that can happen? We get caught, we get a smack on our hands.'

The Italian baker winked at the curator to get support. The old man kept a blank, impartial expression, diplomatic enough not to upset either Enrico or Viviane. He could not ignore the historical value of what they had in their hands.

Viviane glared at Enrico not understanding why he would be so reckless.

'You think you can barter with the police because they covered up the explosion? What if the man after the black azalea finds out what we know? He seems capable of killing.'

She threw the consequences at him and they all hit him hard like stones before falling without a sound on the museum floor.

'I have an idea.' intervened Dr Watkins after a brief pause.

The two turned to him. He stared back and left his work as a curator to join them at the desk.

'I will go to the Chapel House. I know the park and I can get in and out.'

'Agree with that.' added Enrico. 'I almost got lost in the bloody thing.'

'You are not serious, Dr Watkins? Do you want to play with fire too?'

'And don't you want to know if the black azalea exists?' replied the curator with a peaceful face. 'Imagine a rare flower found in Wimbledon. Picture yourself and your flower shop on the news, everyone congratulating you for your green-fingered contribution to such a discovery. Think about me and this museum, getting a renewed attention it deserves. The museum, the WAIS, the whole Wimbledon maybe needs this.'

'You are not serious, are you?' asked Viviane bewildered.

'Practical, I would say.'

'Is that why you want to do this? Fame and glory?'

'We want to help, Viviane.' butted in Enrico. 'Help the Trust. Help Lady of Cannizaro. Help Sergej.'

Viviane bit her lip. She felt outnumbered. She could have just left but she was not talking to complete strangers, at least when looking at Dr Watkins.

'Then if you are going Dr Watkins, I will come too.' she decided.

'*Come?* There is no need to…' protested Enrico worried for Viviane.

'Hold on! You can be reckless but not me? I need to keep an eye on you too.'

Her face hardened again. This time though she was not opposing Enrico but rather challenging him. If he wanted to be reckless, then they would all be reckless, and cry over spilt milk later.

'We go tomorrow to the Chapel House and see if we find anything that could help.'

'What do I do?' said Enrico.

'You have a bakery to look after.' she replied bemused.

The plan was set. Dr Watkins folded back the music sheet carefully and wrote the additional line they discovered on the written transcription left by Lady of Cannizaro. They would carry the transcription with them but return the music sheet to the Duchess Hotel. The museum did not have a safe and it was better not to run risks.

When Enrico and Viviane both left together, they walked side by side along the narrow pavement on the Ridgeway. The breeze pushed them closer, almost pushing them to brush each other's arms while left alone with their thoughts. They came up to the first roundabout of Wimbledon High Street and stopped outside Enrico's bakery. Little traffic pushed up and down the street.

'I still think it is a bad idea.' Vivian said before leaving. 'If we keep running around in circles like this, we will need to go to the police. You know that, right?'

'I do.' replied Enrico.

He took her arms to reassure her they were doing the right thing.

167

'I wish Dr Watkins had not given away all those clues,' sighed Viviane. 'making you and himself believe you will find something. A black azalea…ah! It sounds like a perfume.'

They kissed each other goodbye on the cheeks. Two times since according to Enrico this is what Italians did. They then parted to return to their shops. The street was strangely quiet considering a storm had been brewing over Wimbledon for a while.

Lawyers. Lawyers. The word echoed in Baynard's head while he massaged his temples and reclined in his office chair. He stared at the ceiling above to clear his head. The blank staring back at him did not inspire. He thought of the many people suing for damages or negligence. All of them calling their lawyers after everything that had been happening at the Duchess Hotel.

'Paracetamol, inspector?' rang Jeremy's voice.

Baynard blinked to wake himself up and return to the harsh reality.

'Will it enlighten me on all this and make it all go away?' blurted out Baynard. 'Anything new from forensics?'

'No. They simply confirmed again the near-fatal poisoning of Sergej Vernikoff. A neurotoxin mixed in his tea, called gra… granayo…toxin. Granayotoxin. It sounds like taken from an Agatha Christie novel. We already rounded up the waiting staff and the bar men. Nobody says they touched it.'

'What was the poison made with?'

'They are still debating. And the Chief Superintendent called, asking what is going on.'

'We will get grilled by the Chief Superintendent if we don't get a hold on this. What is the word out there?'

'The media are asking rhetorical, speculative questions. Things are slowly coming to the boil. We don't have much time before we need to come clean with the Chief Superintendent and the Council.'

'What's the latest from the Duchess Hotel?'

'We isolated the meeting room, so we are ok in terms of keeping the crime scene untouched. But we would need to interview all the guests…'

Baynard groaned in seeing his idea of subtlety vanish like a mirage. Jeremy changed topic.

'Did you get anything out of Mr Vernikoff's statement before he…you know…'

'His statement is not really hard evidence.' recalled the inspector. 'I was onto something though. When I was mentioning Eric Quercer and what he babbled to that baker …Lorrova or something, Mr Vernikoff became a little stiff and wary someone may be spying on him.'

Baynard's image of the white chef jacket disappearing over the wall had not left him. It was still a flashing memory nagging him at the back of his head.

'The baker?' exclaimed Jeremy. 'You think he is involved?'

'I don't know. But he must know something. I am telling you.'

'Were you meant to question him further?'

'I was not planning to, but I do now. I will pay him a visit. Where is his bakery again?'

Jeremy gave him the address. 9b High Street. Baynard picked his light coat ready to leave.

'Why would he want Sergej Vernikoff out of the picture?' quizzed Jeremy.

'I am going to find out.' replied Baynard.

'What if the Chief Superintendent calls?'

'We still have around thirty-six hours before we have to go public. If Vernikoff pulls through, and I damn hope he does, I can finish with him

169

what I started yesterday. Do we have a guard in front of his room twenty-four-seven?'

Jeremy nodded.

'Anything from forensics on the explosion?'

'Nothing new. The bomb was home-made, a very basic one. Amateur work.'

'Amateur work? That thing caused more pandemonium than an earthquake. Someone is pulling my leg and I don't like it. And if I look at my suspects, I have an opera singer, a baker and a horticulturist. It sounds like a joke!'

The inspector was about to make his exit when he added one more request for his favourite and only sergeant-turned-assistant.

'Put a tail on the baker and the horticulturist until tomorrow evening.'

'Is that safe?'

That was a question Baynard had not been able to put off his mind all day. He had wondered if Wimbledon was in danger of something bigger they had not foreseen. He realised he was in no position to guarantee anyone's safety until the case was solved. The inspector did not waste any more time. He left the police station and took his car back out into the streets. He drove up the hill to the first roundabout and parked it on one of the side streets, from where he could see the location given by Sergeant Jeremy.

Enrico sat at one of his tables with a calculator. Behind him, the bloomers had all been baked and ready for a promotional sale on the high street in the next few days. Enrico struggled to focus, his mind filled with Dr Watkins's promises of historical discoveries and Viviane's warnings of danger from an hour before. Staring at the financial paperwork had been rather tiring and cumbersome for the last hour or so, and his eyes drifted off easily to watch Wimbledon Village taking its course towards the end of the day. He peered to the right, across the bay window, where traffic slowed down around the roundabout with so many cars and public transport coming from all directions through that small intersection. He suddenly noticed a police car had jumped out from beneath the hill, normal speed, no siren. Recollections of his recent encounter with the local police made Enrico shiver, if not feel a pinch of embarrassment. He followed the police car slowing down, turning on a left indicator blinking, and parking in a side street visible from the bakery. A policeman got out and Enrico recognised the inquisitive stare of Baynard. He was marching in the direction of the bakery's large shop windows and there was nothing in between to shield Enrico and let him hide. The Italian baker asked himself what the unexpected visit was all about and why he should hide if he hadn't done anything wrong. Well, almost.

The bell rang again. Its twinkle felt gloomier and out of tune as the inspector made way onto Enrico's territory.

'Good afternoon, Mr Lorova.' greeted Baynard in a curt manner.

'LoTrova! And good afternoon!' replied Enrico. 'Would you like a coffee, some bread?'

'Very kind, Mr Latreva! However, since it would be my tenth coffee today, I will pass. Would you be able to spare a few minutes to answer a few questions? We have a few leads since we last spoke and it would be helpful if we could double-check a couple of things.'

'I love the English. It is all so polite!' said Enrico pretending to be excited.

He did not know what else to say without betraying what he knew. On second thought, he was not sure whether being overly friendly would help.

'Never mind. You are not open officially yet, right?'

'No, unfortunately. Licenses to pay and works yet to finish. Getting there!'

'Well, good luck with that.'

'Oh thanks. I can offer you a 20% discount on opening day.'

'Let's stop it there before we end up talking about bribery.'

Enrico was not clear if the inspector was joking or not. His inquisitive stare did not flinch.

'I am listening.' said Enrico putting up a serious face.

Baynard paused for a moment.

'You probably heard of the poison attack against Mr Sergej Vernikoff, the famous opera singer, earlier today.'

'Oh no…' lied Enrico putting a hand over his mouth. 'Is he alright? Who did this?'

'He is in a critical condition at Parkside Hospital. Did you know Mr Vernikoff?'

'Not at all.'

'Are you sure?'

'Opera is not my thing, and I had never heard of him until a few days ago when they announced the opening night.'

Enrico watched Baynard carefully. He listened and then read off from his notebook lifting his head up and then down, and then up again. An ordinary routine of questions, which the Italian baker mistrusted. He expected an ambush question from one moment to the next. He needed to stay calm.

'Would you be able to share your movements from today?'

'Here, most of the time, or downstairs in the lab. Setting up shop as well as I can.'

'Anyone can confirm?'

Enrico started to doubt Inspector Baynard's visit.

'The florist opposite can confirm.' he lied again. 'Is there something wrong?'

'Not at all. I wanted to check again that hunch of yours. The one you told me so passionately in yesterday's statement.' soldiered on Baynard not to lose precious time. 'Why would you think the explosion was deliberate, even arson maybe?'

Enrico thought quickly on how to say it. He wanted to choose words carefully. Seeing Baynard's inquisitive stare though was not helping. His calm was already out in the streets, crushed under the heavy weight of a double-decker bus.

'I think what happened today says it all.' Enrico bragged. 'I mean, the man is not in his room when it blows up and then death catches up by poisoning him...'

'How do you know the room that blew up was Mr Vernikoff's?'

Enrico swallowed hard. He could not tell the inspector he had met the opera singer inside Cannizaro Park. He scrambled for an excuse. Small details are easy to miss when your brain runs so fast, pretending to be ahead of the game. Too ahead.

'Erm...Lady of Cannizaro told me...' he dared.

'You two know each other?'

Enrico nodded with a pursed smile stretching from ear to ear. He did not have to lie. It was true.

'Well, she was not meant to share that information.' reproached Baynard. 'Yet, before what happened to Mr Vernikoff today, you were so convinced it was deliberate. I am curious to hear your method of deduction, Mr Litrueva.'

'LoTrova!' Enrico corrected. 'A hunch. Or maybe I am just too much into mystery novels...'

Baynard grinned.

'Well, leave it to the professionals. A hunch can lead you down the wrong path.'

Enrico could not fathom what Baynard really knew and what he pretended to know. His visit was odd, and full of traps to make him talk. Or maybe the inspector did not like him, ever since the first time they met in the Dutch Sunken Garden.

'I am not following, inspector. Is there an investigation going on perhaps? Am I a suspect in some faulty wires causing a room to blow up?'

'There is no need to exaggerate out of proportions.'

Enrico wanted to bring Baynard into the open. If the inspector knew something was going on, he could not understand why he had come here to question him again. The holes in the story were many and Baynard was probably trying to fill them all as much as Enrico had been trying to. The shop suddenly felt as small and cramped as a prison cell. Enrico needed to get rid of him and warn Lady of Cannizaro the police were starting to squirm. At that point, his mind took a pause. It then became clear to him; the police were playing a similar game as Lady of Cannizaro. They knew there had been an explosion and still no announcement was made, no information given to the press or the Council. Baynard could have been playing on one of the two sides, and maybe playing one against the other.

'I bet' started Enrico. 'if news spread that someone attempted to blow up Wimbledon, or that we had a poisoner in town, it would not go down well with the locals, or even your superiors.'

Baynard's face hardened. The backlash from the cheerful and dramatic Italian baker took him by surprise.

'Defamation is not a good sport, Mr Lereva. Don't cross that line!'

'LoTrova!'

'You wouldn't want me to search your premises for granayotoxin!'

'*Che?* What?'

Baynard bit his tongue and stepped back from the confrontation. He was finding the Italian baker irritating. Everything was getting out of control. The tail on him would help find out more.

'Tell me, do you plan to leave town anytime soon?'

'I am not leaving, not even on holiday, until this place is open. You can come here to question me anytime. Would you like some freshly baked bread to take with you?'

Baynard made a step forward. Enrico felt his icy stare on him, cold and penetrating.

'Listen, do not let me find you in the wrong place at the wrong time again or I will arrest you for obstruction of justice.'

He then went for the door. Upon exiting, Baynard turned around.

'Do not leave town!' he said. 'Better cooperate or you may not have time to open your bakery.'

Enrico followed him walking down the road, until he could no longer see him. The inspector did not wish to return to his car straight away. He strolled thoughtfully on the pavement bending around the roundabout and away towards the Ridgeway. He stopped at an antiques shop, not really looking. He glanced at the shop across the road and through the glass windows saw the florist Viviane Leighwood, busy sorting pots and plants. It crossed his mind he had to verify the Italian baker's alibi. He then saw the owner of the antiques shop stopping at the entrance to give him a welcome smile.

'Is the bakery open?' he asked casually.

'Oh, not yet. I am still waiting to learn the date'

'Are they still working in there? Were they today?'

'Sometimes. They've slowed down a bit, though. Today there was nobody for most of the morning and early afternoon.'

The owner giggled and so did Baynard, but for different reasons. He now knew the Italian baker had lied twice and there is never smoke without a fire.

Lady of Cannizaro sank in her desk chair, exhausted. The vitality that usually wrapped her with an indistinguishable aura, felt shattered. Her whole body slumped, and she closed her eyes to find a corner of inner peace. She shut the door to leave her staff to handle the complaints flooding in. She had heard cries of protest on the Duchess Hotel being unsafe, and the

Council had called an emergency meeting later that day to understand the implications for the Cannizaro Festival. The police held their position to keep the park and part of the hotel off limits until the morning of the day after tomorrow. However, the recent illness of Sergej Vernikoff was unfortunate and they hoped not to find foul play that could give them reasons to extend the lockdown. When Lady of Cannizaro heard it, she was baffled by the position of the police, Inspector Baynard included. She knew her staff had been questioned about who made the drinks and from that she could guess the police too were more than certain someone had made an attempt on the opera singer's life. Someone poisoned Vernikoff and she knew well who could be behind it. It dawned on her the police too may be on the same tracks and yet they were playing as if nothing dangerous was happening. Enrico's claims came back to her. She could not believe the opera singer tried to protect his room with explosives and without her knowing. She wondered what sort of person Sergej Vernikoff had become, and worst of all, what sort of person was hunting him down.

The only positive of the day was that no sponsor had pulled out yet, and the main one, Alberyx Enterprises, confirmed their support until facts were clearer. The emergency meeting from the Council had been adjourned until the morning of the day after tomorrow. For Lady of Cannizaro, it was so little time and there was plenty to go through. The hotel, the festival, the Trust, Hilary Wilson's assets.

Her desk phone rang, startling her. She picked up the receiver in the silence of her own office.

'Hello?'

'Hello. It's me.' said the voice.

'Nice to hear from you.' sighed Lady of Cannizaro.

She would have preferred to avoid having this conversation now.

'What the hell happened?' he asked.

His voice was direct and strangely gentle and quiet.

176

'You tell me? Did you know he was responsible for bombing one of my hotel rooms, just to keep the bad guys away?'

The voice said nothing.

'That man is in hospital, Lady of Cannizaro.' the voice resumed. 'I don't know if he will pull through. At least it is not you, or me, or anyone else.'

'It's still chaos over here. I am sure you know who is behind the poison.'

'What about the music sheet?'

Lady of Cannizaro knew Sergej Vernikoff was meant to keep the music sheet with him at all times. Now he was in hospital, there was no way for the Trust to track the movements or stay in touch. Little they knew, Vernikoff had hidden the music sheet under a stage for Enrico to find. She faltered about mentioning her disclosure to Dr Watkins, Enrico and Viviane. She knew the Trust may not see eye to eye with her about bringing new people into the mix, especially after the dangers pending onto them. However, she felt both music sheet and the notes on the secret message were safer with them.

'Safe. With me.' she lied.

'Good. Make sure it stays that way until we can re-schedule the announcement.'

'Any news about the man looking for it?'

'No. I am sure he still out there so be careful.'

'What about the search?'

The voice hesitated and breathed deeply. She felt the person on the other end of the line was anxious.

'I don't think I will come over. Need time to think what works best.'

'What does the Trust think?'

'The Trust simply wants to ensure we don't lose that music sheet.'

'And the black azalea?'

There was a brief pause.

'We agreed not to mention it over the phone. I thought you didn't believe that story anyway'

'An explosion and a poison attack at my hotel made me change my mind…' she scorned.

'Sorry, Lady of Cannizaro. We will refund you accordingly. Thank you for everything.'

He hung up. Again, she was alone with the dark of the evening. She dreaded going to sleep, not sure if she could catch some shuteye, or perhaps she was scared to wake up to a new tragedy tomorrow. Wimbledon had lived a quiet life for such a long time. She did not want the hotel to go down in history as the place where everything went wrong.

Dr Watkins returned home late. He had been sitting at his desk until after closing time, with only his desk lamp to protect him from the invasive darkness. Its glow flooded his stationery and his papers with a decadent gold. The rest of the small museum stood out there melting in the shadows.

He could not stop reading and re-reading Hilary Wilson's music sheet. It was natural of him to appreciate the value of this document in the same way Vernikoff and Lady of Cannizaro did. He felt the same responsibility on one side but on the other he was starting to itch at the thought of the secrets it concealed. The mythical black azalea was starting to become as interesting as the Stone Age arrows found in Wimbledon Common or the forgotten parchments from the Tudor era collecting dust in a British Library, miles away from Wimbledon. To cast away any doubts, he refreshed his memory about some of the facts known around Edward Wilson. He was happy to find out he remembered well. Yet, when listing Edward Wilson's amazing achievements as a horticulturist, there was no specific mention of azaleas, never mind black ones. Maples, magnolias, orchids, a wide range of trees and flowers were brought to the park and the Wilsons were smart enough to plant them in a way they could fit the harsh terrain of Wimbledon hill. Dr Watkins searched further back in time and a little bit further afield. Nothing in the world talked about black azaleas, no legends, no examples, nothing.

Another thought stunned him. Apart from Dundas's features, no major works had been done to the park as much as the Wilsons had done to turn it into the beautiful park it was today, or what was left of it. Still, there were a hundred years or so to cover and Dr Watkins could not grasp the concept of a black azalea still thriving without being looked after. Most of the trees and flowers had hardly survived since the Wilsons sold the park. Disease, weather. The chances of a single species of flower surviving were very few.

The curator entered his house and brought back light to the abandoned living room. His thoughts went back to Hilary Wilson, the Countess of Wrenbury. She loved art, she loved music, she adored Adela Schuster. Both of them were hedonists. As a matter of fact, they both looked up to the Duchess Sophie of Cannizaro, who was a hedonist herself at the time of the Romantic movement. Music, art, and a coded message in a music sheet. For who the message was intended, Dr Watkins could not tell. He read the poem again and stopped at the last line Viviane transcribed below the original text given by Lady of Cannizaro. The sentence rang a bell. It was how Hilary Wilson described her dog, but he had read it somewhere else, somewhere more important. He brooded over it for a whole half hour, checking online, checking the books he had around. He then came across a summary of Adela Schuster's biography when living at Cannizaro House in the 1890s. She was known then as 'Lady Wimbledon' since she had many artists over for her parties, one of whom was Oscar Wilde. Dr Watkins needed to tap into all his knowledge until he remembered the sentence was an extract taken from Oscar Wilde's 'De Profundis'. He used it to describe Adela Schuster and thank her for helping him at his most time of need. She had been a good friend of the Irish writer until his death and he had been a guest at Cannizaro House before his fall. He was the number one hedonist.

Dr Watkins scratched his head. Perhaps the black azalea was such a beautiful flower, an emblem of perfection Hilary Wilson recognised and was mesmerised by. The coded message, the secrecy did not fit in at all. He rubbed his eyes and yawned. He understood why Enrico and Sergej Vernikoff could not forget the matter. It was a rabbit hole he was just staring into from the edge, waiting for the plunge to happen. He read once more the poem. The first lines showed Hilary Wilson was writing about something personal, something from her youth.

The curator looked at the time and decided to call it a day. Tomorrow was a busy day. It was the last day Cannizaro Park was meant to be closed off. It was also the day he would try and dig out some answers lying around Chapel House, if any. He was planning to meet Viviane at the Rose and Crown in the afternoon.

A creaking sound came from upstairs. Dr Watkins jumped and looked up, alarmed. The house stood still and silent. He slowly grabbed his umbrella and took the short flight of stairs to the first floor. A cool breeze filled the corridor and Dr Watkins followed up to his bedroom. The door was ajar, just as he had left it. He leaned forward and then pushed hard to barge in with the umbrella raised above his head. He flicked on the switch and found the room empty. One of the windows was open and the wind was blowing gently in, rustling his scattered notes from the bedside table to the wooden floor. He could not remember if he had forgotten to close the window properly. He went to close it. Outside he could see or hear nothing. The draught made him shiver and somehow Dr Watkins felt he was being watched.

Reginald Bosham waited in the study. He stood still by the desk, legs slightly parted and arms crossed. Anyone would have thought he was a soldier. His burly figure, his large hands. Yet, he was not an army man but a merciless mercenary, a crook of the worst species. He had been hired in the last six months by a man he had never met or heard of before. A man who had introduced himself as Lord Awlthorp and required his help as a professional bodyguard. Reginald had spent the last few years in Wandsworth Prison and the only bodyguard work he ever did was protection for some of the top dog inmates at the prison. Lord Awlthorp, the man in black, did not want to hear about it. Reginald could only suspect he was being hired for shady business the lord himself would not get his hands dirty with. The pay superseded any doubts or uncertainties. There were only three rules he had to strictly follow.

The first rule was about the strict routine when he arrived at Lord Awlthorp's house. He always had to use the back entrance and slip into the main study upstairs, where he would wait until either Lord Awlthorp or his driver entered the room. The same would apply when he left. He was forbidden to use the main entrance. Ten minutes or so passed and the man in black made his entrance. He did not have his usual black overcoat. Instead, he wore a dark blue velvet shirt and black trousers which made Reginald understand perfectly his new employer was not a fan of colours. He did not look at him and went straight to his desk to check a small leather-bound notebook. He held it open in his hands and did not speak or acknowledge Reginald's presence, as if he did not exist. Reginald's Casio watch beeped, and he quickly glanced at it to check the time.

'Turn it off!' snarled Lord Awlthorp, looking up towards him.

His black eyes narrowed to a slit, sharp like knives ready to stab him if he did not follow what he said. Reginald was a man with no fears, but he had to admit the man in black scared him for his bizarre and meticulous attitude. Rule number two was about the complete absence of any form of clockwork in his presence. No watches, no clocks. His study only had a grandfather clock in the corner and it was stuck at three a.m. with no ticking sound. Reginald did not take notice at first. Now that he had been caught wearing his beeping Casio more than once and witnessed the bad temper of his new employer, he realised Lord Awlthorp did not joke. The row of silent clocks on the staircase was the proof. He did not hesitate to silence his watch for good.

'Good. We got that straight.' added Lord Awlthorp, pleased. 'Now, it is time to get down to business, Reginald. Or should I call you Reggie.'

'Reginald, sir.' he replied uneasy.

It was the fourth time he had asked.

'Good. Reggie it is.' Confirmed Lord Awlthorp, still focused on reading his notebook.

Reginald did not object although deep inside he loathed being called as such. He did not want to contradict the man in black any further.

'Do you require any updates, sir?' followed up Reginald.

'In time, Reggie, in time. I need you to do something else for me.'

'Which is?'

'The mess at the Duchess Hotel is a little out of hand. Too many people getting involved and it is not good for my plans.'

'You should have let me deal with it and not give the job to some crazy gardener.'

'Horticulturist, Reggie. He is a horticulturist. And yes, he is a nutcase, but for the first phase of my plan, our test phase, I needed someone not local. Someone from outside to take all the blame.'

'Blame for what? To find a stupid flower?'

Lord Awlthorp made a clicking sound with his mouth, a sound full of disappointment as he shook his head.

'Reggie, Reggie. The black azalea is not some stupid flower.'

He slammed shut the leather-bound notebook and walked towards him holding it to Reginald's face like a preacher brandishing some holy scripture. The bodyguard took one step back.

'When I read about it, I too thought it was just a legend. Then, when I came across old manuscripts that once belonged to the Earl of Spencer, what

I read was a revelation. It was clear to me it was more than a myth. It was a powerful force to reckon with.'

Reginald could not hold Lord Awlthorp's crazy-eyed gaze for long. He looked away and chuckled. The man in black sneered.

'You don't need to believe. I did not hire you to believe. I hired you to help me get what I need.'

Reginald looked back and straightened his face.

'What are your orders, sir?' he said coldly, pushing down any emotion.

'That's more like it. This is what I heard about you, from when you were in prison. You are the local help I need.'

'I am not from Wimbledon.' said Reginald defiantly.

'But you are from SW19, almost. Not like that useless Canadian.'

Reginald did not understand where Lord Awlthorp's faith and trust lay.

'Do you need me to take care of him and get the black azalea for you?'

'No. He will meet his own demise, I am sure. We are keeping an eye on what he does now that he is close. I need you to tell me how you are getting on with phase two. I heard you found the two boys.'

'Yes. I convinced them to do the job for you. Not sure what you think they could help you with, though. They are not professional scientists, more amateur chemical engineers who have built a few homemade bombs out of soap and crystallised new forms of drugs. Are you sure, sir?'

'Perfect for what we need to accomplish.'

'Which is?'

Lord Awlthorp did not reply. He looked sternly at Reginald and walked back to his desk. He opened his notebook again. Reginald did not know if he opened it on the same page; he did know what was written on it. Lord Awlthorp always consulted it, as if the answers to all his questions could be found in there. The bodyguard knew he was pushing his luck. Rule number three was to never ask about the project. His job was just to fulfil the specific tasks which the man in black provided to the smallest detail.

Time froze for what seemed a very long time. The absent ticking of time made past, present and future merge into a flow with no end and no beginning. The dark silhouette of Lord Awlthorp was a chilling site. His silence was almost deadly.

'In time, Reggie, in time. One day I will unearth power beyond your wildest dreams and you can be a part of it. This black azalea is only the first step.'

Reginald's face hardened. He was close to face the wrath from his employer again. Instead, he should better put his head down and accept the fact it was better being here than behind bars.

'What did you call me to do, sir?' Reginald asked.

Lord Awlthorp smiled. Pure evil seemed to transpire.

'Good.' he answered. 'We have what we need to find the black azalea. The Trust is no longer a problem. However, I need you to rub out Mr Vernikoff at Parkside Hospital and make it look like someone else did it.'

'You want Mr Quercer to be the scape goat?' asked Reginald.

'No. We still need him. What I want is a distraction, and I think we already have one we could easily frame.'

'Who?'

'Fancy some bread?'

It was another fine morning. Enrico was dusting off the counter to clear the crumbs and flour dust from the last batch of bread he had made. He had slept on and off the night before. His thoughts focused more and more on Lady of Cannizaro's story and the black azalea. His hands called for more action, but Enrico wanted first to see if he could sell what he had made before he went to knead more dough simply because he could not clear his head. Maybe the Wimbledon Village Club would buy his fresh bloomers.

Maybe he could sell it to other shop owners on the high street. A little promotion would not hurt now that his stall had been abandoned and technically confiscated by Wimbledon Police. He was following Viviane's advice after all. Perhaps it would show her he listened, and he wanted to be in her good books.

She sat at one of his empty round tables staring out to her shop. They had just had another friendly bickering about the whole thing. Viviane worried about the consequences and worried about herself and Dr Watkins being dragged into the whole affair. She was less feisty though and Enrico too had softened. They still spoke to each other but neither understood, both lost in translation. A double-decker bus passed, rendering the inside of the bakery blood red in an instant.

'You are an adult, Enrico.' sighed Viviane after a while. 'I won't stand in your way. I wanted to help differently, make your bakery known in Wimbledon. Not sure you can do that from a courthouse or behind bars when this whole conspiracy falls on us like a ton of bricks.'

'And I thank you for accepting that. *Grazie!*' he said.

He stopped what he was doing to look at Viviane in the eyes.

'For this reason, I am not going to hang around here with my hands deep in my pockets while you two venture out to do something dangerous. I am taking my own responsibility for dragging you into all of this, and I will go and see Sergej Vernikoff to get some answers from him.'

'What if after all we have done, there is no black azalea?'

'*Colpa mia!* My fault. I will be the first to admit it.'

Viviane looked at him with a coy smile. She then sighed and looked back onto the streets. Enrico smiled too and resumed the tidying up, knowing it would take time to make Viviane understand.

'Have you always been this helpful back home in Italy?'

Enrico slowed down the circling gestures he was making with the rag on the counter. He saw the contour of his face reflected in the surface. He probably knew the answer. He just had to think how to say it.

'I am a curious man, first of all, Viviane. *Un ragazzo curioso*, my grandma used to say. And I stuck my nose in the wrong things sometimes, but that is how I came across people who needed help, people who suffered injustice. I am just a baker, but I can still give my little contribution to help. A contribution to humanity.'

Enrico stood up as he spoke, talking to Viviane's eyes who had turned to listen. She looked less angry, or so Enrico wished. He was about to add something. Then shook his head to himself retracting whatever distracted thought had come into his head.

'What time are you going to Cannizaro Park?' he asked, changing subject.

'Afternoon. Dr Watkins and I are meeting at the Rose and Crown. You?'

'I will probably make my way some time. Where is this hospital Sergej is staying?'

'Head north on Parkside, keeping Wimbledon Common to your left. You may want to get bus 93.'

Enrico nodded vaguely.

'Not sure if Sergej is under guard.' commented Viviane. 'What are you going to say?'

'That I am there to see someone.'

'Just like that?'

'Once inside, I get my way around it.'

'Baker *and* doctor.'

Viviane sneered.

'This is an obsession, Enrico.' she continued. 'What are you going to do? Give him flowers?'

'Not a bad idea. Do you think you could give me a bouquet?'

'Right, and let's not forget to add some bread too, huh?' she scorned. 'I am going to punch you in a minute. But I will be reasonable and let you run off like you are some sort of Sherlock Holmes, handle your own mess, while I ensure at least Dr Watkins stays out of trouble.'

'Ok, hear me out.' reassured Enrico. 'All I want is to go in there, check on him, tell him what we know, that we are on his side. And then I am out.'

'Oh great. Do you know his room number?'

Enrico hesitated.

'Oh perfect! You go in there and play a game of Guess Who?'

'I'll think of something.'

'Perfect! Absolutely perfect! How about the police?'

Enrico winced and looked away.

'I saw Inspector Baynard here yesterday, talking to you. I don't know what he told you, but I don't think he would be pleased if he found out you were meddling in all this without telling the police.'

Enrico thought of Baynard's last word. He remembered his inquisitive stare before he left, almost challenging the Italian baker. Enrico was about to reply to Viviane when the beeping ringtone of his Nokia 3310 went off.

'Oh dear, nineteenth century calling Enrico…nineteenth century calling Enrico…' mocked Viviane with her hands cupped around her mouth like a speakerphone.

Enrico glared at her and checked the small pixel screen. His Nokia 3310 may be old and unstylish, but he felt reassured when little or no technology interfered with his life. He dreaded it.

The Italian baker saw the message. He then placed the call and listened in. Viviane watched him attentively and she noticed his jaw tense.

'Who was it?' asked Viviane after Enrico ended the call.

He was staring at the phone, having not uttered a single word.

'Voicemail. It was the Council. They say they have not yet received neither forms nor payment for the license and the inspection date may slip further if we do not confirm one.'

'Oh no…'

Viviane felt for Enrico in that moment, realising none of her plan had come to fruition after all that had happened at the Cannizaro Festival.

'What are you going to do? Do you want me to organise a fundraiser or something?

Enrico shook his head.

'No need to. We are going to find a way to make it all work.'

'Don't say it!' warned Viviane with a cringe, knowing where Enrico's speech was going.

'We will find the black azalea' continued Enrico. 'and put it on display as Wimbledon's finest!'

The Retreat was one of the most recent attempts to embellish the park and fight back its decadent look as the overgrowth and weather slowly gnawed at the beautiful gardening work by Henry Dundas and Edward K. Wilson. The Retreat consisted simply of a round flower bed with a minimalist brick-like column at its centre. The round space was guarded by a tall hedge, about four-metre high, thick enough to seclude it from the outside world hidden beyond it. If a visitor stood on their tiptoes, they could just about spot the rooftops of the rows of nearby houses which happened to share the border with Cannizaro Park along Chester Road, Sycamore Road and Dunstall Road. The only access to the Retreat was from within the park itself, through a narrow path starting from the Belvedere and the Heather Garden. This path too was lined by tall hedges on both sides which then joined in a circle at the Retreat. It was an odd, cramped shape compared to the other immense spaces in the park. After a century spent selling off land around Wimbledon for building residential houses, this peninsular extension became isolated and surrounded by private developments. From a bird's eye view, it would look like a stretched arm with the Retreat as a hand closed in a fist and calling out to Wimbledon in despair.

A few people knew about the Retreat, or perhaps knew about it but found it a bit too far to venture and not really worth it. The place was empty almost every day, isolated and almost forsaken. Even the flowers around the brick-like column seemed to have lost the will to live. A few still blossomed but only half of what there used to be. Visitors only reached the Retreat if they had intention to do so and were eager enough to walk on the rough footpath which was seldom beaten.

Lady of Cannizaro had been many times to this extremity of the park, more out of necessity than for idyllic pleasure. She still had to check the park map twice to ensure she remembered the easiest way to it. The walk from the Belvedere to the narrow footpath was not clearly marked and bushes of heather and fern covered what remained of the track. She followed the tall hedges rising up and coming close to each other, the only tell-tale sign she was headed in the right direction. When sure she could no longer get lost, she quickly wondered why he had chosen this place. Definitely for its privacy, for none of the police patrols had ever ventured up here, neither would they walk as far as the Belvedere. It was safe enough, but she glanced over her shoulder a few times to ensure she was not being followed. Dr Watkins's message had been concise enough. He wanted to talk to her urgently after yesterday's conversation.

The midday sun was rising but still could not bash through the tall hedges. The direct natural light, hidden from view somewhere beyond them, cast a deep blue aura across the stretch of sky right above Lady of Cannizaro. She could sense the warmth of the day out there and still feel the cool air blow past her, filled with solitude and uncertainty. When she reached the Retreat, a slice of the round square was washed with an intense yellow glow while the rest was clouded by a sombre shade. Dr Watkins was standing in the shade, leaning against the thick green wall of the hedge. He had been expecting her.

'Are you trying to camouflage into the surrounding area, Dr Watkins?' humoured Lady of Cannizaro.

189

She found the curator in his blue navy jacket hard to miss in the green foliage. For a second, seeing Dr Watkins in his comedy look made her forget the mess they were in.

'I heard footsteps. You cannot be too careful.' he replied in a whisper. 'Can they hear?'

He pointed over his shoulder, referring to the nearby houses in the outside world.

'Not if you speak quietly. What did you need to say to me so urgently? Meeting in the park is not safe.'

'I know. I used the entrance from the Herbal Garden, but I felt inside the park I would be safer than outside.'

Lady of Cannizaro frowned.

'What do you mean "safer"?'

Dr Watkins glanced around, double-checking they were alone in that confined round space.

'I think someone has started following me.' he whispered.

Lady of Cannizaro's eyes widened. Her face was alarmed. She had heard this once before, from Sergej Vernikoff himself.

'Are you sure?'

Dr Watkins nodded.

'I have a feeling I have been watched ever since I came back home late last night.'

'Did someone attack you?'

'No…no…I just feel someone is after me. I keep looking back to check. It is all because of the black azalea.'

'I don't understand.'

'Whoever was chasing Sergej Vernikoff is now chasing me, or maybe us. You are not safe, so we need to move quickly.'

'Move quickly? To do what?'

'Here. Take this.'

Dr Watkins gave her back the music sheet and the written note containing the poem decoded from it.

'What does this mean?'

The curator hinted at her to open the note and she unfolded it. She realised something was different. An additional line had been added in a different ink.

'What is this?' she said puzzled.

'We found a hidden text at the bottom of the music sheet. Invisible ink, can you believe it?'

'Well, it makes it even more surprising and confusing than before. I still don't know what this poem means, even if now complete.'

'We may have an idea.'

'Which is?'

Dr Watkins explained to Lady of Cannizaro his theory about Chapel House and his plan to check the place out. She listened carefully, a troubled look twisting her beautiful, tired face.

'I accept your help, Dr Watkins, I really do. Yet, I cannot guarantee your safety. I can hardly guarantee mine. If you are found or if you come across whoever is following us from the shadows, I am not sure I will be able to help. I don't...'

'Don't you worry!' exclaimed Dr Watkins holding her by the arms.

He tried to catch her gaze.

'That is why I wanted to give you back the only evidence we have. If something happens to me, then you need to call Inspector Baynard and show it to him. Tell the whole story. Hopefully, Sergej Vernikoff will recover soon.'

'Why risk your life for this?' she quizzed him.

'The same reason you did. We hold Wimbledon close to our hearts. We are talking about a piece of its hidden or maybe neglected history. I need to know!'

'Well, what do you want me to do?'

The plan sounded simple when put into words. If Lady of Cannizaro did not hear back from Dr Watkins or Viviane before eight p.m., she should get in touch with Inspector Baynard at once. The curator, though, was confident they may need just a couple of hours in the late afternoon. Chapel House was small. He kept repeating it, to reassure Lady of Cannizaro's anxious eyes. She still pondered whether Dr Watkins and also the Italian baker had lost their minds in the same way Sergej Vernikoff had. They were believing in something she could not fully grasp. For her, the music sheet was the true historic artefact, the legacy of Cannizaro House she wanted to carry into the future. It was not the fairy tale of a legendary flower. If she did not have to depend on the Trust, she would have come out in the open a long time ago. Dr Watkins though agreed with her to share their plan with the Trust. They needed all the help they could get, especially when facing the Wimbledon Police or the Council.

Lady of Cannizaro mulled over the right words to say while she returned to the Duchess Hotel. Having left Dr Watkins at his house, she took the short walk on West Side Common to the car park. She tried to act normal and smiled to the police guards buzzing around the hotel and the park entrance in greater numbers. She thought she would have a small lunch and do some admin to put her mind at ease for a bit. She would make the call later that afternoon from her office. Come clean with the Trust about the plan. Tell them and hopefully have a chance to close this once and for all. With or without the black azalea.

That afternoon the day turned a little colder. The sun struggled to push away the clouds and Wimbledon seemed to have fallen into an idle daze after two days of shocking events. The presence of the police did not go unnoticed although mainly confined around the Duchess Hotel. The rest of the town walked up and down Wimbledon Village in a cagey sort of way. Some gossiped on the strangest of theories, while others put faith in the people in charge. Life though went on that afternoon. The high street bustled with business and traffic. Everyone came and went. Parkside Hospital was the same despite the team of policemen huddled around an insignificant door of one of the hospital rooms. They acted as normal as they could, keeping a low profile as requested by Inspector Baynard. Most visitors and medical staff were now used to their presence.

Reginald Bosham observed them from above the open pages of his newspaper. He sat at the end of a row of seats in one of the waiting rooms. From there he had a good glimpse of the corridor where the police guarded Sergej Vernikoff's room. Extra care was paramount. He had been checking the police movements. They were pretty static. He kept note of how many visits the doctor and the nurse made. Enough time in between to slip in and do his trick.

Lord Awlthorp wanted Sergej Vernikoff out of the picture. He had had enough of him constantly slipping away, and now that they were closing in on the black azalea, he wanted to make sure neither he nor the Trust came back to bite them. Eric Quercer though was being too delicate, too cautious. He needed Reginald to play a heavier hand, like giving a stronger dose of granayotoxin to the opera singer and ensuring all evidence pointed to that crazy Italian baker. When the police's eyes were busy looking for Enrico LoTrova, the road would be clear for them to finish what they had started. The burly bodyguard did not think one second his employer's wishes were impossible.

Reginald folded the newspaper and threw it on the nearby coffee table. He went to the nearby vending machine, pretending to check what drinks were available. If he remembered the schematics, the maintenance room nearby looked onto the side road which ran alongside the building and led down to the car park at the back of the hospital. Treading carefully onto the ledge, he could easily reach Sergej Vernikoff's room without having to use the main entrance. A clean job. He took a bottle of Coca Cola and drank almost half in one gulp, then he strolled to the side glancing around casually until he was near enough the maintenance room. He slipped in unnoticed. The room was small, cluttered with brooms, buckets and cleaning products. The only window was a thin slit in the wall. Light hardly warmed up the room, stuck in penumbra. Reginald pushed the window open to squeeze through with his robust physique. The breeze hit him in the face as he glanced to each side of the outer wall. Parkside Hospital was not a tall building, but the second floor seemed high enough from the ground. Reginald did not hesitate. The clock was ticking. He grabbed the window frame, heaved himself up and placed his back flat against the wall to take the short perilous walk to Vernikoff's room. Cars passed by below, unaware of him. He tried to focus on his destination only a few metres ahead.

That afternoon Enrico LoTrova jumped off the bus and made his way to the main entrance of Parkside Hospital. He crossed the front driveaway, holding close to his chest the bouquet of flowers Viviane had given him and the brown paper bag with some bread as a gift. Once through the automatic doors, he found himself in a cosy square waiting room with cream and white walls against a modernist décor made of cold, neutral colours. Two people were sitting down expecting something or someone and the reception was busy talking to a new arrival. Enrico had thought of different ways to get access and thought of the simplest way possible. He was a relative. He was a friend. He was the chef at the Duchess Hotel. He did not know why he picked the last of his options instead.

'Delivery!' he shouted to the reception, moving hastily to the lift.

'Excuse me!' reprimanded the receptionist.

Enrico froze. She interrupted her chat with the customer and slid her chair to the side of the reception closest to him. The Italian baker could not believe it did not work.

'Sign here! All deliveries need to be recorded.'

Enrico sighed and gave an apologetic smile. He put the flowers and the bread to the side on the counter and filled in the delivery form.

'I see you are here to see Sergej Vernikoff. The bread may not be allowed so please hand it to the chief nurse.' explained the receptionist.

Enrico nodded, without saying more.

'Second floor. Room 213. You will need to show proof of ID to the police guards.'

Enrico thanked again and cursed under his breath while waiting for the lift. He hoped to easily fool the guards as a delivery man. His worry was to cross paths with Inspector Baynard. What if he was outside the door, he thought. He stepped inside the lift and felt his hands sweating.

That afternoon Baynard received a phone call and a visit. He took both in one of the small meeting rooms at the police station. The phone call carried a weight Baynard could hardly shake off for the rest of the day.

'Inspector!' called out the Chief Superintendent.

'Chief.' replied Baynard with curt reverence.

It was not a good sign.

'I had a nice chat with Sergeant Jeremy this morning. I could not get hold of you, inspector.'

'I was at Parkside Hospital to check on Sergej Vernikoff.'

'Found any foul play?'

'Not yet, sir.'

'I also had a nice chat with the Council this morning after your emergency meeting last night.'

Baynard tensed and pursed his lips thin. He stood up and walked to the window rubbing half of his face as if to wake up from this dream or this nightmare.

'Are you there, inspector?' said the Chief Superintendent again.

'Yes, sir. What did the Council have to say?'

'They are concerned. They fear the lockdown on Cannizaro Park could last more than they would like.'

'Is that so?'

'Don't be a fool, inspector. Wimbledon needs Cannizaro Festival. We need any doubts about Sergej Vernikoff's poisoning cleared, as well as the fire hazard. Why is it taking so long, inspector?'

Baynard swallowed hard. He was not sure what Sergeant Jeremy had told him. He had to tread on a very thin line.

'There is some contradicting information, sir. I thought it would be wise to take the time needed. The attempt on Mr Vernikoff's life, even if coincidental, threw us off on what is already a delicate matter for Wimbledon.'

He could hear the Chief Superintendent nodding to acknowledge what he said. Baynard repeated the words he said in his head to check it made sense or was convincing.

'I heard something about suspects, Baynard.'

The Chief Superintendent called him by his surname. It was never a good sign. The line between professional and personal was being crossed, and it only meant the Chief Superintendent wanted to share his disagreement.

'I don't know what you are up to, Baynard.' he carried on. 'However, unless you tell me you need a warrant of arrest and you have evidence to show, I will consider this case ready for closure and force you to re-open the park tomorrow at nine a.m.'

'But sir…that gives us less than twenty-four hours…'

196

'Do you know something I don't? Is this "contradicting information" you talk about grounded on evidence?'

Baynard had the evidence but no motive and no culprit. The Chief Superintendent seemed to act in favour of Wimbledon and its community. Two days of shocking news was enough, and it was bad for business too. Baynard could not agree more. However, he was worried about coming out in the open with the few facts he had. If the whole police force announced some form of manhunt, he would put the community at risk.

'I am working on it.' answered Baynard vaguely, to buy time.

The Chief Superintendent sighed.

'You have until tomorrow morning, Baynard. You are a good inspector. Don't make me change my mind!'

He hung up before Baynard could give him some words of reassurance. He cursed under his breath. The Chief Superintendent was getting pressure from the Council, and perhaps from the sponsor Alberyx Enterprises as well. Even Lady of Cannizaro and Mr Vernikoff's agent probably raised a complaint too, he thought. He had nothing though.

Sergeant Jeremy stormed in without knocking. The blinds attached to the door rattled. Baynard was surprised to see Jeremy caught in such a frenzy.

'I am in no mood to argue so I will pass over the knocking. What do you have?' said the inspector.

'Forensics confirmed poison.' said Jeremy in brief.

'Damn it!'

'We also have news on the two tails.'

'You do?'

'Yes. Eric Quercer did not move from the Rose and Crown. He returned yesterday late afternoon and he has not come out since.'

'How about the baker?'

'Well…'

The sergeant wet his lips. He found it hard to tell what he had to say.

'Today perhaps?' blurted out Baynard. 'Before the Chief Superintendent hangs our heads outside the police station for public viewing?'

'The Italian baker left his shop. He took the 93 bus and he was spotted getting off at Parkside Hospital. He had flowers and bread in his hand.'

'What? And you tell me now?'

'This just came in. He just went into the building.'

'We have him!'

Baynard did not hesitate. He needed to seize the moment. They both jumped into his car and raced up the hill, sirens blaring and zigzagging through the moderate traffic at that time of day.

'What are you planning to do, inspector?' asked Jeremy holding himself on the passenger door handle. 'Maybe the baker went to pay a visit to someone, or maybe he is going to see Mr Vernikoff but as a friend.'

'Too convenient, Jeremy. He knows something!'

'Do you think he is behind the whole thing?'

'Time to show our teeth, Jeremy. I know the Chief Superintendent called you and he called me earlier. We have less time than we think.'

'Ok, inspector. Again, what are you planning to do?'

'Have a chat.'

Reginald Bosham finally completed the walk on the ledge and stood by the window to Sergej Vernikoff's room. It was quiet compared to the relative confusion in the corridors. Blinds were drawn to let the light in. Reginald looked inside twice. Nobody. The window was unlocked, and he slowly slid it open. Once inside, the smell of phenol stifled the air. Reginald heard the beep of an electrocardiogram and saw the drip for intravenous fluids. Sergej Vernikoff lay unconscious on the hospital bed, slightly raised. Reginald crept up to his side. It had to look like a natural death as much as possible.

He took a needle from his jacket and quickly detached the transfusion bag from the drip feed to inject a liquid in it. He shook the bag to let the liquid dissolve and then he put it back into place as if nothing had changed. It would kick in ten minutes at most. No traces. Reginald moved back to the window and slid it open. There was a noise outside the room. He glanced back. The police guards were talking to someone. He was not expecting anyone for another thirty minutes. Reginald felt a surge of a panic and took hold of himself. The plan was to go back to that Italian baker's place and plant some evidence like the syringe. Anything would lead back to Enrico as long as Reginald was not seen. He kept his ear to the door. A man was talking to the police. A thick accent. Reginald Bosham leered. The scape goat had arrived. He would catch two birds with one stone. The boss would be happy.

The lift bell rang, and the doors opened on to the second floor. Enrico made a small step forward and stopped at a notice-board next to the nurses' reception. The second floor was more alive with patients, visitors and doctors, and the natural confusion in the corridors was ideal for Enrico. The Italian baker peeked to his right in the direction of the corridor leading out of the reception area. The policemen were outside room 214. Two sitting down and one standing opposite. Enrico tried to catch the attention of one of the nurses.

'Delivery! Mr Vernikoff!' he said.

The nurse eyed him suspiciously.

'Let me check.' said the nurse.

She checked the contents.

'Leave the bread here. No food, I am afraid. You can go to the room with the flowers, though. You have ID?'

Enrico nodded. The less he said, the better. He then moved down the corridor. He could see one policeman talking to one of the doctors. Enrico slowed down his pace, so as not to catch their attention too much. He walked up to the door acting as normal as he could. There was no sign of Inspector Baynard, which was good.

'Delivery!' Enrico repeated for a third time.

He gave out a broad, innocent smile. The two policemen sitting by the door looked up. One stood up, alert.

'Who are you? Please show some proof of ID.'

'I am from the new bakery in Wimbledon. We from the WAIS thought of showing our sympathy to Sergej Vernikoff.'

The policeman gave him an odd look.

'You can call Lady of Cannizaro. They know me. They can vouch for me.'

Enrico could not believe his shameless lies. I am losing it, he thought. The policemen looked at each other.

'Alright. We'll have to search you though.'

'Absolutely!'

Enrico opened his arms wide and handed the bouquet to one of them. He had nothing to hide, no weapons concealed.

'Five minutes!' said one of the policemen.

The Italian baker nodded obediently. The police opened the door and let him in, closing the door. Enrico was now alone with Sergej. He slept profoundly in the only bed in the room. He moved closer and put the flowers at the foot of the bed, unable to find a vase. He then gave a closer look at Sergej and saw the opera singer was not really fit for a chat. Enrico did not know what to do next. He could shake him or whisper his name. He wondered if he could hear anything.

Behind Enrico, there was a large wardrobe against the opposite wall. The door was pushed ajar slowly from the inside. Reginald peered through and he could see the Italian baker with his shoulders turned toward him. Perfect scenario. The burly man sneaked out without making a sound. He tiptoed forward while Enrico whispered loudly Sergej's name. Reginald was swift in his actions, and before Enrico realised, he had fallen into a trap, something hit him hard on the back of the neck and darkness fell over him.

Reginald stood over Enrico's unconscious body. He then glanced at Sergej Vernikoff. The drug would hit soon, so he'd better be on his way out. He pulled the syringe from his pockets and placed them in Enrico's pocket trousers. The evidence had been placed in an even better position. The police would rush in and catch the baker red-handed. Reginald did not delay his escape any longer. He quickly slid the window open, closed it behind him, and carefully walked along the ledge. Further down the building the thin ledge ran along the perimeter of the building and turned a corner. He followed it around and from the corner he could see a couple of metal chutes running down into a secluded courtyard where all waste was dumped. Reginald did not think twice about descending. This was his escape route. He settled his feet on the very thin ledge. To his left, a bundle of old pipes offered another point to grasp and hold onto. Reginald took tiny steps until he could cling to the pipes with both arms. He carefully descended and hung from the ledge until his feet could barely touch the outer layer of one metal chute. The drop was clumsy, but he had safely reduced the distance of the jump. He slid down and came to an abrupt halt by the mouth of the chute. The smell of the waste coming from the large disposal bins below overpowered the fresh air. He quickly jumped down to the asphalt and ran off down the side street of the building to make his exit. The boss would be happy another hurdle was out of the way. Mr Quercer would deal with the rest while Reginald went back to his other assignment.

Baynard got out of his car leaving the door half-open in the middle of the driveway in front of the hospital. He pushed his way through the main entrance of Parkside building, holding up his badge. He eyed the receptionist with his icy stare, a warning not to get in the way. The lady nodded; her eyes widened. Jeremy followed and they both ran up the stairs to get to the second floor in the shortest time possible. Once in the corridor, they dashed towards the three policemen whose faces dropped the moment they saw the inspector running towards them. His inquisitive stare melted away any calm that had reigned until then.

'Where is he?' Baynard cried out.

'Who?'

'The baker.'

'Oh. Inside paying his visits.'

'What?' bellowed Baynard.

The policemen were bewildered. Suddenly, a frenetic beeping sound echoed from inside the room, alerting the whole group outside. Jeremy stepped towards the door and opened it. Baynard slipped through without hesitation, followed by the two policemen. Sergej's body was shaking in convulsion, another seizure. One of the doctors came rushing by and called out the emergency. Inspector Baynard looked around the room, his eyes on alert, and quickly met the confused gaze of Enrico, standing by the window, massaging his neck. The inspector pulled his gun out and aimed.

'Don't move!' he warned.

'Don't shoot!' pleaded Enrico raising his hands, still waking up.

The inspector walked over to Enrico very carefully. The Italian baker was unarmed but Baynard did not like the scene in front of him. It bothered him greatly.

'You!' shouted Baynard again when close enough.

'I can explain…' started Enrico, scared.

'No! I am not taking any more chances!' replied Baynard.

He then hit Enrico hard in the face with the handle of his gun, enough to knock him out of his senses again.

'Take him!' ordered Baynard to his men while he made way for doctors and nurses to attend to Sergej Vernikoff's dying body.

That afternoon the Rose and Crown pub was empty and idle. The seating area felt more spacious and there was a vague sensation any word spoken at the table would echo all around the ground floor. Dr Watkins and Viviane sat at the same table where Enrico and she had sat after the explosion at the Duchess Hotel. It was only two days ago, and it felt already like an eternity.

'Ready for this, Miss Leighwood?' said Dr Watkins after a long sip of his drink.

'For what? Call the police?' she said, her arms crossed in front of a gin and tonic she had barely touched.

'I thought you had time to think it over.'

'I don't want to think it over. It's crazy. Are you seriously going ahead with this?'

'Already did this morning. I went to meet Lady of Cannizaro.'

'What?'

'S-s-s-h!!!' whispered Dr Watkins. 'People can hear you.'

Viviane glanced around with suspicion. The man behind the bar was checking his cashier and the few customers were busy reading their paper.

Dr Watkins wet his lips and smiled to himself.

'Is this a game to you?' said Viviane in shock.

'No but don't you think we have to do what it takes to safeguard Wimbledon?'

'We are not rescuers, Dr Watkins.'

'Maybe. However, we cannot let something belonging to Wimbledon fall into the wrong hands. Half of Wimbledon's treasures have been lost to foreigners or people from not around here.'

Viviane groaned and rolled her eyes.

'Listen, I re-read the poem. I know it does not make sense. You also said a black azalea sounds a bit like fiction. You know what else does not make sense? A man out there, actually no, two men, if you include Sergej, are spending all the resources at their disposal to find it. Why do such a thing?'

Viviane eyed him, not willing to hide how sceptical she still was. Her thoughts went back to Enrico and what they talked about that morning.

'And Sergej is now out of the picture,' she added. 'which makes this mysterious man after him even more dangerous. I wonder why we can't ask for police help.'

'I thought Enrico convinced you. We need to frame this man, whoever it is. We have the advantage. We have decoded the poem, and we have an idea of where to search next.'

'Assuming this thing is in Cannizaro Park…'

'Of course, my dear. Where is Enrico, by the way?'

'He went to Parkside to see Sergej. He was hoping to find out more. I could not change his mind. The Council called him again about the state of his bakery.'

'Do you think he is doing this for fame and fortune?'

'Isn't that what you are doing too, Dr Watkins? I am not blaming you two. I am just worried about the consequences.'

A chorus of sirens blared outside and sped fast down Wimbledon High Street. The quick row of blue lights came in succession like crazy, visible through the tiny window of the Rose and Crown. Dr Watkins and Viviane looked up.

'What is that?' said Viviane.

'It has become normality lately. We need to put a stop to this.'

'So, take me through the plan again? You said you spoke to Lady of Cannizaro.'

'I had to warn her, so she knows what we are up to, and gave her the decoded poem. She is highly visible now and it is best if she looks after it. We are going to the north end of Cannizaro Park. One of my keys opens the red door leading into Keir Cottage. We will then be only a few feet away from Chapel House. Short walk, less likely to be seen.'

'You make it sound easy. And then?'

'We search.'

'And if we can't find anything?'

'Police?'

'Deal!'

'Ok, let's get this over with before I find another reason not to.'

The earpiece clicked at the press of the button. Eric Quercer thought he had heard enough. He was at the back, in the outdoor beer garden of the Rose and Crown. He sat comfortably at a bench behind an ivy-covered trellis. He could not see the two very well, but the bug captured every single word clearly. He asked himself why he had not thought of it before instead of running around. Attaching the bug to Dr Watkins's jacket had opened doors he could not have imagined. The man in black was right. They were doing all the work for them. The music sheet was with Lady of Cannizaro, but it was no longer needed. He could get that later. The two knew already where the black azalea may be, and he had to ensure he did not lose track of them for the rest of the day, until he was sure he could act. He spotted through the foliage Dr Watkins and Viviane leaving their table. He grinned. He almost had the black azalea finally in his hands. Fame and fortune would be his, and no one else's.

Enrico felt discomfort. His hands kept flopping to the left then to the right, half numb and heavy. The pressure on his spine kept him awake, forcing him to sit upright mechanically with knee-jerk movements. Enrico thought he was awake but could not remember where he was. His eyes stayed closed, half-conscious. His body had sensations of discomfort. His memory faded and a sore pain at the back of the neck surged from time to time. He wanted to move his hands, but he could not. He felt his body slouch as he almost slid off the chair, but something held him back. He wanted to wake but he could not.

Baynard looked at him with his icy stare. He was leaning on the dull grey green wall of the interrogation room. He stroked his goatee more than usual, unable to fight his restlessness and also a bit of excitement in front of the unexpected turn of events. Finding Enrico right next to Vernikoff's dying body was something he had never come across in his years of police work and never would have expected. Bless the opera singer's soul, he thought, who was fighting for his life. Another poison, perhaps. He had asked forensics to speed up the reports, including what they had found on Enrico LoTrova. From the way things looked, the Italian baker wanted to rub out the opera singer. He could not think of a motive why the baker wanted to kill the opera singer outright. They must have both been involved in a deal gone wrong. Perhaps a disagreement over something dear to them, if they were working together.

Baynard hit the brakes on his train of thoughts. The evidence was again all too circumstantial. He needed to hear what the Italian baker would come up with in front of such evidence implicating him up to the neck. Everything was happening on the last day before the park was meant to re-open. He had to be sure whether this was the proof he needed to extend park closure, or maybe there was someone who wanted him to close this investigation as soon as possible. The inspector checked his watch. It was just past teatime. He would not be going home any time soon, but he did not want to spend the whole night here. It was time to wake the Italian baker. Time to ask questions and get answers.

Enrico shifted around, without really moving, his hands handcuffed at the back. From his closed eyes and his incomprehensible mumbling, Baynard could tell he was not coming round as fast as he expected. With the care he was known for, the inspector moved to the table nearby. There was a thick file folder on it. Baynard lifted it up, feeling the weight of this case in his hand. He then dropped it again on the table surface and a loud thump echoed in the small square interrogation room. Enrico woke up with a startle, his eyes wide and frightened. The light blinded him, and he closed his eyes again. He pulled his arms up but could not. He turned his head around, left to right, not knowing what held his hands back or what was happening. The loud thump rang in his ears for a while until he heard Baynard's voice roar.

'Wakey, wakey!' he shouted, bent over Enrico's twisted face.

Enrico looked up, his eyes now small, dazed. He writhed in the chair again and realised he could not move at all. Enrico shook his arms and hopped with the chair a few times, but the handcuffs made it difficult to move. He glanced sideways, avoiding Baynard's icy stare. He could tell he was not at home, or any other place he knew in Wimbledon.'

'*Ma che diavolo...?* What the hell is this?' he protested.

'Wimbledon Police Station, Mr Lereva!' said Baynard moving away.

'LoTrova...' mumbled Enrico, weak and confused.

Baynard did not take any notice. He went to the only door and gave it a modest knock. A man in a white coat came in and quickly put a bag on the table. He took a few instruments out, among which a stethoscope. Enrico did not follow.

'Let the doctor do his thing. Just checking you are in good health.' added Baynard standing at the back away from the table.

'What is this? Torture? Why did you imprison me?' shouted Enrico shaking in the seat.

'Always passionate, Mr Lariva.' chuckled Baynard.

'LoTrova!' he said.

The doctor was checking his pulse. He then flashed a small light into each of his eyes.

'You probably wonder why you are here.' continued the inspector. 'Let me remind you how things work. Finding you on the scene of a crime allows me to keep you for twenty-four hours, to clear any suspicions or charge you. Since we had to knock you out to neutralise any danger to Mr Vernikoff, it is paramount to confirm your health is in a good status.'

Baynard wanted to be hasty in his introductions, skip the pleasantries and get right to the chase.

'Scene of a crime?' repeated Enrico. 'I have no idea what you are talking about. Let me out of here...'

The doctor pulled the stethoscope out of his ear.

'He is ok, inspector.' the doctor confirmed putting his tools away. 'Just a knock on the head as suspected. I cannot see any bruises. However, I recommend no more than two hours.'

'Two hours? You need to let me go now!!!' cried out Enrico.

'Thank you, doctor.' replied Baynard, ignoring the Italian baker's plead.

The doctor did as he was told and left the room. The two were alone together. Baynard took the handcuffs off and sat opposite Enrico, putting the file folder to his side. Enrico massaged his wrists and checked his surroundings. The only natural light came from a window behind him with an opaque glass and a grate against it.

'You are breaching human rights, inspector...'

'Please, Mr Larrava...'

'LoTrova!'

'Do you know why you are here?'

Enrico had been gathering his thoughts piece by piece since waking up. His head was still spinning and the pain at the back of the neck stung more than ever. He blinked a few times and focused on his thoughts and memories. The last thing he remembered was entering Sergej Vernikoff's hospital room. Then seeing Baynard's angry face. He then focused on Baynard's words.

'A few hours ago, in the late afternoon, we found you in the hospital room of the known opera singer, Sergej Vernikoff, at Parkside Hospital. Do you remember that?'

'I...I...wanted to talk to Sergej...he knew...hold on, why the handcuffs? Why are you holding me here, inspector? Am I under arrest?'

Enrico's tongue was getting looser at each smack of the lips to moist his dry mouth. He still could not focus. Facts in his heads were all jumbled up. His joints hurt from the uncomfortable position he had been in for a long time he had no recollection of. He wondered how he had ended up there.

'What was the purpose of this chat? What was your relationship with Mr Vernikoff?' carried on Baynard.

'I don't understand. Where is Sergej?'

Baynard's inquisitive stare did not flinch.

'Answer the question.'

'No...' insisted Enrico.

'You are in no position to negotiate. Not when suspected of attempted murder.'

Enrico's eyes widened in disbelief. His mind started to jump through loops back in time, to recall the moment before he lost his senses. He traced his steps from the bus to the hospital, the several checkpoints, the policemen letting him through, the image of Sergej almost in a coma on the bed. He asked himself if they had spoken. Yes. No. Yes. No. Then black engulfed his memories, and the last memory again was Baynard's angry face.

'What did I tell you? Don't cross my path again.' recalled Baynard. 'How come I keep finding you near crucial scenes ever since the explosion?'

'Name one.' challenged Enrico childishly.

'You were at the scene of the explosion. You were on the grounds of Cannizaro Park the day after, sneaking out so to speak.'

Enrico grimaced. Baynard had more eyes everywhere in Wimbledon than he had thought.

'Is this your proof?'

'Let me finish. You were not at your bakery yesterday as you claimed, while Sergej Vernikoff was being poisoned. And today you are in his room right when he is in the grasp of another deathly seizure! All coincidences?'

Enrico's strengths were returning and so his memories resurfaced in hearing Baynard's point of view. He remembered the blow to the neck as he crouched over Sergej to wake him up. Someone killed Sergej Vernikoff.

'Don't make a silly mistake, Inspector Baynard!' insisted Enrico. 'Someone tried to frame me for the murder of Sergej Vernikoff.'

'Attempted murder for now. Mr Vernikoff is still alive but whatever you gave him is as toxic as hell. I still wonder how you slipped in that syringe undetected...'

'It wasn't me!'

'How do you explain this?'

Baynard took out photos portraying the syringe. Enrico stared at them, blinked a few times, and then returned his speechless gazed at Baynard.

'Never seen this before...'

'Oh really?' said Baynard. 'Then please enlighten me. Why is it I always come across you in this investigation? Are you delivering bread each time?'

'It is not what it looks like. I have been trying to prevent things from happening.'

'Prevent what? The explosion? Perhaps Mr Vernikoff's betrayal towards you?' insisted Baynard returning on his line of enquiry. 'What was your relationship with Mr Vernikoff? Perhaps you two worked together but there was something you disagreed on. Something he knew and was about to tell me or the police. That's why you have tried to kill him ever since the explosion!'

'*Oh Maria Santa*...no!' answered Enrico in despair.

The Italian baker's hands had become more agitated, cutting the air between him and the inspector with hand gestures and finger pointing. The inspector's inquisitive stare did not flinch and tried to look beyond into Enrico's face. He did not want to be fooled again. Enrico almost felt his rage as well as his own. This clash had been unavoidable from the start.

'You need to believe me...I mean, yes, we were on the same side. But no, I did not kill him. I was trying to help him find safety from the man hunting him down...'

'What man?'

'The man I saved from the explosion. He was after Sergej.'

'Eric Quercer? The horticulturist?'

The name stuck in Enrico's head forever. He now had a name, but he was probably miles away from anyone to warn them. Viviane, Dr Watkins, Lady of Cannizaro. He wondered if they had already found something at Chapel House or if they had been framed like him. Enrico wanted to shout so loud so they could hear him. Eric Quercer. He was the dangerous man.

'You are accusing Eric Quercer, the man you saved, to be a killer? Seriously?'

Baynard was incredulous. He was at that point where he could no longer tell if the Italian baker was really clever or really stupid.

'I know it sounds crazy. Listen. He is after something Sergej Vernikoff had. A music sheet. This guy must have known I was helping Sergej to hide it or something.'

'A music sheet? Mr Larriva, my patience has a limit. Stop making things up!'

'LoTrova! And no, I am not making this up!'

Enrico let his self-defence hang in the air. He calmed himself down. He had to. He also wished Viviane was there to rein him in, to make Baynard think through. Enrico was astounded by what happened. Eric Quercer was a very resourceful man, enough to frame him so easily with planted

211

evidence. I have been a fool, Enrico thought. His fantasies of heroic grandeur came crashing down in that small interrogation room. Baynard had him pinned down and ready to lock him up if he did not come clean, or worse, failed to be believed. Poor Sergej, Enrico thought. The opera singer was now on the verge of really dying without ever finding the black azalea. And it was all his fault.

'I don't want to fight, inspector, but I have witnesses who can prove what I say is the truth. Eric Quercer is after something valuable. You are wasting your time keeping me here!'

Baynard sneered. The Italian baker was quite impulsive. He jumped up out of his chair, plead after plead, and hoped he could be persuasive using all his dramatic tactics. The inspector found it hard to see through. Motives were just not there, or not enough to close the matter for good. He glanced at his watch. He knew he had to get a confession or a statement if he wanted to wrap the case up before it was late into the night. The Italian baker's version of the facts had to be reported in full and Baynard could then break it down bit by bit the moment he spotted gaps or contradictions.

'Well, Mr Lortova.'

'LoTrova!' mouthed Enrico without uttering the words.

His strength was fading again. The light in the room had changed and the neon had turned on. It was getting close to dusk outside.

'We have at least one hour.' continued Baynard. 'Forensics are completing a thorough check on all the evidence. The item we found on you. Sergej's biopsy. I asked them to complete this before eight a.m. tomorrow morning. Why don't we kill time and you tell me what really happened?'

Enrico crossed Baynard's icy stare, now fixed on him, inescapable. The Italian baker winced again for the remaining pain left in his sore muscles. He winced again under the dull artificial light now casting an even tighter circle where only him, the inspector and the table could fit. Enrico almost felt claustrophobic. He wanted to cry for help even though he didn't know

212

to whom. Baynard's question was a rhetorical one. He simply wanted Enrico to say he was the man behind all this. Enrico understood he had to gather whatever strength he could and convince the stubborn inspector twice as hard. He had to make him believe a mysterious man by the name of Eric Quercer wanted to get his hands on a mythical flower worth, probably a lot of money, and kill anyone in his way in the process.

The man in black did not have a watch on him, not even a clock nearby. He did not need to. He hated them. He hated the ticking of it or anything reminding him of that ephemeral passing of time. He knew his plan was all that mattered, when one day he could rise above what mankind called 'time' and be infinitely more powerful beyond his wildest dreams.

Making sure this night came and went was all that mattered. His driver had just delivered a message from Eric Quercer. It simply said he was on the move to Cannizaro Park and he was sure to find the black azalea very soon without any more obstacles in the way. The man in black grinned in the dark of his study. It sounded promising. He should have considered hiring Wimbledonians from the start, though. They had made more progress than the self-centred Canadian horticulturist. They could easily come in handy in the future, he thought. Still, Eric Quercer turned out to be useful. He was meticulous, ruthless and persistent. He needed him until the black azalea was found before getting rid of him.

The man in black watched the sun disappearing behind the high trees and their dark treetops creating a shapeless dark mass. His thoughts went back to the police who had caught the bait. Reginald did a clean job and now both Sergej Vernikoff and that baker were out of the picture. There were three more pieces of the domino to fall and then the road to success would be open wide. By tomorrow, he would be fully enlightened when

Eric Quercer would hand him over Cannizaro Park's most treasured possession.

Dr Watkins pushed the red door lightly. It stuck fast and it took a strong pull from both the curator and Viviane to open it without making too much noise. Camp Road was empty but it might not be that way for long. Viviane kept whispering to Dr Watkins who had to first fumble through his large key ring to get the right key and then try to gather some of his senile strength to open a door he had probably opened only once every twenty years for maintenance reasons. He grinned to himself in knowing Enrico had clambered over the big wall to get in when he could have asked for his spare key.

When the door finally gave in, the stuffy air of Keir Cottage whirled out onto their faces. Viviane hesitated but Dr Watkins pulled her in and closed the door behind before anyone caught a glimpse of them. The cottage was not in a bad state. Light-coloured walls and furniture decorated in what was a temporary lodgement for Cannizaro Park's gardener, or team of gardeners. The drawn curtains made it look darker than it was. However, Viviane thought it cosy and simply in need of being freshened up. Dr Watkins led her across the corridor without stopping and through the door opposite. It led out onto a small walled garden and he then took a sharp left where an older door was framed in the brick wall. Viviane eyed Dr Watkins with a look of interest and she was intrigued by how easily he knew where to go. The curator took out another key, a smaller one, and slipped it in. The clang echoed in the air as he turned the lock. Viviane and Dr Watkins froze, worried it could be heard far away into the park. They held their breath and then opened the door slowly.

The beautiful rose garden of Keir Cottage stood right before them, guarding the entrance and already showing the first signs of blossom. Viviane looked in awe before she felt her arm pulled again by Dr Watkins who was now on a tiny path shrouded in high shrubs and low trees, hidden from the main footpath running along in front of the cottage. There, they both crouched and stood quietly.

'What are we waiting for…?' whispered Viviane.

Dr Watkins put his index finger on his lips. He showed his eyes, widened and alert, almost reflecting the fainting blue sky like crystal. He then pointed somewhere through the shrubbery. Viviane heard footsteps. Someone was nearby. Not far from them, walking on the main footpath. The florist knew they were inches closer to getting caught. She hoped Dr Watkins could read the same trouble and despair in her eyes as they looked at each other in silence. The footsteps were coming closer and they could hear bits of conversation in between the crunching of the gravel and the chirping of the birds.

'Will Baynard be back here anytime soon?' said one voice. 'How long do we need to patrol here? I am tired.'

'Until we know if the man he has in custody is responsible for the poisoning.' said the other.

Viviane recognised they were from the police. She swallowed hard. The thought of being there, trespassing, was hard to push down, and even if too late to go back, she wanted to be elsewhere.

'You think they will keep the park closed for much longer?' asked the first policeman.

'Baynard knows what he is doing. If that baker has something to hide, he will spill it out and we can hopefully go home soon.'

'My wife has started asking me what is going on…'

'Shut up! Not a word until the inspector's next press statement.'

Viviane and Dr Watkins exchanged worried glances. There was only one baker they could think of, and it appeared something happened on his way to see Sergej Vernikoff. Being in custody only meant jail. Viviane felt mortified.

The two policemen disappeared to the west and then south of the park, their voices fading gradually until they were no more. Dr Watkins traced back his steps to peak out from the rose garden. The two policemen were down Maple Avenue. The road was clear. He re-joined Viviane and for a brief moment they looked at each other, trying to process it all.

'Do you think what I am thinking?' she said.

Dr Watkins nodded with a sigh.

'Enrico is in custody?' she added.

'We don't know.' he said. 'The matter is getting uglier by the day. We'd better act quick.'

He motioned her to follow him. They both ran along the tiny path, covered by thick shrubbery on both sides. The high wall of Cannizaro Park stood stern and solid to their left, while somewhere on the right the rest of Cannizaro Park lived on through this tragedy in all its beauty. The path led them to the back of Chapel House, out of sight from the main footpath. Dr Watkins and Viviane looked in all directions, making sure they were alone and nobody had followed them.

Chapel House was a quiet, ominous building despite its peculiar look. Covered in ivy for the most part, it was somehow hidden from view despite being visible from the main footpath coming from the Duchess Hotel. It shouted a more glorious past, which now faded behind dried flower beds and a few wild bushes that kept the public at distance. Apart from the ogive-style windows reminiscing a perhaps old gothic-inspired past, the whole building had nothing historical or religious to show. At the back, a gated fence led into a concrete pavement acting as patio just outside the building. A modern, light blue emergency door acted as the one and only working entrance.

'How is this a chapel?' whispered Viviane.

'It was a long time ago. It was refurbished to host the Guides' Scouts, so they had to make it habitable and safe. The windows and the roof are probably the oldest features, although they date from the early twentieth century. I have not been here in a while. Not sure what to find.'

'I don't think anyone has been here in decades. Is it locked?'

Viviane cupped her hands to peer inside one of the windows. Dr Watkins pointed at the heavy chain and lock blocking the emergency fire door. He took out the set of keys he had again. They held onto the chain once it was unlocked to prevent it from falling on the ground making a loud clamour.

'So far so good.' said Dr Watkins.

'Too easy, I think.' added Viviane.

She wondered if what they would find in there would help Enrico. Or maybe the man after the black azalea was waiting for them. Yet, once the emergency door was opened, the dark inside Chapel House did not talk to them. No sound, no voices. Only their footsteps as they crunched over debris and chunks of broken glass and tiles. The inside was poorly lit from the windows on the ground floor, a few of which were half-barred with wooden boards from the inside. They could make out a kitchenette definitely out of service and a large room with pale blue walls and some drawings or sketches on one side.

'This is probably where the Guides met.'

'What happened to them?'

'I don't think they use it anymore.'

Viviane grimaced at what was around her. She could see torn pages from books and old worn-out crayons scattered here and there on the floor. There were a couple of half-broken cabinets, their doors unhinged. The sense of decay was permanent, accompanied by a musty smell that prickled Viviane's nose.

'Are you sure this is the place Hilary Wilson referred to?'

'It can't be anywhere else. She convinced her father to turn this place into the Guides' meeting place. She was a scout herself. This is where the summer camps and other outings or outdoor meetings were held. What better choice than the vast space of Cannizaro Park?'

'I get it, Dr Watkins. I just wonder what we are looking for. I don't think any flower could survive the stiff, rancid air in here without sunlight. Let alone us if we stay here for more than a couple of hours.'

Dr Watkins grouched at Viviane's comment and glanced around the empty room. He pictured the lines of the poem. He could feel, as much as Viviane, they were about to hit a wall, if they had not already.

'Books…' murmured the curator. 'She loved reading books. Possibly here somewhere.'

'This place is not that big.'

Dr Watkins looked up. The ceiling was not as high as the building, suggesting there was an attic or some space above to explore.

'I don't see stairs.' commented Viviane following Dr Watkins's gaze.

'Look behind you.' he said.

The wall adjacent to the one from the kitchenette was thicker where they noticed a small entrance from which a narrow flight of steps led upstairs. The first two steps were made of wood while the others had been changed to a more solid structure. The feeble yellow line at the edge of each step was a futile attempt to comply with health and safety, when the place was more popular.

'This whole thing is about to collapse…' warned Viviane on hearing the creaking sound of the first two steps.

Dr Watkins did not listen and was already ahead of her, his pace a little less careful despite his age. She knew the curator was eager to make a discovery, although she was starting to doubt again the reason they were in this empty, abandoned building while the world outside was in danger.

'Come up, come up!' incited Dr Watkins from the top of the stairs.

The top floor was a spacious attic, high enough to stand up straight in. There were no partition walls, making it brighter than the ground floor as the last light of day swept in from all four top windows. The under roof and its beams were exposed. The wood, although solid to the touch, appeared pale and sick here and there, uncared for, almost rotting from the inside. The floor was also wood, layered on top with a concrete slab from more recent times. The creaks echoed less but Viviane doubted the whole safety of the building. She tiptoed from one corner to the other of the empty and spacious attic. There was no debris here, just a few birds' nests now empty. There was nothing here and she wanted to be out as soon as possible.

Dr Watkins was more agitated. He walked up and down carelessly, with heavy footsteps, retracing his steps, peering into corners already explored. He was not worried about falling down with the building. He was more concerned there was actually no black azalea to be found here.

'There is nothing here.' reminded Viviane.

'Impossible!' insisted Dr Watkins.

'Look! We came here on a hunch from interpreting a young girl's poem. Maybe it was just a poem she was too shy to publish.'

'It does not make sense.' sighed Dr Watkins. 'Why go through the pain of encoding it in a music sheet??'

Viviane was not listening. She walked back to the top of the narrow stairs and walked down. She then stopped on the bottom two steps and turned around to check the curator was coming.

'I am going, Dr Watkins!' she cried out.

When the curator did not appear, she stamped her foot to show this time she was being serious.

'Enough, Dr Watkins! This is a dead end. There is nothing here…'

Viviane felt her words slip out of her mouth unfinished and only a slurred, elongated vowel rang in her ears as she felt her body fall like a dead weight into a cold void. She did not feel her feet touch the ground. The wooden steps had disappeared. Instead, her feet floated and danced for what seemed an eternity before she felt her arm scratch against the rough surface of a wall and then her whole body fell flat on a soft sandy floor.

'Viviane!' shouted a voice.

She could not locate it. It sounded like Dr Watkins's, but it was distant. The cold room she found herself in was darker and only a halo of light shone from above. She looked up and she could see Dr Watkins's face framed inside the jagged shape of a hole through the broken wooden stairs.

'Are you alright?' the curator cried out again.

His voice rang loud in the dark room below. Viviane lifted herself from the ground. She felt her head pounding. She rubbed her arms and knees. Nothing broken but the cuts and bruises on her arms and legs stung like hell. Her blouse sleeves were ripped and so were her trousers.

'I'm alright!' Viviane coughed.

She stood up, limping a little until her strength returned. She looked at the wall she hit during the fall. It was rough, red brickwork never sanded before. Her eyes adjusted to the scarce light and moved to the layer of dust and sand she fell on. It covered the whole floor, recreating the miniature version of a desert. Four thin pillars supported the round vaulted ceiling.

'What's in there?' called out Dr Watkins.

'Just a basement…I think. This one's empty too.' described Viviane.

'Let me find a way down.'

'You mean a way out for me, right?'

Viviane looked closely where she had fallen from. The wooden steps covered an old trap door but there was no sign of a ladder, or at least one had not been in place for a very long time. She then noticed a metal hook in the ceiling, near the opening. From there, a knotted climbing rope dangled with its trail ending on the sandy floor.

'I wish I'd seen that before!' commented Viviane pulling the rope towards her to show Dr Watkins. 'Be careful on your way down!'

She leaned on the wall to catch her breath while Dr Watkins descended with surprising agility. Once he checked she was alright, he did not waste time exploring the newly found surroundings. He pulled out a torch he had brought just in case. The dying day was struggling to reach the depths they were in.

Dr Watkins kept muttering to himself in excitement. Viviane looked at him from where she stood, unsure whether to laugh or cry at how absurd the curator looked. He was a believer, like Enrico.

'Is this a cellar or something?' she asked joining him in the search.

'Mmm...this belonged to the original Roman Catholic chapel. Eighteenth or nineteenth century probably.'

'Well, someone took out any form of stairs but kept a way in.'

She pointed at the knotted rope

'That rope has all the characteristics of scout work. Hilary Wilson?' she commented.

'I would not exclude that.' carried on Dr Watkins scraping crevices in the walls and lifting rocks in the darkest corners. 'Hilary Wilson maybe came here to find some quiet and solitude for her reading. Or maybe to hide something...'

Dr Watkins stopped his search repeating to himself what he had just said. There were only one or two places where a young girl could hide something here. Either buried or hidden in a wall cavity. However, the sandy floor had a solid pavement a few inches underneath. The latter seemed more probable. He therefore started checking each brick one by one on each wall until he came across one jutting out a bit more than the others.

'Found something?' she asked the moment Dr Watkins crouched; his eyes fixed to a nondescript part of the wall opposite her.

'You may want to check this out!' he answered.

He grabbed the odd brick with the tip of his fingers and Viviane joined to help him. They edged it out inch by inch until they could each grab a corner with their hands. Behind it, a small cavity had been dug out of the natural soil. Dr Watkins flashed his light and found a small tin box. It bore the décor of Edwardian England except the painted ornaments were now faded and the box showed its humble making. A jewellery box perhaps, thought Viviane. A place where to store your marbles, thought Dr Watkins.

The initials under the lock proved without a doubt both Dr Watkins and Viviane were onto something.

H. W.

There was no need for Viviane to convince Dr Watkins to open it. He was already fidgeting with the lock, rusty and weak. It gave away at once, releasing its content and scattering it over the sandy floor. A hoard of yellowish letters fluttered out of it and spread around their feet. A fine eligible handwriting looked back at them, suddenly making the floor alive with history. Viviane kneeled down to pick a few. She could read dates on the top right corner.

'I think it is a journal or a diary.' she said.

Dr Watkins picked the rest and they started putting the many sheets of papers into some form of chronological order. There were gaps in the timeline, the same way life and memories take twists and turns when the least expected. In just a few minutes, Dr Watkins and Viviane realised they were about to read an extract from the private life of Hilary Wilson, Countess of Wrenbury.

From Hilary Wilson's diary:

May 1926

Father asked me today if the park grounds could be a welcoming place to host the Scout Guides. I said it would be a wonderful idea and I asked him if he had thought of lending the garden to organisers of honourable charity fundraisers. There is something about this place, this park, which summons such a beauty of art and nature you wish to share it with fellow men and women.

222

Father tells me our house hosted famous guests for centuries. When he told me authors like Oscar Wilde and Lord Tennyson, and a string of opera singers and renowned politicians had danced and sung under the roof of Cannizaro House, I was overjoyed. I love Oscar Wilde and I have been reading any book of his I could put my hands on (when mother is not looking). Sometimes, I dream to be Adela Schuster, Lady of Wimbledon, and be the host for all those talented artists that wish to share the beauty of their art with the rest of us. Maybe, someday.

The park is constantly changing. New trees and flowers planted, some of the rhododendrons and azaleas have been salvaged and revived. There is a never-ending traffic of gardeners and carpenters, all managed by the good-hearted Mr Allison. Adele, my lovely dog, is over-excited and she does not stop running all day. I had to put her on a leash a few times so that she would not mess the beautiful landscape garden my father was working on.

My parents love nature. They are doing so much for this place, restoring it to its glory.

June 1926

Father returned from a long trip to Asia. I missed him. He missed me too, and he was sorry to be away for such a long time. He brought me a present. I was very excited. It has the shape of an azalea and it is luminous black in colour. I don't know where my father found it, but it is mesmerising. It almost shines in the sun and I stare at it for days on end. Father says it must be one of its kind. A gift so rare and unique just for me. I now keep it by the side of my bed and sometimes I think there are tiny beads of glitter shining on it on a moonlit night. Or maybe it is the silly imagination through my starry eyes.

It is a fairly hot summer, so I have been looking for a quiet cool place to write my diary. The house and the park are so big and so busy. I tried sneaking inside the gardener's cottage with no avail. I then started exploring nearby, outside the park. Chapel House is the only quiet place when there is no scout meeting. It is on the grounds of the Keir, the house where our butler and his family live. Of course, he does not mind me going in there, being a scout myself. It is a beautiful old style Roman Catholic Church, cool and fresh inside. I even found the old crypt, accessible from a few steps to the side of the presbytery. It is empty, though. Not even an old bottle of brandy the priests may have hidden back in the day. Oh well, at least I can write here in peace. I can read about Oscar Wilde, about beauty through art and music. I wish sometimes there were some frescoes or statues to look at in this forsaken crypt.

August 1926

I have had very bad dreams in the last two months. Terrifying nightmares. About evil creatures and blood-thirsty men. Father thinks I have been influenced by those short moving pictures showing vampires and monsters. Whatever it is, I feel queasy before going to bed and I wake up restless. One night I woke up in the middle of the night and I saw father's gift on the bed side table glowing with a strange blue and violet halo around it. I went to splash some water on my face, and when I returned, the glowing was gone, as if it were all a dream.

I still write in the crypt, but now the summer rain has finally arrived, and my secret place is a bit cold. Soon I will need to find a warmer place. Or maybe the place looks haunted now that my head is tainted with my nightmares. I find that playing with my dog Adele or playing the piano or even admiring some of the old art scattered across the park is very soothing. I cannot help staring at

224

the Diana and the Fawn statue, right outside the house when you come out from the living room. It reminds me of that passage in Wilde's "The Picture of Dorian Grey" about the beauty and the strength of a woman, embodied by the perfection of a Greek sculpture. The statue of Diana personifies the threshold of discovering womanhood. "She was the loveliest thing I had ever seen", said Dorian Gray in comparing the beauty of Gladys to Diana. And then Lord Henry Wotton compares Sybil to Diana as well, saying there was "something of the fawn in her shy grace and started eyes...A faint blush like the shadow of a rose in a mirror of silver, came to her cheeks". When I stare at the statue of Diana, it reminds me of the power of a woman, and then I think of Sophie Johnstone, the Duchess of Cannizzaro, and Adela Schuster, Lady of Wimbledon, both bringing the peace and beauty of arts to Wimbledon. I find myself more and more eager to become a patron of the arts, and when I get lost in this bliss, I forget the nightmares. My lovely dog Adele is a true friend. She sits next to me sometimes and watches me happily as I daydream all this. She is probably the only one that understands me. I think she is the loveliest thing I have ever seen, the most beautiful thing I have ever known. Oscar Wilde would say the same about her.

Father caught me one lazy afternoon daydreaming. He had just come back from a presentation at the Royal Horticulture Society showing the work he and mother have done to the gardens. He told them some of the trees and shrubs around Lady Jane's Wood date back to 200 years ago! He thinks our house and the park should be recognised for its historical value. Anyway, he checked with me that I was alright and he confessed the gift he had brought me is not from an exotic land far away. They found it in the statue. The statue of Diana! I laughed thinking he was mocking me, but he insisted it was true. At the base there is a secret hollow

225

compartment which opens when you press Diana's breast. He showed me. I was embarrassed to see father touch the breast of a statue. I was so scared he would break such a fine piece of art. My imagination ran wild, but my father told me to keep my feet on the ground. The statue was less than 100 years old and the secret compartment was probably one of those old Victorian tricks to hide jewels or bank papers or even opium. He still thought the black azalea he found, as he liked to call it, was an odd finding and it belonged to me and nobody else.

October 1926

The nightmares continue to increase in intensity and disrupt my sleep more often. I realised that when I go camping with the scouts overnight, I sleep like a baby. I told mother and she thinks it could be the air or something I eat. I have my own theories, but mother and father may think I am crazy. I tried putting the black azalea away in a cupboard or a drawer, thinking the glow is disturbing my sleep. I noticed when I did that the nightmares stopped altogether. It is now four weeks since my last nightmare and I think father's gift is poisoning my mind. I don't know. I don't want to upset him, so I decided to put the black azalea back where he found it, back in the secret compartment at the base of the statue of Diana. It is better that way. Now my mind can think clearly. I even got better at my music and I have been entertaining mother and father, and their guests. The idea of lending the gardens to organisers of fetes and fundraisers seems to be growing on my parents. I had the courage to tell them I want to become a patron of the arts, and they were happy for me, as long as I completed my studies and found the right husband for me so I could put up a family. I laughed nervously.

This is probably the last entry for this year that I write at Chapel House. The place is now cold and damp. I can feel it in my bones.

Baynard rubbed his eyes in front of the bathroom mirror. They still looked red from the little sleep he had had in the last few days. He splashed some cold water on his face and then kept his head low, holding steady on the sink to put his thoughts into place and let all the new information sink in.

The Italian baker was still a suspect but with no police conviction yet hanging on his head. His story, the one he had just heard, was hilarious and utterly ridiculous. A perfect smokescreen. Baynard shook his head. He held himself from getting carried away. The deadline imposed by the Chief Superintendent had made him and Jeremy rush too much. The good policeman in him understood already he could not put all the blame on the baker. At least, not yet. Not until he could prove his story as a made-up fairy tale about mythical flowers and secret music sheets. He glanced at his watch. Past seven p.m. He hoped this interrogation would not be an all-nighter. He wondered how long it would take for forensics to give him what he needed.

The inspector slapped both his wet hands on his cheeks to wake himself up and get Enrico's story out of his head before he ended up believing it. The baker did not even ask for a lawyer, he was so sure of himself. He recalled his smug face as he finished telling the complex story. Baynard looked again in the mirror. The icy stare looked at him this time. It told him to stay cool, be rational, but listen. The inspector understood he was close to an answer, but he could not put it into words.

A knock came on the bathroom door. Baynard dried his face, tidied his looks and went to open it. Sergeant Jeremy was waiting outside. The inspector furrowed, eager to know what he had for him. He leaned on the door frame and waited.

227

'We cannot find Eric Quercer at the moment.' said Jeremy nervously. 'He is not at the Rose and Crown. The moment we find him we will bring him here so we can prove or disprove Enrico LoTrova's story.'

'Disprove, more likely. How about Lady of Cannizaro?'

'Not yet. We will call her soon. We cannot get hold of the florist, Viviane Leighwood, and Dr Watkins, from the Wimbledon Museum.'

Baynard grunted.

'We could go and check the Chapel House?' added Jeremy.

'Do you believe him?' asked the inspector in the open.

Sergeant Jeremy was careful about contradicting Inspector Baynard. The latter knew his job. Yet, they both had to see things clearly and not make mistakes.

'The timings, the movements, even the motives. They fit well. Maybe too well.'

Jeremy kept his position vague enough to avoid a reproachful look from his superior. He quickly added something else.

'The Chief Superintendent called again…'

'Again?' exclaimed Baynard flabbergasted.

'He seems to know we have an investigation for attempted murder on our hands we preferred not to announce. I think news is starting to leak here at the police station, or maybe people are being more suspicious after all we have been through in the last two days. He asked to see the reports.'

'We are on it!' dismissed Baynard.

It was clear the Chief Superintendent was getting pressure from someone or something. Maybe the Council. Maybe Lady of Cannizaro. The scandal would be out in the open before he knew it if he did not get some results. Not an ordinary week for the quiet town of Wimbledon.

'He knows we are holding a suspect as well…'

'Why are you telling me all this, Jeremy?'

'You know I am here to keep our feet high up from getting too wet. You are a good detective, inspector, if not the best. You follow protocol and you carry it out thoroughly, as it should be. Now, we are up against a crime we have never faced and it is all moving pretty fast. Someone may be playing us.'

Baynard did not smile or flinch at the compliments. He appreciated without showing. He listened, and he read between the lines. He had to take a step back and look at the big picture again.

'Ok. Get in touch with Lady of Cannizaro. The baker said she is involved so she can confirm it.'

'Shall I bring her here?'

'Either way. How about forensics?'

'Fingerprints match Enrico LoTrova's.'

Baynard nodded, unsure how to take such incriminating evidence. After hearing Jeremy's spiel, he thought whether everything in this investigation had become too easy.

'The team had to run the test twice for the poison, inspector. That is why it is taking so long.'

'What is the problem?'

'Well, they kept having a mismatch.'

'A mismatch?'

'Both on the first and second poisoning.'

'What do you mean?'

He shrugged his shoulders.

From Hilary Wilson's diary:

October 1934

Gilbert is impressed with father's work. The park around Cannizaro House is not just more beautiful and lusher than ever before. It is even bigger. We bought the Keir two years ago and now the park extends further north right onto Camp Road, making Chapel House part of our estate.

Ever since that first idea years ago, we have had many events on the park lawn and offered the grounds for charitable events to the public. We still hold the Guides' summer meeting at Chapel House and probably more frequently than before. Since I married Gilbert, I have hardly been to see the crypt where I used to hide and write this diary or read my books. I look back at the entries and there have been less and less of them. Music is probably my passion now, entertaining Gilbert and my parents, giving piano lessons, playing at public events. I feel more and more like Adela Schuster now than ever before, and I could probably accomplish something greater. Gilbert is supporting me every day.

May 1935

I have not slept well in the last two months. Gilbert has been very busy in Parliament, especially since the Abyssinia crisis has worsened. I can feel his agitation sometimes, or at least this is what I thought was upsetting my sleep. Because of this busy schedule, he stays over at our apartment in Central London, and I often take the opportunity to go and see mother and father.

It took me a while to recognise the pattern of my sleepless nights, identical to those I had years ago. Bad dreams haunt me again. I see stone circles surrounded by a bluish fire and rivers of a crimson colour flowing underneath. In the last one I remember well, I think I saw something resembling the black azalea. I know it is just a figment of my imagination but still one very early morning I went to check the statue of Diana. The lever mechanism concealed under the breast still worked and the black azalea was still intact and surprisingly shiny. I think seeing it again, after such a long time, upset me even more and worsened my nightmares. My dog Adele barks at the statue more often. She is not happy I hang around it. Sometimes I joke she wants to compete with Diana and be the loveliest thing. Upon hearing me, she then circles around with her happy face.

I confided in Helda Seligman, the sculptor who lives nearby. She has been visiting Cannizaro House often lately and expressed many times, in her libertine fashion, her dismay at how Abyssinia, or Ethiopia, as she likes to call it, is being treated by the Western Powers. She said my bad sleep is perfectly normal, a side effect of the negative and extremist forces plaguing Europe. To be honest, it does not help hearing father and Gilbert talking about it in the garden. However, I am still not convinced. Maybe I need to throw away the black azalea without letting my father know. Call me superstitious.

June 1935

Father said he is thinking of moving the statue of Diana to put it somewhere else in the park. Normally something like that would fly over my head. Father is always changing something on our estate. He spent so many years fixing this park with no plan to stop. It is the jewel of Wimbledon and father's monogram at the entrance gate is a sign of his, of our legacy.

I think about the black azalea from time to time. What it may be. Where it may have come from. It scares me, as much as war breaking out again in Europe. One night I made the decision to bury it somewhere, somewhere deep underground. The only place I could think of is the chapel's crypt where nobody goes and digs things out. Somehow, I feel I cannot leave and take it away from the estate or even destroy it. Something tells me not to. Maybe because it is gift from my father. Hiding it is probably best.

May 1936

I have not written in this diary in months. My family life is taking most of my time while I still practice my music. I know I am no longer the young girl looking for a quiet place to write about my life and my personal secrets here at Cannizaro House.

What has changed? Well, I sleep better, and my nightmares have gone despite the current affairs in Europe not improving that much. I am into music though, not politics. Hilda on the other hand is an artist so politically engaged. She even built a bust for the Emperor of Ethiopia after welcoming him into her home as an asylum seeker. He had to flee his country, invaded by Mussolini's forces. I prefer playing my music, reading Oscar Wilde, using the arts to find what is beautiful and improve ourselves and make us better persons.

Chapel House in the meantime is being rebuilt. It needs necessary work to make it safe and habitable. I must say I am worried someone could find the black azalea. Whenever I visit home, I never miss a chance to go and have a look. Last time I checked the crypt had been boarded up, but I don't know if anyone has ventured down there to snoop around.

Sometimes I wonder whether someone could still find it in the crypt, and I ask myself if I should move it again and hide it elsewhere. I don't know why I care. Perhaps the strange power it had on me and my dreams, if true, still mesmerises and haunts me. It may still have an effect on me. I can't even consider destroying it with a hammer or throwing it off Putney Bridge. I then worry about if someone else found it in, let's say, ten, thirty, hundred years from now on. Should I heed them with a word of warning? Should I tell them where it is so they can find it, research it and ultimately destroy it?

232

Ah - what am I thinking? It is nothing. It is just a beautiful black azalea.

Eric Quercer kept a close eye at the back of the Chapel House building and its back door wide open. The Canadian breathed heavily after the rush to climb over the tall northern wall. The moment he had seen the curator and the florist disappear behind the tiny red door, he knew he had to scramble in order not to lose them. With the earpiece turned on, he used a nearby low building to climb over and leap towards the wall. He was able to get into the park unseen, but he had to slow down to catch his breath. The voices from the curator and the florist had gone quiet for a while until whispers came back. Then whispers turned into conversations. Eric knew they were in a safe place away from prying eyes or the police beat.

Chapel House. He chuckled at the thought the black azalea may have been inside here all this time, and he was just over at the Duchess Hotel nearby playing silly dirty games. He sat in the bushes just outside the concrete patio at the back of the building. He waited, catching snippets of the conversation through the earpiece. He then took a few small steps forward and kept a watchful eye on the entrance. The two could come out at any time. He was only a few metres away when shouting and a loud fracas boomed from inside. Eric jumped to the side of the open door and hid flat against the outer wall. He held his breath. Then the old man's voice called out. Eric heard the double echo from the earpiece and from inside the building.

'Are you alright?'

Eric waited again. The florist's voice was fainter, distant, and both their voices became fainter as if the two were moving away. The frequency buzzed and crackled a little. Something made it hard to tune. Eric bit his lip and faltered before stepping inside. He took out his gun. The decision had come to use it. It was the easiest option in case he had to face the two and force their hand more easily.

The ground floor was empty. The voices still sent a faint echo throughout and Eric felt they came from inside the wall. He followed them and it did not take him long to spot the hole in the two cracked wooden steps. He crouched next to it and eaves dropped on the conversation in the underground room below. He listened in. Dr Watkins and Viviane had found something. Eric smiled to himself for they were truly doing all the work for him.

'This diary explains a lot!' concluded Dr Watkins as he piled all the loose sheets together. 'Putting aside its historical value for Cannizaro Park, it confirms the existence of the black azalea.'

'Confirm is a big word, Dr Watkins. Assuming you are right, where is it if she hid it down here?'

Dr Watkins searched around where the content of the tin box laid scattered around. He then peered inside the cavity in the wall. The torchlight shone on something. It glinted feebly in the dark humid alcove, sealed for more than fifty years. Dr Watkins reached in and grabbed a smooth curved shape. His nail made it tinkle at the first touch. He frowned and pulled it out slowly. They were both surprised to see a small glass bell with a wooden base. It was tall enough to hold something erect inside. Except it was empty and the dust and soil covering it proved it had been hidden there untouched for a long time.

'Another dead end?' groaned Viviane.

'Hold on.'

Dr Watkins lifted the glass bell and on the wooden base there was another sheet of paper folded and yellow-coloured like the others.

'It feels like a treasure hunt.' commented Dr Watkins.

'I'd say more like a scavenger hunt.' bit back Viviane, who clearly had enough of the cryptic clues they were coming across.

Dr Watkins quickly unfolded the paper and flashed the light on it so both he and Viviane could read it.

From Hilary Wilson's diary:

January 1948

I don't know what made me write this last entry in my diary. Somehow I wish to write one last message, for posterity. Perhaps the solitude after mother and father passed away, or the memories of my lovely dog Adele, who died a few years back. Or perhaps the fact I sold the house and the park to the Council. I really don't know. There are so many things to do before I leave this place. Maybe I need to leave a warning before these green meadows and old maple trees are no longer mine. Wimbledonians need to know of the beautiful treasures this park holds now it is theirs. Even the black azalea, although it may be too much for them to bear. I need to move it, take it out of the crypt and hide it with the loveliest thing I have ever seen.

'What?' blurted out Viviane.

She was stupefied. The cat-and-mouse search for this flower was becoming ridiculous. She was more and more convinced there was only smoke and no fire at the end of the road. She could not believe they had gone through all this without getting anywhere. And for all they knew, Enrico was probably rotting in jail because of this charade.

235

'Dr Watkins,' she continued. 'can we really believe this to be Hilary Wilson's diary and not a prankster's clever joke to make us, everyone, run around like idiots? A flower cannot survive that long without light, let alone in this damp crypt or under this glass bell for so long. Even if it had dried up, it would be worth nothing.'

'I cannot make an official statement of the authenticity of the letters here on the spur of the moment. All I can say the people and events mentioned really existed. Even by looking at the layer of dust, or the age of the box, the letters, the glass bell. If it were a prank, it must have been planned more than ten years ago for it to have been faked so well'.

The curator with his expertise scrutinised everything they had found in the wall cavity as it now lay neatly displayed on the ground by the wall. Part of him wanted to believe they were close to the truth, while he knew perfectly why someone else like Viviane could not be convinced. He re-read the last letter and skimmed through the others. Then his face lit up.

'Hold on. The clue has been here all along for us to see.' he said.

'I am not following. Did you find something?' said Viviane.

'We do have a lead to follow…'

'Which is?'

'We know where she moved it last.'

Eric listened attentively, half incredulous to what he was hearing, and half poisoned by the greed inside him. He made no sound, so as not to miss a detail. He riveted in hearing the two had found the diary of Wilson's daughter. Her story proved the music sheet was right. She was the one who knew about the black azalea and was the only one who knew where she had hidden it for safekeeping. Until now. In the end, she wanted someone to find it. Otherwise, why leave these cryptic clues around. Eric Quercer grinned in the penumbra of Chapel House. He would soon be rich.

'It is all in the text, Viviane. Both texts, actually.'

Viviane looked at Dr Watkins puzzled.

'Here. "The loveliest thing I have ever seen".' he explained. 'Mentioned two, three times. And then when she says "The most beautiful personality I had ever known". They are all quotes from Oscar Wilde's work.'

'And?'

'And? All references to beauty and perfection, like the Greek goddess Diana. She hid it back in the statue itself!'

'Are you sure?' quizzed him Viviane.

She re-read the passages.

'I don't see any other explanation.' continued Dr Watkins. 'The statue of Diana and the Fawn has been in the north, north-west part of the park for years. Sitting there, half-covered in moss and misery, little is known about who brought it here to Cannizaro Park. Everybody just glances at it and moves on. Hilary's story fits in. They too did not know much about the statue.'

Viviane looked askance at Dr Watkins. It made sense, and at least they would not have to stay in this humid crypt for longer.

'All we need to do is go to the statue, find the secret lever…on her breast, right? And the black azalea will magically appear in a secret compartment.'

'Precisely!' he exclaimed, bringing back his historian's enthusiasm once again.

'You really think it is there, don't you? You don't have the slightest doubt it may be another dead end?'

'This is not a dead end.' he commented waving his hands at the clues to show what they had found.

Viviane did not hide her perplexity. She nodded vaguely at Dr Watkins and thought it best to make a move.

'Let's get going and climb out of this place. We find this thing and then we contact Lady of Cannizaro and find Enrico. We'd better be quick.'

The crypt was getting colder and claustrophobic. She walked towards where the rope was but could not see it in the semi-darkness. Her hands fumbled at nothing and grabbed nothing. It was no longer there. She spun around and then looked up. She did not realise something was odd until she saw the last inches of dangling rope disappear through the opening.

'Hey! That rope is our way out!' she shouted in panic. 'Who is there?'

Dr Watkins heard and he too was in shock to see their only means of getting out completely gone, sucked up by an unknown force.

'Who is there? This is not funny.'

'I think it is. And I am afraid your search stops here!'

Eric Quercer's voice echoed in the crypt, greedy and malignant. He did not show himself straight away. He leaned on the wall near the stairs, staring into the void as he told Viviane and Dr Watkins the way things would run from now on. Viviane though did not have to see him to realise the horror. She knew who they were finally up against. The dangerous man that Sergej Vernikoff had been fearing all this time. They listened to his creepy voice in the semi-darkness.

'You two were very clever.' he carried on. 'I wish I had known that before. It would have spared me chasing Mr Vernikoff and that stupid music sheet. Messy job, I know. All I can do now is look forward to holding the black azalea in my hands. Thank you sooo much!'

Eric peeped in. He then peered down into the gaping hole. He met the desperate gaze of Viviane looking up with Dr Watkins by her side. They are both scared like rabbits in the headlight, thought the Canadian. His face was against the backlight, barely visible. Viviane grabbed the torch off Dr Watkins to flash it on Eric. She wanted to know who he was. He shielded his eyes from the bright light. She scowled.

'I have seen you before…'

'Clever! While I let you figure that out, if you excuse me, I have a flower to pick and money to make. Would love to stay here and chat. Bye bye, my friends!'

He let out a spiteful chuckle.

'Come back!' shouted Dr Watkins in vain. 'You can't leave us here…'

Eric Quercer moved out of view and turned off the audio tracker. He needed to move fast before those two started shouting for help. Someone may find them at some point eventually, maybe a patrolling policeman, but hopefully by then he would be long gone, and on a plane back home. He had all the advantage now, knowing where to go and what to do. No stops allowed.

Back in the crypt, Dr Watkins and Viviane stared in silence at the beam of the torch aiming up where Eric's face had been. He had now disappeared, and his footsteps faded quickly as he left Chapel House in a rush. Viviane was speechless and her lips trembled. She felt cold, she was furious. All this effort to see everything stolen from under their noses.

'Do you know that man, Viviane?' asked Dr Watkins while checking if the rough brick wall nearby was good enough to climb to reach the only exit.

'I have seen his face and heard his voice on the media. He is known in my circle of professionals. Eric Quercer.'

'Eric who?'

'He is a Canadian horticulturist. And not a very nice one. Although they are all rumours, he loots rare specimens of flowers and plants for his collection or the black market. I thought he was just a big mouth...'

'He is the man who has been threatening the Trust and Sergej Vernikoff?'

'Apparently so. Too bad we found out too late!'

'What do we do now?'

Viviane knit her brows. It was obvious there was no way out. They were trapped.

'We need to get help...somehow...'

She hardly believed her words.

'That man...Eric Quercer...will stop at nothing to get what he wants.' she added.

'We've seen that. What are you trying to say?'

'If he is involved, then he is after the precious flower to steal it from here and take it away from Wimbledon. The black azalea is what he is after and now he knows where to look for it!'

She paused exchanging a worried glance with Dr Watkins. He was astonished, not sure what to say.

'What happened to Enrico?' she prayed.

The cold walls of the interrogation room made Enrico shiver. He slouched on the chair with his half-opened chef jacket. His pride and credibility had reached rock bottom. He stood up and walked to the dark window looking into the evening. He massaged his face and pulled back his wavy hair. He thought of Viviane, Dr Watkins, Lady of Cannizaro. He wondered why they were not here yet, why they had not heard about what had happened to him and come to the rescue. They could come and pay the bail, like he had seen on TV. The police had taken his phone, so he had no way of contacting anyone. His thoughts shifted to darker places. Maybe Eric Quercer, the dangerous man, had won and made them all disappear. He gulped. He could not live with that, especially after all their help and how they had made him feel Wimbledon was his home.

He thought again about where he was and the trouble he was in. All of a sudden, the thought of how Eric Quercer had framed him made his blood boil. The dangerous man had been so clever in pulling the strings all along the way, as if nipping and shaping the flowers of his conservatory into an evil masterplan. A rogue horticulturist. Enrico could not come to terms with how to explain the absurdity of it all. Eric was no hired gun, no burglar. He was a rogue, mad horticulturist in search of his holy grail, the black azalea. A rare flower, unique in the world for its colour. Enrico could see Baynard pulling faces as he told him everything from the explosion to the decoded poem. He did not know if the inspector believed him. He started walking around, eyes fixed on the dull floor where its monochromatic shade changed into deceitful, colour patterns under the neon light above him. Enrico kept his head low and massaged his neck with one hand. He was still sore here and there. His head though was now clear. He knew he had to get out of there before it was too late. Unless his friends showed up the same time as Baynard, he had to assume the worst.

The door clanged open, stirring Enrico's thoughts. Baynard walked in with Jeremy right behind him. The inspector's face was stern as it was his habit. He watched Enrico from under his eyebrows.

'Hello again!' mumbled Baynard.

'*Buonasera!*' said Enrico.

'So, did you have time to think things over?'

'About what?'

Baynard smirked.

'Your story.'

'I am not changing it.'

'We found your fingerprints on the item.'

'Brilliant!' exclaimed Enrico in exasperation. 'I told you. Someone knocked me out when I was in the room. I was unconscious for most of the time. Anyone could have taken them.'

'Have you thought about a lawyer?'

'No.'

Baynard held his gaze at the Italian baker, unable to grasp his stubbornness.

'Did you call the people I mentioned? Did you find this Eric Quercer?'

'Not yet. We are on it.'

'They will tell you everything I told you.'

'We'll see. You seem pretty sure.'

Baynard moved to the table to put his phone and the room key next to the open file folder. He pulled his chair out, ready to continue the session.

Enrico looked at him and stood up, tired of the charade. The inspector motioned to Jeremy to close the door when a woman appeared in the doorway.

'Inspector Baynard?' she called out. 'I am forensics. You should see this.'

'No need to come all the way here. I could have joined you later.'

'Believe me. You need to see this.'

Enrico moved near the table, listening together with Baynard and Jeremy, who were also taken aback by the unexpected arrival.

'It is Sergej Vernikoff.' she exclaimed taking a few steps into the room and closer to the two policemen.

'Oh no!' blurted out Jeremy. 'Don't tell us he is dead?'

'No! He'll live. But you may want to know he is not the real Sergej Vernikoff!'

'What?' cried out Baynard and Jeremy together.

Enrico mouthed the same. He had his eyes though elsewhere. The door was open. The room key and the phone were there on the table. He wondered if it was worth the risk.

'Young lady, tell it to us straight. What are you talking about?'

'The man who was poisoned is not Sergej Vernikoff, the famous opera singer. We found out by chance when his DNA did not match some we found in the hotel room.'

Baynard wavered, feeling he was about to lose balance.

'Who is it then?' he asked.

'I don't know. Sure, he does look like him, but he is not the man we thought. An impersonator, perhaps.'

'That son of…'

Baynard finally realised Mr Vernikoff had always been one step ahead in order to protect himself. It had occurred to him Mr Vernikoff was definitely escaping from something or someone. It could have been the baker, and the inspector's plan was to grill him on the basis of this new information, now that the attempted murder had failed.

However, before Baynard had time to think all of this through, Enrico had already grabbed the phone and the key, and moved fast against the table. He pushed it with all his might across the floor. He only needed those few extra seconds. Enough to push the inspector and the sergeant away from the door as much as possible. Baynard heard the screech of the table and the chair. He and Jeremy were hit by it before they could turn. Just a few extra seconds, enough for Enrico to leap towards the door.

'Stop him!' he cried out, getting back his balance.

Enrico grabbed the handle and closed the door behind him as he swept by out into the corridor. He turned the key in the lock and heard the thud of Baynard's fists banging against the door. The voices were muffled and must have been difficult to hear but the Italian baker knew the inspector was fuming more than ever. He looked to the left and right. He had to get out before he crossed paths with anyone. The corridor seemed to be in the basement of the police station. He spotted a tiny window at the end of the corridor and made a run for it.

Baynard and Jeremy tried to open the door without success. The inspector had a face like thunder, close to exploding in an array of insults at the man who had tried to fool him before. He slammed his fist a couple of times before turning to Jeremy.

'Do you still have your phone?' he asked.

'I left it upstairs.' gulped Jeremy in embarrassment.

Baynard's icy stare had never been colder.

Lady of Cannizaro entered her office and checked the time. Almost eight p.m. and still no sign of Dr Watkins. Something was wrong. She thought he would have been in touch hours ago. She went straight to the window and looked out into the car park from her office. It was dark and the streetlamps had been turned on to keep the shadows at bay. Lady of Cannizaro had the ugly sensation someone was watching her. This feeling had followed her all day while trying to run a normal day at the Duchess Hotel. Clients were disgruntled to a point they were all leaving as hopes of things getting fixed soon waned. She had to agree with them, whether she liked it or not.

She went back to the desk and picked up the landline phone. The plan was to call Inspector Baynard as Dr Watkins had instructed. She asked herself what she would tell him, what would make Baynard listen. She had barely thought her story through. The office was silent around her. All lights were off except her desk lamp. She felt something hanging in the air. A presence. The dial tone suddenly came to life, startling her, and she pressed the combination of numbers on the keypad. She let the phone ring but then hung up straight after, unsure. Lady of Cannizaro bit her lip and pulled her drawer open to get the phone number she needed in case of emergency. She dialled that number instead.

'Don't move!' boomed Eric Quercer from a far off corner.

Lady of Cannizaro jumped. The phone slipped out of her hand and onto the desk. Next thing she heard was the click of a gun pointed at her. She could see the barrel emerging slowly and the silhouette of a man standing behind where the feeble light of the desk lamp reached.

'Who are you?' she cried out.

'Don't shout, miss. Or I will shoot! Like I did with that florist and museum geek of yours!'

Lady of Cannizaro's eyes filled with fear. The man had a vaguely familiar look. Surely someone she had crossed paths within the hotel. Eric emerged from the shadows but kept his distance.

'You are…' muttered Lady of Cannizaro upon recognising him.

'…Eric Quercer.'

'What are you doing? What do you want?'

'I want to know where it is. Where did you move it?'

'Move what?'

'The black azalea.'

Lady of Cannizaro knew then who she had in front of her. Eric's fame as the man behind the tormenting of Sergej preceded him. The dangerous man behind it all, standing right there in her office.

'I should have known it was you who was lurking around my hotel…' she hissed at him.

'Where is the black azalea?' interrupted Eric.

He showed the loaded gun.

'Don't you dare shout, or I swear to God, I will shoot!'

Eric's eyes were fiery and angry.

'I…I…I don't understand.' she answered desperately. 'I thought it did not exist…I have no clue where it would be…'

'Well, darling, it is not where it was supposed to be…'

Lady of Cannizaro was at a loss and the sight of the gun, pointing straight at her face, made her fear for her life. She did not understand what Eric Quercer was saying.

'Chapel House?' she queried recalling where Dr Watkins was heading.

She could not believe Eric Quercer had shot the curator and Viviane. The news was too much to bear. The emotions were overwhelming, and the thought of coming to the same end worsened it all.

'See, you knew those two were going there. You probably knew already about the diary and the statue.'

'Diary? Statue?'

Lady of Cannizaro was genuinely confused. She was at an impasse though. There was no way Eric would believe she had no idea what he was talking about. Her eyes fell on the phone on the desk. She could not tell if someone had answered and was listening in.

'Don't take me for a fool, Lady of Cannizaro. I should have known you were involved in this as much as that annoying opera singer, friend of yours. You know where the black azalea is. Where did you hide it? Tell me now!'

Lady of Cannizaro held her breath. Tension was rising. She failed to find the right words, to explain she knew less than everybody. A moment of pause passed between them. It could have been as short as the blink of an eye or as long as a human life. It did not matter. It was over when a phone in the room rang. It was her mobile phone.

'What is that? Give it to me! Slowly!' blurted out Eric.

His attitude was edgy and out of control. Lady of Cannizaro did as she was told and picked up the mobile phone from her purse on the desk.

'Slide it!'

She did so, without breaking eye contact with Eric. He picked it up and saw the name on the screen. The caller's name said 'Inspector Baynard'. It did not sound good, thought the Canadian horticulturist. He pulled an irritated face. Nothing was going to plan and he was running out of time. He had to think quick and find out where the mythical flower was. Before the police came rushing to Lady of Cannizaro's rescue. Before the man in black pestered him to give him what was rightly his. Eric felt his head exploding. A circle was starting to close in and there was little he could do to wriggle out of it.

The phone kept ringing. Eric thought quickly. He then answered, holding the gun at Lady of Cannizaro and watching her crazy-eyed from behind the barrel.

'Yes...?' mumbled Eric to keep it vague whether he was a man or a woman.

'Lady of Cannizaro. It is me. Enrico!'

Eric's eyes widened. That buffoon of a baker. He was calling using the inspector's phone. He did not like that.

'Still there?'

'Yes...'

246

Eric put the phone on mute and turned on the speakerphone. He then took two long steps forward. He moved closer to Lady of Cannizaro and the gun looked even bigger in her frightened eyes.

'Eric Quercer is the dangerous man.' Enrico kept saying. 'He is the one who has been trying to get his claws on the music sheet and eventually the black azalea. I am now on my way to Cannizaro Park to find Viviane and Dr Watkins. I just managed to escape Baynard's clutches. He thinks I am involved. Meet me at Chapel House.'

Eric hinted at Lady of Cannizaro to agree. He put the cold barrel of the gun on her forehead, to be sure she would comply. He then unmuted the phone.

'O…ok…Enrico. See you there!' said Lady of Cannizaro.

'We'll get this *figlio di…*'

Eric terminated the call, uninterested. He threw the phone away into a corner of the room.

'Now, darling, we go for a walk. Undisturbed.'

His eyes glinted with spite. He waved the gun and Lady of Cannizaro followed the direction, moving ahead of him and towards the door.

'Avoid crowded places. And no stupid moves or…bang!'

He pressed the gun into her side, well concealed between them. Lady of Cannizaro's heartbeat faster. She was scared. She also had hope. She realised the landline phone on her desk had connected to the number she had dialled as it had fallen. She hoped that the person on the other end of the line had picked up in time and had heard the whole conversation. She hoped they realised Eric Quercer was the man behind it all. She hoped they knew what they had to do. A few seconds after Eric and Lady of Cannizaro left the office, the landline phone clicked. The conversation ended. Someone had been listening.

Enrico knew the taxi ride to the Duchess Hotel was less than ten minutes but for him it seemed an eternity. He kept looking behind, worried a police car would be chasing them before they reached the designed destination. The black cab raced up the hill and flew past Enrico's closed bakery. He looked to the other side and Viviane's shop was closed too. Enrico told himself not to rush to conclusions. It was late evening. The streets were less crowded and window lights dotted the darkened high street.

The most surprising revelation so far was that Sergej Vernikoff was not Sergej Vernikoff. Enrico was somehow relieved the world was not with one opera singer less as he had previously thought. The biggest question though was actually knowing where the real Sergej Vernikoff was, assuming he did come to Wimbledon. A great double, thought the Italian baker, although he had never met the real one before, so it was easy to fool him. He pondered whether Lady of Cannizaro had spotted the difference.

And then there was Eric Quercer, the man he had saved and could have easily done without. The dubious horticulturist had orchestrated a very complex trap to try and get his hands on what he wanted. He even framed Enrico in the process, and poisoned Vernikoff's double twice. Eric Quercer was a resourceful man not to underestimate. Enrico needed to catch up with Dr Watkins and Viviane and warn them about him as soon as possible. The two must have found something by now, or at least be able to confirm there was nothing to be found at all. Chapel House was probably smaller than Cannizaro House.

Enrico looked eagerly down the road ahead as the black cab swerved to the left and onto the road cutting across Rushmere Green towards the Duchess Hotel. The dead of night was set and the wilderness of the Old Park lived on, away from the lights of Wimbledon Village. He asked the black cab to park further on, away from the entrance, and shortly after he was alone at the entrance on Camp Road. He recognised the place where he had jumped over the wall, almost beckoning him in this hour of need. Enrico thought he could use the door between Dr Watkins's home and the Herbal Garden but the thought of crossing the whole park, without a map, and with a mandate from police hanging over his head, advised him to find a quicker way in. This time, though, it was less painful. The shrubs and the trees felt softer and more docile in the pitch dark of the park. Enrico squinted in the dark. The place looked more eerie at night. He could make out the rose garden he went through. That led to the left, past the statue of Diana and then down the slope towards the walls of the Italian Garden. He remembered that. Chapel House, according to Dr Watkins, was along the wall he had just climbed, and so Enrico instinctively crawled into the night to his right. He could not see flashlights shining in the distance. He saw it as a reassurance he would not bump into a policeman patrolling at night, if they ever did. The Italian baker walked over the grass, off the public gravel path, until he came across a large tree and behind it stood a quiet, ominous building. He could not tell if it looked like a chapel, but it was nowhere near anything he had been used to back home.

The Italian baker circled around to check it out. There were no other buildings nearby as the park curved south towards the Duchess Hotel. At the back there was a blue emergency door ajar. He stood there in silence. The park had little to share. No birds chirping, no breeze blowing. He could only hear his heart racing and wondering whether Eric Quercer or the police may be hiding in the bushes, ready to leap on him. He vaguely heard faint cries coming from inside the silent building. Enrico crouched and moved closer, through the gate leading onto a concrete patio, and went to open the door. The cries were clearer. Two voices but not sure to whom they belonged. Calls for help from the pitch-black inside. The echo appeared to be bleeding out of the wall. Enrico followed it until he caught a beam of light flashing occasionally on the ceiling to the right. Enrico followed it and found the stairs. The beam was coming from a gaping hole into the bottom of two broken stairs. The voices came out of it, now loud and clear, and

Enrico recognised Viviane's voice with joy. Enrico looked inside the dark, cold room below.

'Viviane?' he called out.

'Enrico?' she replied.

The torchlight hit Enrico in the face blinding him on the spot. He covered his eyes. Viviane lowered the light and put it above her head. Enrico could then finally see Viviane's face washed by the light of the torch.

'Enrico, is that you?' added Dr Watkins, emerging next to her.

'What are you doing down there?'

'Eric Quercer trapped us here. He knows where the black azalea might be.'

Enrico cursed to himself. He had arrived late.

'How?'

'No time to explain, Enrico. We need to get him. Find him!' she shouted.

Enrico had questions popping into his head one after the other. They had to wait.

'Where is the black azalea?'

Viviane and Dr Watkins took turns to explain the location of the secret compartment, sometimes talking over each other. Enrico was surprised to hear Hilary Wilson had apparently hid it there in the end, under everyone's nose, or so Dr Watkins believed. There was only one way to find out.

'Where is Lady of Cannizaro?'

'We don't know.'

'She did not come here?'

Viviane and Dr Watkins shrugged. They both looked worn out and Enrico felt the same way. If she was not here, she was either late or something had happened to her.

'Ok. I am going after Eric Quercer.' said Enrico. 'He may be at the statue of Diana or at the Duchess Hotel, or worse he may have left Wimbledon already with the black azalea.'

'Enrico, take this!'

Viviane launched the torchlight. Enrico grabbed it at the first attempt. 'Thanks. But what about you two?'

'The rope, Enrico.' she explained. 'Throw it down and we will get out of here to find help. It is time to get the police involved.'

Enrico gulped at her comment. By the state of things, he knew this was not the safety he had promised Viviane. On the other hand, he hoped Baynard would not hold a grudge on him and would finally see through all this. The Italian baker felt he owed it to them.

The Italian baker lowered the rope and disappeared. He dashed out of Chapel House and ran back to where he had come from, remembering where the statue of Diana and the Fawn was. Enrico ran through the rose garden outside Keir Cottage and wound around a path of beech trees. The bark of the trees, lit by the torchlight, shone like safety lights showing the way.

Enrico did not know what to expect. He had not thought of how he was going to face Eric Quercer, and he was more puzzled when he emerged into the open round space, clear of trees or shrubs where the statue sat in the middle. Alone, undisturbed. Her moulding grey seemed a splendid white under the effect of the torch. Diana had her pursed, tranquil smile on her face slightly bent over the fawn. She gave out a peace Enrico struggled to reckon with. He slowed down as he shortened the gap between him and the statue. He dabbed the sweat from his temples. He felt exposed despite the darkness of the park around him looking nothing but desolate and abandoned, as if he was the only person left in Cannizaro Park or even Wimbledon. He stood in front of the statue. At a closer look, even with the flashlight, the white stone acquired its pale grey colour again mixed with faded green moss. A splendour long gone. Enrico located the breast Viviane had mentioned. He wet his lips and reached out to press it, hoping he would not look like a fool. His palms were now feeling sweaty. He grabbed the breast, putting aside the awkward contact he felt with the lifeless smooth skin of the Greek goddess, and pushed it hard. He pushed twice until a clacking sound echoed from the pedestal on which the statue stood. Enrico

251

pointed the torch to the ground and saw that something had opened to the side of the pedestal. So far, it had worked exactly like Hilary Wilson described it. The Italian baker had forgotten the world around him, the moment of truth had arrived, the moment he would finally put his hands on the black azalea. He kneeled to pull open the small hatch, now slightly ajar, and flashed his light inside the tiny secret compartment. Inside was a hollow space, the size of a football. A thin layer of black dust and ashes was at the bottom of it. Beyond that, the secret compartment was completely empty. Eric Quercer had been here already. The black azalea was gone.

Enrico was clueless. He kept the light fixed inside the hollow space and then shifted it on Diana's mocking smile looking down on him, perhaps bemused. Her motionless posture did not give further clues to go on, nothing about what happened to its most guarded secret. Eric Quercer could be anywhere now. He sighed and shrugged in defeat with his head lowered. He felt stupid too after all this running around playing detective. For what, he thought.

The Italian baker pulled himself up by the edge of the pedestal and stood up. He pointed the torchlight downwards, in his limp hand. It cast a round halo around his feet and let the darkness fall on him. Enrico listened to the silent park. He frowned. It was not the same silence. He froze upon hearing a faint breathing. There was a presence. His ears strained to listen in all directions. The silence was deafening. Enrico pulled the torchlight and flashed to his right, half-turning to face whatever was there with him.

'Right on time, Mr LoTrova!' said Eric Quercer.

He turned his own torch and flashed it in the Italian baker's eyes. Enrico saw him edge out from behind a tree. He was not alone. Someone walked slowly next to him. Lady of Cannizaro stood there, hands up and gun pointed at her head. Enrico shivered. He had not considered until that very moment a mad horticulturist may very well be armed.

'It is you again!' Eric continued. 'You have been a thorn in my side from the beginning. I should have seen it coming!'

He moved a few steps to the side and pushed Lady of Cannizaro, keeping the same distance between them and Enrico.

'Next time, I won't save you from an explosion….' said Enrico with disdain.

'Ah!' mocked Eric. 'So, you *were* involved from the beginning. All this was no coincidence. How much did Sergej Vernikoff pay you?'

'What?' said Enrico baffled.

'Or maybe you played both me and Sergej Vernikoff to get your hands on the black azalea. You and those two crazy friends of yours. Clever!'

'*Pazzo!* You are talking nonsense…'

'Shut up, stupid baker.' he cut him off. 'Tell me where the black azalea is. Where did you move it?'

Enrico tried to look into Lady of Cannizaro's eyes. She did not seem to understand either what Eric Quercer was waffling about. It did not look promising. Madness seemed to have caught up with him. Reasoning with him would be trickier, and Enrico was already thinking what on earth he could do to come out of this alive. No policeman in sight, he thought. They had all disappeared. Dr Watkins and Viviane were probably his only ace up the sleeve. Time. He needed to buy time.

'I don't know what you are talking about.' explained Enrico. 'I came here, found the compartment and there was nothing in it.'

'And how do you know about the compartment? Perhaps you have been here before me?'

Enrico may have been crazy to believe in Sergej Vernikoff's stories on the black azalea. However, he had in front of him an even worse example, paranoid and delusional. He held Lady of Cannizaro's gaze. He realised then she was not looking into his eyes, but somewhere to the side of his head.

'Hilary Wilson's diary.' carried on explaining Enrico. 'Dr Watkins and Viviane just told me. Plus, I had never heard of the black azalea until a few days ago. Maybe we need to accept we have all been on a wild goose chase…'

253

'No!' cried out Eric. 'It must exist, and I will find it. Whatever it takes.'

'Then we cannot help you. Let us both go, and we will let you disappear...'

'Let's agree to disagree. You should have let me die in the explosion. Goodbye, Mr LoTrova!'

Eric Quercer was quick to load and shoot, or so he thought. As a man whose delicate hands were probably better dedicated to handling flowers, his aim was below average. Still, Enrico knew he stood no chance. Lady of Cannizaro knew she did not either, especially at such close range. She would have been the first victim of Eric Quercer, and feisty as she was, she simply could not accept that. She leaned back just in time and the bullet never hit her. Enrico imagined the Canadian would then try to shoot him. Instead, Enrico saw the mad horticulturist fall backwards, his eyes wide and lifeless, his mouth open. A deep red blotch appeared on the upper-right of his torso. All in a matter of seconds.

Enrico froze and focused on the body spread-eagled on the grass. He then touched his body and could not find any wounds anywhere. Not sure what had happened, Enrico followed Lady of Cannizaro's gaze; she had slumped by the tree nearby, exhausted. She was looking behind him. Enrico spun around, and a cluster of torches lit up to clash with his. Inspector Baynard stood a few feet away from him, his guard still up, his gun still smoking. Enrico thought he could feel the inspector's inquisitive stare in the penumbra. The rest of the torch lights moved forward as Baynard's men went to check on Eric Quercer's body. A couple of paramedics arrived shortly after to assist Lady of Cannizaro. Enrico was still in a trance and expected Baynard to make a comment. He walked to him and patted him on the shoulder, without saying anything, and moved on to help setting what would be the third or fourth perimeter the police would setup in Cannizaro Park, hopefully the last. One of the policemen escorted Enrico away, back to the Duchess Hotel where the lights of the orangery welcomed him in warm, open hands. The Italian baker was dazed and believed he was in some sort of dream.

'Enrico!' shouted Viviane.

She stood up from one of the tables where she sat with Dr Watkins and threw herself at Enrico in an embrace the Italian baker found overwhelming.

'You are safe!'

'Am I?'

Enrico could still not believe what had happened.

'Glad to see you are ok, Enrico!' said Dr Watkins.

He came forward to shake his hand and gave him a strong pat on the shoulder. The Italian baker pulled a half-smile, unsure how to take the cries of joy. Another hand grabbed him on the shoulder and Enrico turned around to meet once again Baynard's inquisitive stare.

'Eric Quercer is dead.' he confirmed nonchalantly. 'I believe the case can be closed.'

'I guess I owe it to you, Inspector Baynard.'

'Owe what?'

Enrico hesitated. Baynard simply did not warm up to him.

'That I am alive and well.' explained Enrico. 'Eric Quercer was about to shoot me and Lady of Cannizaro. If you hadn't arrived on time…'

'Part of me wished I hadn't arrived on time…' Baynard replied.

Enrico gulped. Baynard kept a serious face. His words did not give away a single hint of sarcasm.

'…and the other part is glad we received a visit from a very important person that confirmed everything you told me.'

He then beamed at someone behind them to come forward. A tall man, elegantly dressed, stood from a distant table. Enrico knew him. He had seen him many times. He walked differently though, more self-confident, and at first sight he had an impeccable sense of fashion wearing the same clothes his double had. Sergej Vernikoff joined them and for Enrico it felt like an old acquaintance if it weren't for the better-mannered, more soft-spoken way he introduced himself. Completely at odds with the person he had met a few days ago.

'Allow me to introduce you to the real Sergej Vernikoff.' said Baynard.

Dr Watkins and Viviane looked at each other confused.

'*Piacere*, Enrico!' said the Italian baker shaking hands.

'Great to meet you.' he replied with a more evident but milder Russian accent. 'Thanks to you, the Trust and its legacy is safe. We, and I speak on Lady of Cannizaro's behalf, are in debt to you and Dr Watkins too. I had been in touch with her these last few months, keeping a low profile, hearing what was going on. When she tried to call me tonight, I overheard this man Eric Quercer threatening her on the phone. I knew things were completely out of hand. I went to see Wimbledon Police immediately where Inspector Baynard, here, told me you had a story to tell similar to mine.'

Enrico eyed the inspector who looked back. Again, he did not flinch once.

'We have a long discussion ahead of us Mr Leriva…'

'LoTrova!' added Enrico.

'…to clarify all the loose ends, finalise the paperwork and put this behind us. I hope we don't come across a situation like this again. Stay out of trouble!'

Inspector Baynard left to join Sergeant Jeremy and the crowd of policemen and paramedics for a quick briefing.

'Did you make a new friend, Enrico?' joked Viviane. 'I overheard you were in custody…'

'I'll tell you another day. It is embarrassing. Last thing I want now is being asked what the hell I was thinking…'

Viviane chuckled.

'Being alive is what is important.'

Dr Watkins, who had been thoughtful but restless all this time, could not self-control himself from asking the question.

'Was it there, Enrico?'

Enrico knew what he meant. He breathed a deep sigh.

'No, Dr Watkins.' he replied sadly. 'I think we have been chasing fairy tales.'

'Are you sure Eric Quercer did not have it?'

'He was as clueless as us. Trust me, the black azalea does not exist.'

'Funny, hearing you say that.' added Viviane. 'I was just starting to be a believer…'

'I must say I probably believed too much in it.' confessed Sergej. 'Now, I know I don't have to worry about something missing from this beautiful park. I did not want a nobody to take away something from this place. It was a way to protect not only the Countess of Wrenbury's legacy, but Wimbledon's too.'

'Well said!' added Dr Watkins, still unsettled about the failed quest. 'We will probably never know what this black azalea was. Probably withered in the cold British weather or squashed among dead leaves ready for burning. Who knows…'

'I do like though the idea of reading the diary you found.'

Sergej pointed at the stack of yellow-coloured letters on the near table.

'It must tell us more about our patron of the arts.'

'It does.' added Viviane. 'She is worth the title. An impressive woman, like the legacy of women here at Cannizaro House. She saw beauty everywhere, even when grey days were onto her. Very positive. It was funny at one point when she joked that her dog is the loveliest thing she had ever seen, better than that lifeless statue…'

She laughed to herself. Enrico glanced at her, surprised to see Viviane so laid back as she talked about it. The fact they had got caught up in this mess to find nothing in the end did seem trivial to them at that moment. At least the nightmare was over. All that was left was a piece of history, about Hilary Wilson, the park, Chapel House, the statue, her dog. The dog. Enrico thought about it for the moment.

'Did you say the dog was the loveliest thing she had ever seen?' he commented.

His thoughts were fuzzy. Something was not right.

'Yes, it is weird.' joked Viviane.

'Weird, huh?' repeated Enrico with a frown.

Enrico remembered the dog, Adele, in that black and white picture he kept looking at the museum, as he heard Mr Watkins's stories. Adele, Hilary's faithful companion. So important to get a mention in her diary. Probably so important to be mentioned in the poem concealed in the music sheet, the one that had been source of curiosity and grief. So weird, now that Enrico remembered.

'What happened to the dog?' he added.

'It died, I suppose. Poor beast.'

'And where was it buried?'

Dr Watkins was again thoughtful, and his eyes had narrowed onto Enrico to try and follow what he was thinking.

'Who cares, Enrico? It was decades ago.'

'No time to fool around over dead dogs.' added Sergej.

'They are buried here…' murmured Dr Watkins.

They all turned to him, dazzled.

'What do you mean, Dr Watkins?'

'There used to be a pet cemetery in the park…it is still shown on some maps…'

Enrico jumped in.

'Yes, Dr Watkins. I definitely need a map this time.'

The curator pulled out his smartphone and tried to bring up a digital overview of Cannizaro Park. He found one which pointed out all the sites to see. Enrico could not believe the sheer amount of it and the odd shape the park had from a bird's view. To the north, half-way between the Duchess Hotel and Chapel House, a cluster of dots was labelled as 'Dogs Graves' right off the public path. Enrico tried to remember if he had seen it on the way here, but he could only recall thick bushes and trees lined up in that part of the walk.

'Come with me!' he shouted.

Sergej and Viviane stared at each other.

'What are you doing?' said Viviane. 'Enrico, you may want to explain. I don't think we have the strength to run again.'

'The black azalea is still here.' claimed Enrico. 'It never left.'

Viviane gave Enrico a dirty look.

'Seriously, after all that's happened, you keep banging on about this?'

'Mr LoTrova!' said Sergej annoyed. 'Our hopes have been shattered a few times already. We should not be playing games, let's just leave things to rest in peace.'

'*Ascoltate!* Listen!' said Enrico catching their unconvinced stares. 'You said Hilary loved her dog. It was her true companion. And you said she kept quoting Oscar Wilde's idea of beauty, that she even quoted in the poem. It could have been a hint to the statue, but don't you remember what Dr Watkins said at the museum? Hilary used to refer to her dog Adele as the most beautiful thing she had ever known, the loveliest thing she had ever seen... Can't you see? The black azalea is with the dog!'

Viviane still looked confused. She glanced at Sergej. His frown shared the same position as hers. Dr Watkins's face instead was now lit up. She instantly recognised that same schoolboy excitement the curator had felt in Chapel House and in the crypt.

'Follow me!' Enrico said.

'OK, let's go!' said Dr Watkins.

'What?' shouted Viviane in disbelief.

'Dr Watkins, lead me to the Dogs' Grave!' added Enrico.

Sergej and Viviane gaped in shock at both of them as they left the orangery. Baynard, who had heard the animated conversation, seriously hoped the Italian baker was not going to create more problems than he already had.

The park was in pitch darkness. It felt quieter and less threatening than it had been as Enrico dashed out of the hotel and headed north. Dr Watkins held the torch and showed the way. The darkness felt heavier as they moved away from the warm lights of the Duchess Hotel.

'Stop here!' cried out Dr Watkins.

Enrico stopped and looked at the curator who was pointing at something to their right. There was no path leading off the one they were on. Wilderness simply stared back at them with a thick undergrowth and thick low trees. There was no sign or monument or headstone, or even a simple marker, indicating where to look or where to go. The Dogs' Graves was a personal memory of the Wilsons rather than something of historical value.

'Definitely ahead here' confirmed Dr Watkins. 'Probably beyond the undergrowth. Just walk as far as the park wall.'

The Italian baker turned on the torch and stepped on the grass, feeling the softness under his feet. He bolted forward, jumping into the hedge. Dr Watkins lost sight of him just as Viviane, Sergej and even Inspector Baynard joined them, gasping for air. They could only hear the violent rustling through leaves and branches.

Enrico felt the branches scratching his arms and brushing against his trousers. He soldiered on, the beam of light his only guide in this maze of wild shrubbery. The distance to the high wall boundary was short but messy. He could see the mouldy bricks almost picking back their colour under the artificial beam of his torch, after years and centuries without sunlight. He moved the torch sideways and then to the muddy ground. A tiny semi-circular clearing seemed to form between the wilderness and the wall. Something ordinary. He made the last leap over some dead branches and stood with both feet in the small space, casting the light of the torch to the ground. A bed of leaves and humid earth stood there. Enrico thought no graveyard would ever be defiled. He just hoped his luck had not run out. Enrico knelt down, put the torch down next to him, and started to move away the leaves and branches frenetically. The cold earth rubbed against his hand, sticking to his palm like glue. He started digging his nails into the ground and pulling mounds of earth to the far sides. A few creaks behind made him stop and turned to flash the light towards the noise. Viviane was struggling in the dark to trace Enrico's path.

'Are you looking for what I think you are?' she shouted.

She picked up the torch to help him see better.

'Adele's grave!' he answered.

The Italian baker furiously dug out a medium sized hole and it quickly grew wider. The earth felt less cold as they went deeper but nothing other than soil, worms, gravel and dead leaves kept heaping up next to them. At some point Enrico felt ridiculous, almost to the point he would hit the wall of frustration.

'Enrico, this is ridiculous! Stop it!' said Viviane over his shoulder.

Enrico was having none of it. The dig continued, never-ending, until his fingers were black beyond recognition. He brushed some of the earth away and finally the ground revealed a piece of dark brown rough wood. It was definitely something man-made. Enrico took it out of the hole. Its weight was light and the inside felt hollow with the faint sound of something rocking inside. A brass plaque on top of a wooden rectangular box said it all.

To my dog Adele. My dearest friend.
The most beautiful thing I had ever known. The loveliest thing I had
ever seen.

The coffin-like box could only mean they had finally found the pet cemetery, long forgotten under the shade of these low trees and bushes.

'What are you expecting to find in there?' asked Viviane. 'A flower dead for fifty years?'

Enrico did not falter or doubt himself further. He lifted the small coffin and opened it. Viviane peered over with the torch, eaten alive by curiosity.

The inside of the coffin was almost empty. A thin layer of ash was scattered on the bottom surface. Two tiny leg bones shook freely around and a rock the size of a fist lay wedged in one corner.

'No flower!' said Viviane in shock. 'Unless the ashes are all that remains... What is this rock?'

Enrico picked it up. It was a smooth and dense rock, black and slightly dusted. One side was a flat base and the opposite showed carved edges with soft spikes and delicate grooves displayed across its surface in a neat symmetry. They looked like man-made decorations simply eroded by time. Enrico polished it with the hem of his chef jacket sleeve and it brought back the original shiny black colour with blue-like veins glittering under the torch light. The rock felt soft to the touch. The material was nothing they had ever seen in the grounds of Cannizaro Park. Enrico and Viviane looked closer at the decorative elements and both dropped their mouths in disbelief. There were five arched rims stretching outward from the centre as if they were the blossoming petals of a flower. They spread out in a star-shape fashion, as a corolla chiselled with its small stigma and filaments in the centre, and now almost worn out by time. They could almost see the veining of leaves sculptured perfectly in the smooth rock. It took them a while to bring the features all together and realise they were staring at the delicate representation of an azalea. A black azalea.

Viviane and Enrico re-emerged from the wilderness with their newly found treasure. The coffin had been left behind, locked and buried back under the cold earth. This is what Hilary would have wanted for her beloved dog Adele, a mere messenger for a special gift she could not part with. Enrico gave the black azalea to Sergej who held it in his hands, caressing its smooth surface. Simple. Decorated. Meaningful. The black azalea glinted a blue hue in their eyes.

'Another treasure of Cannizaro Park!' smiled Enrico holding the torch light above the rock for everyone to see. 'To be returned to its rightful owner.'

'Is this the flower we have been looking for?' asked Dr Watkins astounded. 'A rock?'

The shock in their faces turned slowly to a solemn contemplation of the stone flower.

'Looks like it.' confirmed Sergej. 'I am not sure what to make of it. Does it have anything written on it?'

'I don't think so.' said Enrico observing the rock from all sides.

'I knew it could not be a flower!' exclaimed Viviane looking at Dr Watkins, who had picked the stone in his hands for a better scrutiny. 'Is this the rock that Hilary Wilson mentions all along in her diary?'

'Yes, it is.' concluded Dr Watkins. 'The blue glint across its surface is the same she references throughout. It is a carefully sculptured azalea. Brilliant masterpiece! I don't think Eric Quercer knew either that he was looking for a rock and not a flower.'

'Do you see anything special with it?' asked Sergej keen to know why it had been hidden so secretly.

'Hard to tell here on the spot. From what Viviane and I read, its origins are shrouded in mystery. I can tell you, for starters, this rock is not from here. It has nothing to do with the soil from Wimbledon hill.'

'What is it made of?' asked Enrico.

'It is a volcanic lava rock. Quite old actually. Look at the black smoky density!'

'Are you a geologist now?' commented Enrico. 'Well, that does not surprise me!'

'I would tell you more if I could. I need to make some phone calls and see if we can learn more about this piece. It is tantalising!'

'Just don't lose it. After all we've been through… You are the history buff around here, Dr Watkins!'

'And what about you Enrico?' interjected Viviane. 'Are you the treasure hunter?'

She gave him a crafty look.

'I am just a baker, Viviane. I am just a baker.'

Still late in the evening, the police cars and emergency vehicles were gathered around the front car park of the Duchess Hotel. Their sirens were silent but their red and blue lights cast an intermittent game of lights and shadows visible from further afield. Any Wimbledonian passing by at that moment in time, on a serene spring evening, would have stopped and stared, and wished the heavens it was the last time they would see any of them around the famous hotel. Lord Awlthorp gazed at those lights from across Rushmere Green and then looked up into the starry night above, all from the half-opened black tinted window of his black saloon car. He sat there, thoughtful. He played over and over what he had heard through the different earpieces. Both Lord Awlthorp and his driver had been able to link up to Dr Watkins's earpiece. They even had a bug tracker on Eric Quercer, and his nefarious last attempts to win sounded pathetic over the radio waves. He had been a bad choice, and in the end, it was good the mad horticulturist was out of the picture.

A rock. All this time it had been a rock. A lava rock, to be precise. He had not expected that. Lord Awlthorp recalled when he was given access to the Earl of Spencer's manuscripts. Old, dusty, forgotten. The written evidence, though, from as far back as the 1500s, was all there to see. It told the story about great power hidden underneath the placid top of Wimbledon hill for millennia. A power strong enough to move seas and mountains. Lord Awlthorp knew there and then he had to have it, but he had to be sure the fairy tale was true. This was the test, the first phase. The first manuscript he read spoke about a 'black azalea' filled with the hate of the world. The writing did not describe it, nor did it provide drawings or sketches. Cannizaro Park had to be the first place where he should search, famous for its rhododendrons and azaleas. Stumbling in the secret conversations between the Trust and the Duchess Hotel, only fuelled the man in black's imagination and ambition. If someone else was looking for a black azalea, then the tale could be real. And now, Lord Awlthorp knew the black azalea existed. A rock. A special kind of rock he had to learn more about.

'Is it all over?' said Reginald in the front passenger seat.

Lord Awlthorp did not reply. He held his thoughtful gaze outside.

'The test almost worked...' dared adding the driver.

Lord Awlthorp snorted.

'It could have gone better.' he finally commented. 'Too messy for my taste. Eric Quercer was not as reliable as I thought.'

'You do not seem pleased the black azalea has been found.' observed the driver. 'In the end, it does exist. Just like you predicted.'

'I wish the rock was in my hands and not in the hands of those amateurs who do not know what they could be holding.'

'It is just a rock...' mocked Reginald.

The click of a loaded gun echoed inside the car. Reginald glanced sideways, thinking it was the driver's. He then glimpsed Lord Awlthorp aiming at him with a gun of his own.

'Don't you dare, Reggie, or you will be behind bars sooner than you think! Rest assured we can always link our disposed audio trackers, or the traces of granayotoxin, to your name and hand it over to the police. You may be lucky and not get shot like Mr Quercer did.'

Reginald exchanged glances with the driver who looked back impassively at him, reminding Reginald they were in this together and there was no easy way out. He then recalled he was being paid well enough for this job. Don't be a fool, he told himself.

'My bad, sir.' Sighed Reginald.

A pause and then he glimpsed the gun being lowered.

'Good!' resumed Lord Awlthorp. 'It is imperative we keep tabs on the lava rock and ensure it does not leave Wimbledon.'

The driver nodded.

'How about this Sergej Vernikoff, the real one I mean, and this other group of spoilsports?' asked Reginald.

'Let them return to their business while we proceed with phase two of our plan.'

'Is that where I come in?' asked Reginald.

'Precisely. There is an old mansion not far from here I am close to gaining access to.'

'Paperwork almost complete, I heard.' added the driver.

Lord Awlthorp smiled to himself with evil pleasure.

'Reggie, I need you to bring the chemical brothers there when the time is right. Set base and get to work.'

'I know what I need to do.' complained the burly bodyguard, trying to ignore the childish nickname he was being called with. 'But one thing I don't understand is why. What do you need them for?'

The man in black did not answer. He was already putting the cogs into motion for phase two. The contents described in the second manuscript would be his next test. Together with the black azalea they would put him an inch closer to a power beyond his wildest dreams. Lord Awlthorp saw for a moment everything he wished for shaping into a near future. It materialised before his eyes in the shadows that engulfed the inside of the car. For an instant, he believed everything evil was possible.

Wimbledon resumed back to its ordinary life as if nothing had happened. In a week or two, the explosion would be just a blip of a rare thrill long forgotten. The days of mystery and attempted murder lived on only in the minds of a selected few who in turn preferred to return to their lives and to their real line of business, much to Baynard's appreciation. Everyone went back to normality, under the protective cocoon of the tranquil Wimbledon Village.

Enrico was one of those selected few. The moment Inspector Baynard dropped any charges and any hint of suspicion, the Italian baker could not wait to return to his daily breadmaking. His hands and fingertips missed being in action. The reality of things hit him hard from the start. He realised his finances needed to catch up on the sales missed from the fair. Fortunately, the Cannizaro Festival did go ahead in the end, a bit off schedule than usual, and much owed to Lady of Cannizaro's strong will to rise again. The real Sergej Vernikoff did make an appearance to the joy of all Wimbledonians attending, who were worried about his health. Enrico heard he paid his double an absurd large sum of money to keep him quiet and cover all the trouble he went through. Enrico was blown away by Sergej's lyrical voice and he was still baffled how he had managed to baffle everyone with his double stunt. All for something not even resembling a flower but something far more mysterious.

Sergej and Lady of Cannizaro agreed on the last day of the fair to announce the discovery of Hilary Wilson's papers and celebrate once again her legacy as a patron of the arts. The news was welcomed by Wimbledon with great enthusiasm. There was no mention of the black azalea, not for the time being. Instead, Lady of Cannizaro won an award from the Council for her work, in honour of the great female residents who shared the same premises as hers. Sophie Johnstone, Adela Shuster, Hilary Wilson and others. Enrico imagined how strong these women had been. As he rolled the dough in his basement, his thoughts wandered to the florist from across the street. Despite Enrico's stubbornness, Viviane had not backed down once and left him to his own device. She may have been reluctant, but Enrico never felt let down. He was not sure how she felt after the rollercoaster adventure they had been through. She was probably happy to bear with his foolish curiosity, as long as it did not mean being chased by police or dangerous men. In the end the case had been solved, or at least that is how

Inspector Baynard wanted it to be, without asking too many questions. For the inspector a criminal had tried to blackmail the Trust for money and steal its historical assets. He kept it all vague and dismissed any claims on the value of the black azalea whatsoever, which had been the main cause of trouble and embarrassment. Dr Watkins, on the other hand, dreamed about putting his hands on an historical artefact such as the black azalea and putting it on display at the Wimbledon Museum. His excitement had not waned ever since. Enrico and Viviane could see the glint in his eyes when they chatted with him at the WAIS meeting. They started talking about the weather and somehow the discussion led to lava rocks, the soil of Cannizaro Park, the origins of the statue of Diana and the Fawn. Enrico was not really interested. He had a business to rescue.

As he sprinkled some salt over a flattened piece of soft dough, Enrico heard the ring of the tiny bell on the ground floor. He was waiting for Mr Wyczenski to come and apply the last touches to the bakery and in particular one last change he had asked of him at the last minute. He hoped it was not the Council reminding him of unpaid license and threating him with closure. The Italian baker ran up the stairs and wiped his hands. To his surprise, three guests waited for him by the till. He recognised them straight away. Lady of Cannizaro wore a blue and yellow long summer dress, comfortable but elegant and kind to her shape. Dr Watkins, next to her, wore his usual blue navy tweed jacket. His hair looked whiter, freshly cleaned and combed. The third was Sergej Vernikoff, wearing a fine Italian suit Enrico looked at with envy. The opera singer had his luggage next to him. Outside, Enrico could see the curved shape of a black cab.

'Dearest Enrico!' Lady of Cannizaro greeted him with open arms. 'Lovely to see you. I hope we are not interrupting.'

Enrico kissed her on the cheeks. She looked healthy and bright, compared to the last tragic occasion when Enrico had seen her. He then shook hands with Dr Watkins and Sergej.

'*Nessun problema*! I was just kneading.' he replied.

'Oh, the master baker at work. It sounds as exciting as "The Great British Bake Off" on TV…'

Enrico nodded vaguely. He had never heard of it or had any idea what it was about.

'What brings you here? Are you leaving?' he asked pointing at Sergej's luggage.

'Yes, Mr LoTrova. It is time to go back home.' admitted Sergej with a curled lip. 'However, I told Lady of Cannizaro I could not leave without saying goodbye and visiting your beautiful establishment. I hope it works. I tried your pastries at the fair. Divine!'

'Also, Sergej and I wanted to thank you and Dr Watkins on behalf of the Duchess Hotel for helping us get to the bottom of this and let us reopen the park before things worsened.'

Enrico blushed. He was not prepared for such kind words. It felt like he was being accepted into a circle of trusted friends, a sort of family of his own. He wished Viviane was there to witness it.

'I…I…I don't know what to say…' stammered Enrico.

'Say yes!' blurted out Dr Watkins.

'Yes to what?'

'Dr Watkins here,' explained Lady of Cannizaro. 'may be more in overjoy than you, Enrico!'

Enrico frowned.

'Mr LoTrova,' continued Sergej. 'you will be happy to know the Trust has agreed with the WAIS to fund the remaining costs to open your bakery. We heard from Dr Watkins and also Miss Viviane Leighwood that you need a hand so please take it as a token of our appreciation!'

The Italian baker stood and stared in disbelief. His jaw dropped; he could not believe his ears. He shifted his gaze from one to the next of his three guests two or three times muttering unintelligible words that could not convey the ecstatic joy growing deep inside him.

'*Fantastico! Che notizia!* Thank you, thank you…'

He reached out to each one of them, giving them a hug. Dr Watkins could not stop grinning from ear to ear.

'This is great news. I don't know what to say…'

'There is nothing to say.' said Sergej. 'You actually need to thank Alberyx Enterprises, one of the local sponsors. Upon hearing what you did to save the festival and also what you discovered, they immediately contacted Lady of Cannizaro to put forward more than half the money. You are a special man today, Mr LoTrova. We can only wish you the best of luck with your bread. Dr Watkins and Lady of Cannizaro say it is quite a delicacy.'

Enrico gave a shy smile to Lady of Cannizaro for the compliment. Enrico in that moment felt over the moon and suddenly the opening day no longer seemed a faraway dream.

'And you will be pleased to know,' resumed Sergej. 'the Trust has agreed to hand over the black azalea to Dr Watkins here, for display at the Wimbledon Museum. Under my recommendation and also the influence of Alberyx Enterprises, the Trust thinks it deserves a place in the local museum. Dr Watkins, with his great interest in Wimbledon history, is the best choice to safekeep Hilary Wilson's legacy.'

'This is great.' rejoiced Enrico. '*Complimenti*, Dr Watkins! You will need to find a good spot for it.'

Dr Watkins nodded with an amused look bursting with self-satisfaction.

'I know, Enrico. Isn't it wonderful? In the end we reaped the rewards we wanted.'

'Did you find anything more about the black azalea? Where does it come from?'

'The rock is a mystery.' replied the curator. 'I got in touch with the British Museum for some advice. However, they have not picked up on it. These things take time and can be a bit slow. All we were able to confirm with a local expert is that the rock is indeed of volcanic origin. Very old.

Pre-Jurassic maybe. Most surprisingly, the closest source of volcanic rocks here is Northern Scotland!'

'How did it get inside a Victorian statue? And find its way all the way to Cannizaro Park?'

'The statue dates back to when Sophie Johnstone and Francesco Platamone lived at Cannizaro House. Apart from that, I guess we will only know in time.' sighed Dr Watkins.

'Perhaps sometimes it is best to let sleeping dogs lie.' concluded Sergej. 'I offered Lady of Cannizaro my help though to support the restoration of the statue of Diana and the Fawn to its original splendour. It is the least the Trust and I can do for now. If you excuse me now, I have a plane to catch. It's been a pleasure meeting you, Mr LoTrova.'

They said goodbye one more time. Lady of Cannizaro and Dr Watkins reminded Enrico to send them an invite for when the opening day would be on. The Italian baker reassured them they would be the first to know and accompanied them out onto the side of the street. Sergej returned to the cab under the anxious look of the driver and waved goodbye once more before jumping in. The other three waited for the cab to make a U-turn and kept waving. The busy traffic of the high street swallowed the black cab in a gulp.

The new bakery that opened at 9b High Street on a pleasant Saturday morning was already at its full capacity by the time it was lunchtime. Enrico did not expect such a turn out on opening day. The day before he had even considered delaying it as he found imperfections in the décor or the taste of his bread dough. Viviane reassured him everything would come off perfectly and she even gave him some Mediterranean flowers from her shop as a gift such as sunflowers and lavender. Something to bring back colour to those walls that had been empty for too long. The final result was a full house.

Enrico realised he had given a twenty per cent discount to more people than he could remember. Yet, it was bringing in more profits than he could have ever imagined. Now, he was struggling to fill the paper bags as quickly as the people coming into the shop. Viviane saw him struggle and was quick to arrange for some members of the WAIS to help by taking orders or serving the tables. Even Lady of Cannizaro was giving her share of help, bringing her hotelier's experience and checking each customer was happy or if they needed anything. In the space of that unforgettable morning, Enrico saw plenty of Wimbledonians coming and going. Faces he knew, faces he didn't. Dr Watkins introduced him to Reverend Green, from one of the local churches. Apparently, he organised a charity fair almost every month and the curator had the great idea Enrico LoTrova should be there with his bread and pastries.

'Thank you for the introductions!' he said to the curator.

'Don't mention it.' replied Dr Watkins gladly. 'You have something good here going on. Time to let yourself be known. You can't wait for the next Cannizaro Festival.'

'You're right! How about you, Dr Watkins? Have you heard from the British Museum at all?'

'Not yet. I've tried again and again. Getting a response has been frustrating. They hardly take any interest in trivial local discoveries like this one.'

'Where is the black azalea now?'

'In the museum. I found a space for it, to put it on display. I also found a place for Hilary Wilson's diary – another great donation from the Trust!'

The curator yawned.

'Tired, Dr Watkins? You did not wake up at five a.m. to make bread.' teased the Italian baker.

'I tell you what. This whole experience has made me feel young, rejuvenated, but it has really drained me. I've had trouble sleeping lately. Not sure why.'

'Must be too much excitement for your age.'

'Maybe.' he replied vaguely, yawning again. 'I was re-reading Hilary Wilson's diary the other day. She suffered from bad sleep, and she kept blaming it on the black azalea.'

'Do you believe her claims?'

'Bah! All mumbo jumbo to me. She was just superstitious and listened to too many ghost stories around campfires. Objects sometimes influence our behaviour. The way they look. What they represent. I don't believe in such folklore tales. Pretty, yes, but they are not real.'

He yawned again, and Enrico made another coffee for him. Until two in the afternoon, the bakery was a constant flow of customers. Families, friends, couples, children, everyone wanted to taste Enrico's bread and take it home, or maybe savour his pastries with a nice espresso on the side. Every once in a while, though, Enrico glanced at the clock or asked the time. There was something he was waiting for. By three, most of the bread prepared since four a.m. that day was almost sold out, and the Italian baker found it the right moment to take a break. He was exhausted and seized the moment to step outside for a quick breath of fresh air. He looked at his watch. His man should be here soon. The bell at the door tinkled behind and he turned to see Viviane join him outside. She wore a headscarf around her hair making her look like a woman from the Fifties. Her soft pale skin had flushed from the heat inside the bakery.

'Is fame too much for you?' joked the florist.

'What a day!' exclaimed Enrico incredulous. 'If the days are going to be as stressful and hard-working as today, I'd better get ready!'

'You won't have time to chase mythical flowers or funny-looking rocks.' Viviane laughed. 'You must be feeling proud though, aren't you?'

273

'I am. It is nice to see people in there trying my bread. It is an achievement!'

'What happened to the sign?'

She hinted at the empty strip above the shop entrance where the shop name used to be.

'It was not ready in time.' explained Enrico. 'I had one last change to make. Surprise!'

Enrico peeked through the window of his shop and even without sound the scene inside the bakery filled his heart with pride and satisfaction. He then looked back at Viviane.

'Listen, I wanted to say thank you.' added Enrico. 'And maybe apologise?'

'Oh, listen to this…' chuckled Viviane.

'What?'

'Mr LoTrova,' started Viviane. 'You are a curious man, and even though you may be troublesome, you showed a good heart towards the inhabitants of Wimbledon. I cannot hold a grudge against you.'

Enrico was about to lean forward to hug her and she leaned back.

'But if you let me go through a similar experience again, we do it my way!'

Enrico stepped back and held his hands in surrender in response to Viviane's sombre but playful expression. They had an understanding, as all friends do.

He was about to suggest to Viviane to return inside the shop when a large man tapped on his shoulder. He turned and recognised the helpful face of Mr Wyczenski in his overalls. He had a long, rectangular sign under his arm and a tool case in his hand. The sign was wrapped in a heavy bottle green sheet.

'Mr LoTrova, I think you have been expecting me' said the Polish man.

'Mr Wyczenski! Good to see you!'

He shook his hand warmly.

'Can I start?' asked Mr Wyczenski.

'Sure. Please start getting ready while I get the audience ready.'

Enrico looked at Viviane who seemed confused by the conversation. He winked at her with a hint of mystery about it. He then looked at the shop entrance and started to wave his hands inviting everyone in the shop to join them outside.

It took a few minutes to gather the small crowd outside. It felt like those small celebrations at villages during religious festivities or civic events, when you think the whole town is there. Enrico stood in the middle of the shop front, just as Mr Wyczenski finished putting in place the shop sign one last time.

'Ladies and gentlemen,' Enrico announced when he found the right time to speak. 'Thank you for coming today. I just wanted to take a minute to say thank you to the WAIS for their help, and in particular Miss Leighwood and Dr Watkins. My bakery, my dream, has finally come true and it is now open for business!'

The Italian baker waved his hand above his head, like a magician ready for his trick. On cue, Mr Wyczenski pulled a set of strings attached to the green sheet. The cover around the sign fell in one swift movement behind Enrico and the magic was revealed. The audience rejoiced in amazement. Above him, everyone could read in grand capital letters the way the bakery would be named for future days to come. A local name so simple but not obvious. Enrico turned to read it in his mind again and again.

The Wynnman

Enrico will return in:
"The Wynnman and the Crimson Paths"

November 2015 – September 2018